SAVAGE MOUNTAIN

JOHN QUICK

For Richard Laymon, who showed me how to do this with no holds barred, and for some folks who made me shake my head while on vacation one day; you know who you are.

ONE

THE PLACE WAS PACKED, JUST like she knew it would be, but Ami was too tired to point out she had already tried to warn her friends of this fact. Just because it was the off-season did not mean the hotel would be any less full over the weekend, especially when you added in the unseasonably nice weather they'd been having. When it was warm enough, as January turned into February, that you could walk around outside in shorts and even consider going whitewater rafting, it was a safe bet other people would have a similar idea about outdoor activities. She said all this once before, and after four hours cramped in a car on the drive from Nashville to the foothills of the Smoky Mountains, the allure of letting her muscles relax in the hot tub was more appealing than the satisfaction of an "I told you so."

She hadn't expected the communal hot tub to be empty, but she also had not counted on it being nearly full this late in the evening. It was nearly nine, local time, but the nearby indoor pool was still full of screaming kids, and the hot tub seemed to be the place for their parents to set up shop to keep an eye on them. For a moment, she considered turning around and just going back to the room she was sharing with Benny, but the sight of her friends coming down the stairs behind her made her pause. They would just think she was being silly and unsociable. That they would be somewhat correct was not the point. She'd been looking forward to soaking for a while ever since learning the hotel had a hot tub, and it didn't make any sense for her to turn back now just because there were a few strangers who had the same idea she did and got there first.

At least there were a couple of empty chairs next to a wicker table along the railing separating the pool room from the corridor that led back outside. She went over to one, dropped her towel onto the table, kicked off her flip-flops, and stripped out of her shorts and shirt, revealing her modest bathing suit beneath. When she turned back around, she was somewhat relieved to see a pair of women climbing out of the bubbling water and heading to their own table. She couldn't stop the involuntary thought of how some women should be more careful about the bathing suits they picked, since not everyone cared to see that much hanging, dimpled flesh, but then she immediately felt guilty for it. She supposed there was every possibility once she got to be of a similar age to those women, her body would have lost the litheness granted to it by youth. They had just as much right to relax and be comfortable and content with their own appearance as anyone else did, and she had no right to judge them for that.

Still, their departure left a gap along the edge of the tub, where a submerged bench encircled. That could give her a leg up over the rest of her friends. She waited politely for the two women to move away, and stepped carefully down the built-in steps, giving her body time to adjust to the glorious heat. When the water closed over her thighs, she nearly sighed aloud. She looked up and saw a pair of young boys to one side of the gap she was headed toward, their features sharing enough similarity to mark them as brothers. If she had to guess, she would put them at somewhere in the neighborhood of thirteen to fourteen years old. Her mind classified them as relatively harmless.

When she looked over to the other side of the gap, she found herself meeting the curious gaze of an older man, maybe late thirties to early forties, with a crooked grin and hair that cascaded to his shoulders and floated in the water around him. He had his arms spread out on the edge of the hot tub and appeared more relaxed than anyone in such a crowded space had any reason to. He glanced to the side, apparently noticing the empty space between him and the two teenage boys that would be her only place to sit and dropped his arms to his sides beneath the water.

"Sorry," he said, looking back to her. "Had a second to stretch and took advantage of it."

She gave him a polite smile. "Looks like that's not an easy thing to have tonight. A chance to stretch in here, I mean."

His grin solidified. "Yeah, but it feels so good that it's worth the lack of personal space. At least you've got a little, for now. I'd enjoy it while it lasts."

That actually made her laugh. Any concern she might have had about this guy being unsavory dissipated into mild embarrassment at her own foolishness. They were in a public place, surrounded by people. The very concept anyone here would try anything untoward was ludicrous. She waded over to the open area and turned, settling into the water until it reached her neck. There was a jet almost directly behind her, pulsating into the small of her back. The gentle, persistent pressure on her muscles actually did make her sigh contentedly this time.

"Told ya," the longhaired guy said. "Feels great, doesn't it?"

A loud bustle of conversation interrupted her before she could reply. She looked over to the door and saw her friends coming through it. Benny caught sight of her first, a smile starting to form on his face until he noticed the longhaired guy sitting near her. The smile faltered briefly before returning, though not as wide as before. He quickly pulled his shirt over his head and tossed it onto the chair where her own clothes lay and then stepped into the water, moving toward a seat that would place him between her and the guy. Ami resisted the urge to roll her eyes and shake her head. At first his possessiveness had been cute, even welcome after the disaster of her last boyfriend, but now it was beginning to feel suffocating.

She wished that was the only thing wrong with their relationship.

"You disappeared on us," Benny said, settling down beside her. "I was starting to wonder where you ended up."

"I told you I was heading on down here," she replied. "You nodded at me. I thought you knew."

He grunted. "Must have missed that."

She thought she heard the longhaired guy chuckle, but with Benny blocking her view of him, she couldn't be sure.

She looked over as Jay settled into the spot on the other side of her, his expression blank, his eyes locked—as always—on

3

Christy as she talked animatedly with Eric about whatever idiot person at their mutual workplace had gotten under their skin most recently. Christy had to know Jay was carrying a serious torch for her, but if she cared at all, she never showed it. In fact, it seemed like she went out of her way to ignore him, which only drove him further into himself and his near-constant moping. Ami wished she knew what to do to help him, wished even more she could make him give up his unrequited infatuation with a girl that was only going to be bad for him in the long run, but so far she'd had no idea how to pull that off.

A loud splashing drew her attention to Teddy as he entered the hot tub, obviously not caring he might be disturbing anyone else around him. He stopped in the middle, scratching his considerable chin, and shook his head.

"Hot tub's full," he said. "Okay then, trivia time. Who here's under eighteen?"

The two teenage boys gave each other a confused glance, then looked back at Teddy and gingerly raised their hands. Teddy nodded.

"Right then," he said. He waved an arm toward the steps leading out of the water. "Get out."

The two boys tensed up, unsure of how to respond to this obnoxious bluster. Ami guessed they had been taught to do what their elders told them to, but had no idea how to react to such a direct order from a complete and total stranger. She felt a flash of pity for them and thought about chastising Teddy for being such an asshole. Ultimately, she didn't. She knew that would only end up getting him angry and starting a fight with Benny later about being mean to his friend.

"He's joking," Eric said, stepping into the water behind Teddy. "Ignore him. We all do."

"Anyone ever tell you how rude that is to broadcast to people we don't know?" Teddy asked, looking at Eric over his shoulder.

"Just you," Eric replied. "Every time I do it."

Eric looked around and found no clear spot for him to sit, so he moved to the edge near the steps and sat on the concrete, only his feet and calves submerged. Teddy continued to look at him for a moment, then turned and crossed to where Ami and Jay were sitting. Ami should have known what was coming next but was still somehow surprised when he pushed his way between them and took a seat.

"Hey!" Ami said, trying to shift closer to Benny without scraping her ass on the rough liner beneath it. "Watch it!"

Jay only glared at him, but said nothing.

Teddy gave her a toothy grin. "Just getting comfortable."

Again, Ami forced herself to bite down on her more aggressive comebacks and keep them unspoken. She understood Benny, Eric, and Teddy had all been roommates in college. What she could not understand was how Benny and Eric could continue being friends with such a colossal, obnoxious prick when they were no longer stuck living with him thanks to a trick of fate and a student housing office. That they'd both graduated well before him only added to her confusion. She'd asked Benny about it once, and he only shrugged and said Teddy was fun to have around sometimes. He'd said nothing more on the subject, and once she realized she wasn't going to get any straight answer from him, she stopped asking.

"I hate this suit," Christy said.

Ami looked up and saw the girl standing next to Eric, her bottom nearly in his face. Her suit was pink and, at first glance, seemed perfectly decent until one noticed the shirt top was too small, allowing the bulge of her belly to be visible to anyone who chose—or even those who didn't choose—to look. At least the girl was not grossly overweight, only slightly, so the vision was not nearly as scarring as it could have been. From what Ami could tell, the bikini bottoms were not even, one side creeping into the crack of the girl's ass. All in all, it was not something Ami cared to see, and she momentarily remembered her earlier thought about appropriate bathing suits.

Christy's eyes shifted to Eric's face. "Is my ass showing?"

He turned to look, a slight smile on his face. "A little. It's one cheek though."

"Damn," Christy said, twisting to try and see it for herself. "I can't see where. Can you fix it for me?"

Ami rolled her eyes. It was obvious to everyone there Christy was putting on an act, everything she said and did designed with the purpose of having Eric touch her in mind. Teddy and Benny both snickered. Jay looked more miserable. Eric shook his head, still smiling, and gently pulled the fabric over Christy's exposed ass cheek.

"Better?" he asked.

"Much," she replied. "I don't feel like I'm flossing now."

Unsurprisingly, the two teenage boys chose that moment to stand as one and make their way out of the hot tub. An older couple seated next to Eric also apparently decided they didn't want to see any more of this particular show and got out as well. Christy giggled and somehow managed to look like she was prancing as she got into the water and took over the spot the two older people had vacated. Jay immediately took the chance to move closer to her as well, but Teddy remained where he was, pressed up against Ami. She gave him a dirty look.

"You have room," she said. "Can you move over now?"

"But I'm comfortable," he whined. "Why don't *you* move?"

"Teddy," Benny said. His voice made his feelings on the matter clear: the joke was over, time to act like an adult.

Teddy let out an exasperated breath and shifted over a bit. It wasn't as much as Ami would have liked, but at least she could stop practically sitting on Benny's lap.

"I swear, Teddy," Eric said, laughing. "Sometimes I think you never bothered to grow up."

"Of course I did," Teddy replied. "I'm about to be twenty-five. In a year and a half."

Ami groaned silently. Christy got a confused look on her face and leaned forward.

"Wait," she said. "You're only twenty-three?"

Teddy sighed. "You don't have to say it, I already know. I'm the baby of this group. Go ahead, get it out of your system."

Christy shrugged. "I don't really care, just thought you were the same age as Eric and Benny."

"Oh, no," Eric said. "Don't do that. Don't think we have anything in common with that retard."

The longhaired guy barked a laugh. Every eye turned to him.

"Sorry," he said. "You guys are funny. So where're you all from?"

Ami could not help but notice the scowl on Benny's face as he looked at the guy. She might think the man was harmless, but Benny obviously thought he was some kind of competition for her affections. One more thing she could add to her list of reasons they shouldn't be together anymore.

"Nashville," Eric said. "You?"

The man shrugged. "Nowhere in particular. I travel a lot. But if you want the address that's on my driver's license, it's Boulder, Colorado."

Eric nodded appreciatively. "Long way from home."

The man smiled. "Home is where you lay your head, that's what I've always thought. But yeah, it'll be a couple days before I can check my mail again. You guys down for the weekend?"

"That we are," Eric confirmed. "Supposed to be a nice couple days, so we figured we'd head out and get some nature. From what I hear, that's good for you, you know."

"I have heard that," the man said, laughing. "Anything exciting in mind or just playing it by ear?"

"Whitewater rafting," Teddy put in. "The threat of drowning makes the nature intake more challenging."

"No shit?" the man replied. "Me and my friends finished a run yesterday. You ever done it before?"

"Um, yeah," Teddy said, his tone making it clear there was probably not a more stupid question the man could've asked. "We come down here a couple times a year for it. Hit a couple other places in Tennessee, too."

"Let me guess," the man said, smiling broadly. "Here, Chattanooga, maybe an excursion into Georgia once or twice."

"And North Carolina," Eric said. "I take it you've been a time or two, yourself?"

"All over the country," the man confirmed. "It's why I moved to Boulder to start with, but after a while everything gets too repetitious. Had to start looking other places for the challenge to come back. What class you guys normally go at?"

"We did a class four a couple months ago," Teddy said, his voice filled with pride. "For only doing it a couple years, that's not too bad."

"No, that's respectable for only a couple years at it," the man agreed. "And around here it's the best you're going to get with a guide along."

Ami blinked. "You don't use a guide when you go?"

The man smiled and shook his head. "Nope. If you know what you're doing, and plan it out the right way, you don't really need one. Like I said, it's all about the added challenge for me nowadays."

"So you've been here before, then?" Eric asked. "Know any

good places?"

He shrugged. "A few. But like I said, if you're using a guide, you're pretty much going to be stuck with the same old, same old."

"And if we didn't use a guide?"

Ami looked at Eric and frowned. They had discussed doing a run without a guide before, but ultimately, they'd decided against it. Those conversations had revolved around running a class one or two river where the risks were at a minimum. They'd never even considered hitting a class four, since the one time they'd done one *with* a guide turned out to be the most terrifying experience of their lives. She was starting to get the feeling this entire conversation was turning into a competition now, and that meant whatever Eric was thinking was probably not going to be even remotely healthy for them in the long run. As long as it only remained conversation, everything would be fine. But from the look on Eric's and Teddy's faces, she didn't think it would.

"I know some places, yeah," the man replied. "But they're not easy ones. You want a class two or three with no guide, you're not going to find it here. There's a place down in Chattanooga that's a class three, and there's a few out of state that run the scale, but around here it's all fours and fives at the least."

Ami shivered despite the heat of the water she was sitting in. A class four river was bad enough. A class five would be beyond dangerous to even consider without an experienced guide along with them. And a class six? There was no way any of them were ready to attempt something like that. She didn't think they'd be ready for a class six run even after another ten years of gearing up for it.

"Okay, where are they?" Benny asked.

Eric and Teddy she was expecting. That was the kind of guys they were. Benny was a little shocking. Ami thought he had more sense than this. She gave him a horrified look.

"Benny," she said, shaking her head. "No."

"What?" he asked, shrugging. "We're just talking. No harm in that, is there?"

The man's face was no longer smiling as he looked from her to Benny and back. Finally, he shook his head and sighed.

"Look," he said. "I'm not about to contribute to you folks killing yourselves. Your girl there doesn't seem that into it, and I'm starting to think maybe you should pay attention to her."

Teddy was nearly bouncing in his seat. "Wait, you've been on these runs, right?"

The man gave him a skeptical look. "Yeah, what's your point?"

"What if we hired *you* as our guide?" Teddy asked, his grin nearly big enough to split his face. "Then we'd have someone who knew the run along with us, and we might be able to make it through without any issues."

"You don't even know me," the man replied.

"What's your name?" Eric asked. Ami was alarmed to see he seemed to have caught some of Teddy's excitement.

"Rob," the man said, narrowing his eyes.

"Well, Rob," Eric said. "I'm Eric, this is Christy, and that's Jay, Teddy, Ami, and Benny. Now we know each other."

Rob sighed and shook his head. "Yeah, we know each other's names. That doesn't mean you *know* me."

"You planning to kill us and take the girls as your sex slaves?" Teddy asked.

"What?" Rob said, giving him an offended look. "Of course not!"

"You just said you don't want us killing ourselves," Teddy continued. "So that's off the table. And you've run those rapids? More than once?"

"Yeah, I've run them. That doesn't mean it's not dangerous as hell to do it, though. I'm fine risking my own ass every time I go out there, but that's a huge difference from risking all of yours right alongside me. Besides, you just said the hardest you've run is a class four, and with a guide. How many times have you made that run?"

"Once," Ami said. Rob looked at her and she offered him a smile, grateful beyond words he was on her side and attempting to talk the rest of them out of this crazy idea.

"Once," Rob repeated. "That doesn't mean you've got the experience to try this. Even if I was willing to do it, I'm only booked here through tomorrow morning. I'm supposed to leave and meet my friends in Wyoming in a few days for our next run."

"Okay," Eric said. "Let's deal with that, then. We've all got money we were going to use to pay for this, so what if we pay for your room for another night, pay for a plane ticket to Wyoming for you, and give you the rest for your trouble? That should be a couple hundred in your pocket, unless the plane ticket's higher than I think it would be."

"That's great," Rob said. "Still doesn't change the fact you don't have the experience we'd need to make the run safely."

Eric was nodding, and Ami could almost see smoke coming out of his ears from how hard he was thinking. She was starting to get more and more nervous. It was obvious they were starting to wear Rob down, and Eric did not want to lose his advantage.

"Well," Eric began. "What if we stuck to the class four, and agree that any time you feel like it's getting too dangerous, any time you feel like we're not capable of going further, we head to the riverbank and call it quits right then? We'll even lug the raft and oars back to the starting point so you don't have to. Plus, you keep whatever money we gave you. *Then* would you consider it?"

Rob sighed and hung his head. Ami felt her heart skip a beat. He was ready to cave.

"And what's stopping me from deciding that very thing right after we get started?" he asked. To Ami, it sounded exactly like the last-ditch effort it was. "I could take your money and run, and you couldn't say shit about it."

"We pay for your room tonight," Eric said. "A show of good faith. We give you half the cost of the ticket tonight. You don't get the rest until we're done tomorrow. We don't think you gave it a chance, we don't pay you. But we'll still carry the raft and equipment out on our own."

Rob sighed again and ran a hand over his face, leaving droplets of water to trickle off the end of his nose. He shook his head and stood.

"Fine," he said, starting toward the steps. "I'm in room three twenty-four. Meet me in the breakfast room at eight-thirty with proof you've re-upped the room. You're not there, we don't go, money be damned. And if anything goes wrong, you better not blame me for it."

As Ami watched him snatch a towel off a nearby chair and walk away, she felt her heart beating in her throat. Her friends were all laughing and joking about what an awesome time they were going to have, but she could not help feeling like they had just negotiated their own deaths.

TWO

IF THINGS KEPT GOING THE way they seemed to be, Ami wasn't going to have to worry about getting killed on an insane rafting run tomorrow morning. She thought they would end up getting kicked out of the hotel before that happened. Of course, it was not yet eleven, that magical witching hour in hotels where excessive noise ceased to be acceptable and became taboo. At the rate Teddy, Eric, Benny, and even Christy were pounding beers, they would be long passed out by then. On the plus side, that would mean she wouldn't have to fend off Benny's drunken over-tures toward sex. On the other hand, she would have to deal with his beery farts all night as she tried to sleep in the limited space his unconscious sprawl would leave her. It made her more thankful than ever they had decided on a room with a single king bed instead of the two queens. The latter would have granted her the opportunity to sleep completely on her own, but that small victory would not be worth an argument that would last the rest of the weekend.

She leaned against the railing outside the adjoining rooms and shivered. The days might be unseasonably warm, but the nights gave her a constant reminder it was still a couple of months before spring or summer would be coming to stay. She hadn't noticed it so much walking back from the hot tub, since she was nice and warm from the water she'd been submerged in minutes before. Now that she had changed into a pair of pajama pants and a light t-shirt, she was definitely feeling the final grasp of winter's chill. She considered going back in for her jacket, but she'd managed to slip away without being seen once and didn't feel like pressing her luck.

Another sharp gust of wind ruffled her still-damp hair and made her realize it wasn't that bad out here when she wasn't directly in that cold breeze. Moving might not be such a bad idea, especially since the only view she had from the railing just outside their rooms was a spectacular one of the parking lot and the back of the front office. She checked behind her to make sure no one was watching through the window or anything, heard another braying burst of laughter that sounded like a very drunk Teddy, and made her way around to the back side of the hotel.

The building blocked the worst of the breeze. The temperature on this side felt easily ten degrees warmer than it had on the other side. The view was an immediate improvement as well, even with the near-complete darkness beyond the reach of the streetlamps. She could see the lights' beams reflecting in the wide creek that ran behind the hotel, shimmering and hypnotic as the water flowed away into the trees at the far side of the property. Off to the left she could see a fire burning merrily next to the covered picnic area, and for a brief moment, she could almost forget she was off the main thoroughfare in a busy tourist town. She could imagine she was in some fabulous retreat somewhere in the mountains, taking a break from the world for a while. Maybe she was there with some wonderful man who treated her as his equal, who trusted and cared for her, and whom she was so madly in love with she never wanted to leave his side.

Someone *not* her current boyfriend, but that was a sad state of affairs she really didn't want to dwell on. She'd come out here to get away from his annoyances, which somehow magically seemed to magnify more and more with every sip of beer he took. If she let them take over even this small patch of peace and quiet, she really would lose her mind before they got back to Nashville, where she fully intended to break up with him.

She crossed her arms on the rail and leaned on them, willing those bad thoughts away and trying to replace them with something more comforting. Every time she thought she was close, she would remember what they were planning tomorrow and the illusion would shatter like spun sugar in a strong wind. She sighed. She'd been trying to come up with a good way to bow out of the entire adventure ever since Rob left for his own room after begrudgingly agreeing to be their guide, but nothing she came up with would allow her to escape without having the confrontation with Benny she was doing her level best to avoid for now.

"Thought that was you up here."

She turned and saw Jay walking toward her, a cigarette held casually in his fingers. It was cupped back, the tip hovering dangerously above his palm but shielded from the wind. She smiled and gave him a welcoming but slightly confused look.

"Where were you?" she asked. "I didn't see you when I walked over here."

He gestured toward the creek with the cigarette before taking a drag and exhaling a slow stream of smoke nearly blue in the harsh glow of the light in the parking lot.

"Communing with nature," he said. "The ducks and geese might technically be wild animals, but they're a lot tamer than those assholes back in the room. Guess you finally had enough, too, huh?"

"Something like that," she replied. "If Teddy hee-hawed in my ear one more time, I was going to strangle him."

Jay snorted. "Yeah, he can be a pain sometimes. *Most* times."

She nodded her agreement and the two of them lapsed into a comfortable silence while Jay finished his smoke. Finally, he flipped the spent butt over the railing and leaned on it in a position nearly identical to her own.

"So," he said. "I guess we're doing something stupid tomorrow."

"Looks that way," she said, sighing. "I've been trying to figure out how to avoid it, but I'm not coming up with anything. Are you okay with doing it? I know this isn't really your thing to start with."

He shrugged, not looking at her.

"Christy's going," he said softly.

"And that means you have to?"

He shrugged again but said nothing. Ami shook her head.

"I don't get it, Jay," she said. "You're a smart guy, you're good-looking, so why are you so insistent on chasing after someone that's going to do nothing but break your heart?"

"Pot, meet kettle," he muttered.

His voice had been low, but she was still able to pick out what he said. At first, she felt a flash of anger, but it quickly turned into shame. In retrospect, she probably wasn't the best person to be doling out relationship advice.

"He wasn't like that at first," she said. There was a note of defensiveness in her voice she knew made her sound desperate, but she couldn't seem to help herself. "It's just been the last bit that it's gotten bad."

He shot her a disbelieving glance and went back to looking out toward the creek. "You really think that, or are you trying to justify staying with him to yourself?"

She opened her mouth, closed it, opened it again, closed it again. She genuinely had no idea what to say. She and Jay had been friends since elementary school, had even dated briefly back in middle school before deciding they didn't want to ruin a good friendship by doing so for any length of time. No one alive knew her better than him, but his desire to avoid confrontation at all costs meant he would only rarely point out anything she did he thought was bad. For him to do so now meant he hadn't cared much for her relationship with Benny for a long time but was trying to spare her feelings.

And if she really thought about it, his question was perfectly valid. Her defense of Benny was nothing more than a bad habit she'd been practicing for most of their relationship. He wasn't terrible—it wasn't like he beat her or anything—but she had little doubt he could become that way at a moment's notice. She'd seen him angry before and had been dreading the day that anger directed itself at her for months.

"Would you believe me if I said I didn't know?" she replied at last.

Jay let out a humorless laugh. "I actually would. You do seem to wear blinders where your boyfriends are concerned. At least until things get so bad you can't ignore it any longer."

"Pot, meet kettle," she said, smiling.

She saw him roll his eyes. "Sure, throw my own words back at me. But there's a big difference, you know. Christy *isn't* my girlfriend. She barely even knows I'm alive. She's too busy throwing herself at Eric to notice me."

"So, why so hung up on her?" Ami asked, putting a gentle hand on his arm. "Why waste your time wishing she'd pay more attention to you when she acts like she does?"

He sighed. "I have no idea. There's something about her, something I can't put my finger on, that draws me to her."

"Maybe you're horny and there's some part of you that thinks she's easy?"

That actually got a chuckle out of him. "Yeah, maybe. It has been a while. I don't know. I'm starting to think it was a bad idea for me to come along on this trip. I could be at home, relaxing, but instead I'm here watching the woman I've got the hots for trying to dry-fuck someone else and getting ready to risk my life to satisfy that same someone's stupid ass pride."

"You could be back home," Ami agreed. "But then I'd be stuck here all alone in the middle of the idiot brigade."

"So I'm your sanity preservation device?" he asked, smiling.

"It looks that way," she said.

An idea suddenly came to her. "You think if we went and talked to Rob we might be able to convince him not to do this thing tomorrow?"

Jay considered it, then shook his head. "He seems like a decent enough guy. I'm betting the first thing he'd ask is whether or not they'd made good on paying for him to stay here another night. Soon as he found out they did, he'd feel too guilty about taking their money to back out."

"He might," she said. "But we could still try."

"We could," Jay replied. "Tell you what: if he's still awake, we'll give it a shot. If he's already asleep, we bite the bullet and either back out as gracefully as we can or get our asses killed on the river tomorrow."

"Deal."

Ami lead the way to the stairs up to the third floor, Jay following close behind. She was hoping to see Rob leaning on the balcony outside his room like they had been, but the walkway was empty save for a lone old man with a plastic ice bucket in one hand and a grumpy look on his face. The man's scowl deepened as he passed them, and for a moment Ami thought he might have the room above the one the rest of her group was partying in, but then she remembered they were on the opposite side of the hotel so that would be highly unlikely. She tried to offer him a smile, but the man only shook his head and pretended he hadn't even seen them. She waited until he disappeared into the breezeway where the stairs were before leaning over to Jay.

"What happened to Southern hospitality?" she asked, her voice pitched low.

"We're at a hotel," Jay replied. "He's probably one'a them damn Yankees, pissed off 'cause everyone looks at him funny when he orders a 'pop' at the restaurants."

She giggled. "Maybe his wife wouldn't put out tonight."

Jay shook his head. "He'd be smiling he didn't have to pretend. More likely his mistress backed out so he had to bring the wife instead."

Ami slapped him playfully on the arm. "That's mean!"

"Like what you were saying wasn't?"

"No, it wasn't," she said, mock offended. "Slightly off-color maybe, but not mean."

"Uh-huh," Jay said. "We're here. Knock, you mean bitch."

Ami rolled her eyes and turned to face the door to Rob's room. She hesitated, one hand partially raised to knock, then looked back at Jay.

"What if we wake him up?"

"You're only knocking this one time," he said. "If it wakes him up, we apologize, and then ask him if he's willing to listen to us. He didn't seem overly thrilled with the idea either, remember? He might be willing. If he keeps sleeping, or if he's not willing to listen, it's back to plan 'B'."

She sighed, nodded, and rapped her knuckles lightly on the door three times before taking a small step backward so she was completely visible through the peephole if Rob checked it first. Jay chuckled behind her.

"Not much chance of *that* waking him up," he said.

"I can't help being polite," she scolded.

"Yeah? When did that start?"

She gave him a look of annoyance she could not hold onto very long before it dissolved into a smile. "Hush! I think I hear footsteps."

She turned back to face the door, and a moment later it opened. Rob stood framed in the doorway, his long hair now pulled back into a ponytail. Ami hadn't gotten a very good look at him while they were in the hot tub, since he had been sitting down, submerged underwater for the majority of the time. When he got out, she had been too nervous about the deal they'd all made with him to pay any attention. Now, though, she could see how toned his muscles were. They looked hard and tightly corded across his bare arms and chest. He didn't have a six-pack, but there was precious little flab on his belly, giving him a lean, lithe appearance. He reminded her of some of the old eighties rock stars that managed to age gracefully over the years.

"What's up?" Rob asked. "Coming to ask if I'm willing to throw you all off the side of a cliff somewhere?"

Ami jumped when he spoke, realizing she'd been staring. She felt her face grow warm and hoped he couldn't notice her blushing in the dim light.

"No, nothing like that," she said. "We were hoping you could help us figure out a way to stop the trip altogether."

His head cocked slightly to one side. He looked like a dog that heard a strange sound and was trying to figure out what it was. Finally, a slight smile crossed his features as he nodded.

"That's right," he said. "You were the one who actually seemed to have some sense, and your friend there was the one that never said or did anything besides stare at the other chick."

If Jay possessed Benny's temper, Ami was sure she would be in the middle of a fight right now. As it was, she looked back and saw him blushing as furiously as she was, his eyes staring intently at something on the ground between his feet. He might be carrying a torch, but he wanted to keep it underneath a blanket the whole time. She wondered if he realized it had burned through and was visible to everyone, whether he wanted it to be or not.

"Yeah," she said, turning back to Rob. "That's us. So, can we talk to you for a minute?"

Rob shrugged and stepped to one side, allowing them to enter the room. As she stepped inside, Ami thought somehow it was even darker in here than it was outside. The only lights she could see were the floor lamp behind the table and a faint glow coming from the bathroom. As Jay mumbled something behind her on his way through the door, she saw the papers laid out across the table. She leaned over to study them and immediately recognized them as maps of the rivers nearby. She wasn't sure where Rob had come up with them, but she was immensely thankful that Eric, Benny, or Teddy hadn't found such things for themselves. If they had, it was likely they would have already attempted what they were planning for tomorrow, and to disastrous results.

"Planning the route," Rob said, brushing past her as he went to his chair on the other side of the table where the light would be shining over his shoulder onto the maps. "Trying to figure out the best run to take that keeps everyone the safest."

"Any luck?" she asked.

"Not really," he said. He gestured to the laptop lying closed on the nearby bed. Ami noticed he had a room with two queen beds instead of the one king she and Benny had to share. "I went online and checked the river conditions, and thanks to the snowfall from last weekend melting, everything's roughly a full class higher than normal. Your friends couldn't have picked a worse weekend to try this crazy stunt. And my dumb ass was stupid enough to get dragged into it with you."

"Why not leave?" Ami asked. "We're supposed to meet you at eight-thirty, so leave at seven or something. I'll be honest, they paid for your additional night already, but you can't feel that bad about making them waste their money if it keeps us all alive."

Rob shook his head. "It's not the money. I didn't agree because of the money, anyway. I couldn't care less what you guys do with it. Give it to me, cheat me, really doesn't matter. I agreed because I get the impression once those knuckleheads get an idea going, they're not letting go until they see it through. Am I far off with that?"

Ami considered lying to try and improve their bargaining position, but Rob had a valid point. She was positive, if he backed out, Teddy would become the ringleader and convince Eric or Benny to try it anyway, with or without someone who had more experience along for the ride. Once one of them fell, they'd convince the other and that would be that.

"You're right," she said. "Especially since they've already lost their chance at going with a guide by paying for your room. If you didn't go, they'd do it themselves."

"And you and your friend there would back out, wouldn't you?" Rob asked, fixing her with eyes that seemed to see straight through her.

"Absolutely."

Rob sighed. "Which would leave me with four deaths on my conscience instead of six. Not really much of an improvement, no offense intended."

"None taken," Ami assured him. "Guilt is guilt. Somehow, I think you'd feel bad even if only one person died because you backed out."

"You guess correctly," Rob said, nodding. "If I go, at least I can try to keep you all alive. I still might fail, but at least I'll know I did my best. And if I die in the process, well, I don't suppose I'll care one way or the other at that point, will I?"

Jay snorted a laugh. "No, dying would be a good way to get out of feeling guilty."

"I do have an idea though," Rob said. "It's not perfect, and I can't do it if I'm alone, but if you're willing to help, I might be able to pull it off."

Ami frowned at that. "What's the idea?"

"Look here," Rob said, pointing to a line on the map. "This isn't the channel I was telling you and your friends about, but it's not far from it. Tell the truth, I'd forgotten about it. It breaks off from the Pigeon River and then forks a couple miles further down. This one fork here is wider and absolutely insane to try and raft down. Easily a class five in the best of circumstances, probably a six in present conditions. But this other one, it's normally a four. The current's going to draw the worst of it to the other fork, which means it will probably stay a four, even with the added runoff. Here's the fun part though: I've run that slower fork a dozen times at least, and I'm convinced it's only classified as high as it is because of a few patches. You take those out, and it drops to a three, maybe even as calm as a two. If the runoff's making the currents harder to the bigger fork, this one might actually be negotiable."

"So what's the problem?" Jay asked, peering at the map over Ami's shoulder. "Just take us on that one and call it a day. Say it was rougher the last time you ran it or something."

Rob took a deep breath. "The problem is one of accessibility. There's no starting point along the calmer fork. The closest is a couple of miles before the fork even happens. We'd have to put in there, stick close to the bank, then fight the draw of the current to go down the right side. If it's just me, there's no way in hell. If it's me and four idiots I can't count on, it's freaking insane. But if it's me, four idiots I can't count on and two I can, it'll be tricky but manageable. Well, so long as at least one or two of the idiots actually does what they're supposed to as well, anyway."

"Okay," Jay said, his face scrunched up in thought. "I think I'm missing something here. You want us to go since you want everyone to have the best chance of making it out alive. We don't go, why are you still going anyway if it's such a big risk? It's not like those other dipshits have seen these maps or anything. They're not going to know where that channel is, so what's the issue?"

"They don't know about this specific channel, that's true," Rob said. He laid a hand flat over a large portion of the map that included the offshoot in question. "But they know it's off the Pigeon since that's where all the runs are around here. And all these other channels? Fours and fives with nothing to cut the added current from the runoff. That means all fives and sixes tomorrow. That means if they try any one of them on their own, there's a ninety-nine percent chance they're dead and lost in the river. They might wash up somewhere down around Chattanooga if they're lucky. Realistically, though? Their bodies will never be found."

Jay considered this, sighed, shook his head, and looked over to Ami, one eyebrow raised questioningly. She didn't know if Rob had the heat on in his room or not, but she doubted if it would do anything to cut the chill that suddenly gripped her like an iron fist. What he was saying boiled down to a simple fact that made her want to punch every one of those assholes that had gotten her into this mess in the first place: either she and Jay went to help out so they had a slim chance of making it back in one piece, or they didn't and everyone who they'd come here with—plus Rob, who had never asked for this in the first place— were almost guaranteed to end up dead.

She sighed and looked back to Rob. "I guess we do it your way, then."

THREE

TEDDY WAS DRUNK, TEDDY WAS tired, and worst of all, Teddy had to piss like a racehorse. The first of those was, of course, his own damn fault, but it was also the one that didn't bother him much. It was the desire for sleep and the almost unbearable need to urinate bringing him to the edge of frustrated panic. Once Eric reached his own personal level of inebriation where that bitch Christy actually looked appealing to him, Teddy had been summarily ejected from the room. Benny had already gone to the room he was sharing with Ami, and none of Teddy's attempts to rouse him received any response. Either he'd somehow managed to convince Ami to let him have some tonight, or he'd collapsed onto the bed and passed out straightaway.

Teddy was betting on the latter. Benny could claim nothing was wrong all he wanted to, but Teddy saw the dirty looks Ami had been shooting his way all night and knew sex was not going to be on the table for those two in the foreseeable future.

He stopped in front of the door to his own room and patted his pockets again, hoping desperately one of the two key cards he and Jay got when they checked in would materialize out of thin air. All he came up with was nothing, nothing, and for good measure, a little more nothing. Same as on the previous half-dozen or so attempts. He could blame himself—after all, he was the idiot who didn't bother to pick one up off the dresser before heading over to Eric and Christy's room for the party. The problem with doing so was that he would have to admit he'd been the one to make the mistake, and that wasn't something his beer-addled mind was willing to let him do. After his desperate knocking went unanswered here as well, he decided he was going to blame Jay for it. He should have reminded Teddy to grab his key even if that wasn't exactly his responsibility. Where the fuck could he be at nearly eleven o'clock in this piss-pot town anyway?

Teddy wasn't surprised Jay had abandoned the party. The little shit never said anything unless it was to be condescending to him or to point out the flaws in whatever Benny or Eric said. The only person he actively seemed willing to talk to was Ami. Maybe the two of them had run off together or something. They claimed to be just friends, but Teddy had a hard time believing a guy could be "just friends" with a girl he'd known for as long as those two had known each other. He could make a valid case for it, if not for the goo-goo eyes Jay kept making toward Christy.

Fat lot of good that had done him. That nutty bitch wasn't into the brainy, sensitive types Jay tried to portray himself as. She wanted someone with confidence, someone who was willing to throw her ass down and stretch her insides sixty ways from Sunday. Teddy had given it some thought, but the way she acted all but screamed "skank" and that was one headache he didn't care to deal with.

His bladder constricted painfully, reminding him he had more pressing issues than who sluts chose to share their unspeakable charms with. He needed to find someplace he could relieve himself, and he needed to find it pretty damned fast. He clamped one hand over his crotch, hoping maybe if he pinched the end of his dick closed he could keep himself from pissing all over his pants until he could find a suitable place, and quickly made his way to the stairs.

He glanced toward the front office but could not for the life of him remember if there'd been a restroom in there or not. He supposed he could always hit up the person working the desk to make him a new key card, but the combination of his extreme drunkenness and his overwhelming imperative to relieve himself meant he would not be able to spare the time it would take to do so. Better to not take any chances. If he got in there and they didn't have a public restroom, he was going to end up making a mess of the carpets before he could get back out, he was sure of it.

Instead, he hurried down the stairs, a low groan emerging from his throat as the motion jostled his bladder and very nearly made him lose what little control he had over it. Even if he found a place, he was going to be damned lucky to get his equipment out and aimed before the waterworks began.

As he rounded the corner at the bottom of the stairs, he saw the small grouping of bushes down near the creek on the other side of the parking lot. If he positioned himself right, and if this was coming as hard and fast as he felt it would, it might be good enough to stave off disaster. Another brief spasm in his groin decided the issue. It was going to have to do.

He rushed across the parking lot as quickly as he dared, moaning as he went from the added challenge the activity gave toward keeping his pants dry. His free hand already had his belt and the fastener on his jeans undone before he even stepped off the pavement onto the grass surrounding the bushes. He thrust his hips forward and hoped he was hidden well enough. He undid the zipper as fast as he dared and was already letting fly before he even had his penis completely freed.

His entire body shuddered with relief. There was something about that moment when you finally got to pay the rent on all the beer you'd been drinking that was almost more pleasurable than sex. He considered trying to remember that thought long enough to check online whether or not the endorphins released at times like this were the same as the ones released during an orgasm, but knew he was much too drunk to remember anything so fleeting. He'd never had a full-fledged blackout when he was drinking, but that didn't mean his memory was what it used to be. Too much pot in college, maybe.

Or maybe he really was as dumb as people thought he was.

Either way, it didn't matter. He was thrilled he'd managed to piss before he had an accident. And he was going to kick Jay square in the nuts for not being in their room to let him in, which was how things got so dire in the first fucking place.

After a few moments, he started to think he would have to spend the rest of his life urinating into a bush. Then, finally, the stream began to slow to a trickle before finally stopping altogether. He let out a long, pleasurable sigh and tucked himself away before taking a step from his makeshift toilet. As he fastened his pants, his eyes fell on a nearby sign. He squinted but still couldn't make it out between the drunken haze and the dim lighting. Once he was somewhat decent again, he ambled over to it for a closer look.

"Please keep off the grass," he read aloud. "We have completed extensive landscaping to better provide you with a pleasurable environment for your stay, and need time for the seed to take root. Thank you for your cooperation."

He chuckled. "Yeah, about that. I think I washed a bit away. So sorry. If it makes you feel better, that bush won't need watering for a couple of months."

Snickering at his wit, Teddy stumbled back onto the pavement and started toward the hotel again. He guessed he would need to go ahead and hit up the front office to try to get a new key. He had no idea whether Jay was in the room or not, but if he was and he was asleep, Teddy would end up sleeping in the breezeway outside their door unless he got a new key. Now that his bladder was empty, the desire to sleep was starting to take over as the most prominent thing in his mind.

When he heard soft voices, he looked up, more out of instinct than any real desire to see who was speaking. From his vantage point, it looked like a couple was emerging from a room up on the third floor, speaking to someone else still in the room. Teddy smiled, imagining he was seeing the aftermath of a torrid threesome. When he realized two of the people were male, his smile grew wider. So it was a *devil's* threesome, then. Not something he cared to partake in, but hey, whatever got yer rocks off.

The girl laughed, and Teddy stopped walking, his head cocked to the side with one ear facing the group. She said something to one of the men and Teddy smiled wider. Her voice was familiar, only filled with considerably more good humor than he'd heard in it so far on this trip.

He crouched down and duck-walked farther until he was reasonably well hidden in the deep shadows next to some massive SUV, his eyes straining to make out enough features to confirm his suspicions. Finally, the girl moved closer to the railing and into the light. Teddy nearly laughed out loud. It was Ami, all right. And the guy who emerged from that room with her looked quite a bit like Jay.

At first, he had no idea why they would be coming out of some strange person's room, but then he remembered that the hippie looking guy they swindled into being their guide for what promised to be a killer rafting run said his room was three hundred something, which meant it was on the third floor. He leaned forward and was rewarded with a brief flash of a long ponytail as the guy upstairs pointed to something off to the side.

Teddy could vividly remember the rant Benny launched into about how that douchebag had been undressing Ami with his eyes in the hot tub and how she'd been eating it up and practically flaunting herself to him. Teddy didn't really remember seeing anything remotely like that happening and also didn't think Ami was the type to go running off to meet some old freak she didn't know from Adam, but the idea of what might happen if Benny were to hear about this was too delicious to ignore. He wanted nothing more than to run upstairs quick as he could and pound on Benny's door until he answered, but this would be better to share with the group.

It was a character flaw, one among many, if he was being totally honest with himself. It was also one he couldn't ignore out of hand like he could the others he'd been accused of having. He liked to stir up shit. He had no idea why, other than the resulting explosion amused him, but it was something he did almost every chance he got. If he played his cards right, he could even get Jay caught in the backlash. It wouldn't take much. Benny wasn't too fond of Ami's childhood buddy to start with. Drop some hints that Jay was trying to give Ami a way out of their relationship and Benny would probably end up pounding the little shit into the ground like a post.

There'd be time tomorrow before they set off on the adventure. Then again, maybe after would be better. That way there'd be no risk of them losing their guide. Teddy wasn't opposed to going without one altogether, but they didn't know the channels where they wouldn't end up running into some official group or two that would report them to the authorities, and that could end up bad for them. He wasn't exactly sure how, but even a fine would be a disaster considering they'd spent a small fortune on this trip already. Teddy knew he was already looking at a month of overtime to make sure he could pay his bills before everything got shut off. If he had to pay a fine on top of that, he might as well give it up and move back home with his mommy and daddy like a helpless little dumbass.

Then again, he could always say something privately to Benny right before they got in the raft. That way they'd be all set to go, the explosion would happen, they'd get their awesome adventure with no guide, and they wouldn't have to fork over any more money than they already had renewing the hippie's room for another night. Yeah, that would be the optimum time to say something.

As soon as Ami and Jay had their backs turned again, Teddy cut across the parking lot at nearly a dead run. He would take the stairs on the other side of the building and hopefully make it back to the room either before or at the same time as Jay. He couldn't let on he'd seen them, of course. He'd embellish the truth a bit, say he'd pissed in the bushes next to the covered picnic area or something. Jay would believe it because it wouldn't be that far off from what really happened. Only the location would change.

And once he got back into the room, all he had to do was figure out exactly what to tell Benny in the morning to achieve the maximum effect. He smiled. Tomorrow was shaping up to be an interesting day.

It was not at all uncommon for Christy to find herself wide awake after sex, no matter how tired she'd been before the act started. It was just how she was wired. She'd heard some of her friends talk about falling into some of the best sleep of their lives afterward, especially if it had been particularly good, but for her, she felt energized, rejuvenated, even.

What was strange, however, was to find herself wide awake and energized after *not* having sex when she thought she was going to.

Things had been progressing so well with Eric. She'd finally managed to get him interested shortly after Benny made his grumbling exit. She'd sent Teddy packing and then started working on not only holding Eric's interest, but trying to actively seduce him as well. He'd been responding better than she could've hoped, too, right up to the point where he lay back on the bed in the middle of her lap dance for him and began snoring as soon as his head hit the mattress.

For someone who talked such a big game, he sure couldn't hold his beer that well. Of course, she'd long since lost count of how many he'd had. Maybe she should have made more of an effort at regulating his intake so he wouldn't have passed out on her at the crucial moment.

She made a couple of half-hearted attempts to rouse him, but she knew better than to think she was going to be able to finish what she'd started. She might be able to get him completely on the bed so he'd be more comfortable, but she wasn't going to get any relief for how horny she'd made herself. Well, not unless she took matters into her own hands, so to speak. She gave it serious consideration but ultimately decided against it. Not out of fear that Eric might wake up and catch her at it, not precisely, but more out of the chance for annoyance if he woke up, caught her, and interrupted her when she was nearly there.

Even for all that, she was nowhere near as disappointed as she might've expected to be. Had it been Benny, on the other hand, she would've been beyond furious right now. He'd been her real target for this weekend, after all. When it became crystal clear he and Ami weren't going to implode before the trip, though, she had to rework her plans. Eric had been nothing more than a consolation prize, the best of the three remaining options open to her. The very thought of trying to get with Teddy was enough to make her laugh herself into a heart attack. There was always Jay, of course, but that presented its own set of problems she wasn't willing to deal with.

She wasn't blind, and she wasn't stupid. She knew he had a thing for her, and while it was flattering, it wasn't what she wanted right now. From the way he looked at her, he wanted something for a long haul. She only wanted to have some fun and was nowhere near ready to consider settling down yet. It wouldn't work.

That wasn't stopping her from taking advantage of the situation and scratching her current itch, but she couldn't do that to him. Deep down, she was touched someone could hold her in such high regard. No one else ever had, not even herself. She couldn't knowingly hurt someone who saw something in her she could not see in herself. Maybe one day, but not today.

Sitting here propped against the bed wasn't doing anything to help with her alertness, nor was it doing much for her irritation. She glanced over at Eric sleeping deeply next to her and shook her head. She thought she'd calculated things so well, yet here she was, unfulfilled and antsy while he slept the sleep of the drunken buffoon. Life wasn't fair sometimes. She bounced on the bed as she swung her feet around, not caring if it disturbed him and feeling a minor thrill at the way her breasts jiggled from the motion. She hadn't bothered putting her shirt back on after her failed attempt at seduction, afraid the cloth rubbing against her nipples would only frustrate her more than she already was. Their sensitivity faded as she sat there, but that jostling was enough to tell her it had not gone away altogether. That wasn't a good thing. She was either going to need to take care of this or somehow get to sleep immediately, before she found herself watching the sun come up while still so horny she couldn't stand it.

With a sigh, she stood and headed over to the small fridge nestled under the microwave the room provided for them. She opened it and peered inside, momentarily annoyed at the number of empty beer bottles she came across. What idiot had been putting his empties back in the fridge? It was probably Teddy, thinking it would be funny if anyone wanted another drink before crashing out. Finally, she managed to find the last two remaining from their hoard, tucked away in the back behind all the empties and the bottle of vodka they were saving for tomorrow night. She didn't know why they'd bothered. They could always stop somewhere and pick more up. Still, she hadn't exactly seen any liquor stores around, so maybe it was better to be safe than sorry. And it wasn't like Eric was the only one who was holding. She knew Benny had a bottle of Jagermeister and some Red Bulls in his own fridge.

After considering, she pulled out both beers and let the door slip closed again. She twisted the cap off the first and wrapped her lips around the neck before upending it and swallowing rapidly. Her buzz was reduced, but it wasn't gone yet. Killing the first beer this fast would go a long way toward bringing it back full force. By the time she finished drinking the second one normally, she should feel nice and mellow again and ready for bed.

She winced as the final drops of the beer trickled into her mouth. She'd always hated the taste of the last bit but could never figure out why. It probably had something to do with the yeast settling in the bottle, but it had never interested her enough to find out for sure. She let out a long, loud belch and dropped the empty bottle into the waste can. It clinked loudly, fell off the stack and rolled across the floor, bumping gently against her foot. She realized why the empties had been ending up back in the fridge. There was simply no more room in the garbage. She sighed, twisted the cap off the last beer, and dropped it onto the countertop near the microwave before moving over to the table next to the window.

She should probably put on a shirt or something if she was going to be sitting by an open window, but the idea seemed like more trouble than it was worth. After all, she was planning on finishing her beer and then going to bed. Why get dressed only to turn around and get undressed again? Besides, unless she turned the lights on and opened the curtains wide, it was doubtful anyone could see her. She smiled as she settled into the seat. It was kind of cool that anyone passing by outside could not see her, but she would be able to see them.

When she heard voices approaching, though, she felt a quick flash of panic. She hadn't really expected to see anyone out there, and now she was self-conscious about sitting topless in front of a public window. Trying to preserve some thin thread of dignity, she pushed her chair back until the shadows consumed her. It cut her view of the outside down to the barest strip, but if she guessed right, it would hide her completely from whoever it was passing by.

Surprisingly, she saw Jay and Ami pass by, talking softly amongst themselves. Christy frowned. She was sure Ami had gone to bed a long time ago and vaguely remembered Jay leaving not long afterward. Instead, it looked like the two of them had gone off somewhere together, leaving the rest of them to wonder where they were. Well, leaving Benny to wonder where Ami was, at any rate. She certainly hadn't cared one way or the other. Neither had Eric or Teddy, at least so far as she knew. But Benny had been royally pissed that Ami ditched him. If he found out she was off with Jay, it might be the push he needed to get rid of her. He'd be upset, naturally, but there might also be a small part of him that wanted to get even with her for whatever he imagined they'd done. If she played her cards right, *she* could be that revenge.

Christy smiled and knocked back another swallow of her beer. Suddenly, she no longer felt the urgency to get laid tonight. After all, why waste your time with the appetizer when you had the chance to jump ahead to the main course? She'd waited this long for Benny to be free. What was one more day?

FOUR

CONSIDERING HOW HUNG OVER EVERYONE except for Jay, Rob, and herself was, Ami expected it to take much longer than it did for them to get everything ready to go for their adventure. Surprisingly, things fell into place better than she would have thought, even if her friends had gotten plenty of sleep and had been up for hours beforehand. There was never any question they would be taking two vehicles since, according to Rob, they would need someone at both the starting and ending points of the run, but even choosing from Benny's, Eric's, and Rob's had been easier than anticipated. Not that there was really any hard choice to make; Eric's Toyota wasn't exactly suitable for transporting seven people a block down the street, much less the eight miles or so Rob said it would be.

Even choosing who would be riding with who had gone smoothly. Naturally, Benny would be driving his truck while Rob drove his, so that part was easy. Ami knew better than to try to avoid riding with Benny for fear of a confrontation. Christy and Teddy fell in along with them, while Jay and Eric both volunteered to ride with Rob. Ami had to fight down a smile when Jay chose not to ride in the same vehicle as Christy. Maybe her talk with him the night before had done some good.

Or maybe he was afraid he'd end up having a conversation with her that might let him see she wasn't what he'd built her up to be in his mind.

Whatever his reasoning, once transportation had been arranged, the rest kind of fell into place. There wasn't that much to pack, just a couple of smaller bags with a change of clothes for each of them, a bag with their life jackets, and a cooler with some drinks and snacks in case they got hungry along the way. Beyond that, they only needed to make sure there was ample space for the raft itself, which would ride to the river attached to Benny's luggage rack and back attached to Rob's. Rob also brought along a pack of his own that contained his maps of the rivers she saw the night before, a flare and flare gun, matches, and a first-aid kit.

However easy the preparations had been, it was more than made up for by the excruciating tension that lasted the entire drive out to the ending point. Benny had to follow Rob there, which to Ami wasn't that big a deal considering Rob was the one who actually knew where they were going. The entire concept chafed at Benny's pride and rendered him practically unintelligible whenever he chose to try and speak. Any time Ami asked him something, he would respond with nothing more than grunts or sounds of irritation. Teddy seemed to find this hilarious and even Christy seemed amused by it for some reason, but Ami only felt building apprehension and constant annoyance at it.

She was sure it had something to do with her ditching him at their impromptu party last night, but the only thing he'd said about it was to ask where she'd gone. She said she'd wandered around for a while before coming back to the room and finding him passed out in bed. He grunted and moved on, focusing on loading up the vehicles, and that had been the end of it. Or at least she thought it was. If he had something to say, she wished he'd come out with it so they could get the argument over with. She didn't really want to have it out in front of Christy or Teddy, but it had to be better than this simmering silence he had adopted.

It was all she could do not to let out a cheer when Rob finally turned off the highway and onto an access road that cut up through the mountains before they reached the Pigeon River itself. She checked her watch and was surprised to see it wasn't even eleven o'clock yet. They'd set out around nine-thirty, stopped for gas, and actually gotten on the road for good around ten. If things kept up at this pace, they'd have time for a quick lunch from the cooler before loading up and setting out on the river. Based on what Rob told them, they'd be riding the rapids for around two or two and a half hours, then they should be able to get everything loaded up on Rob's truck, get changed, and be back at the hotel by dinnertime. She'd been planning to have her talk with Benny about ending things once they got back to Nashville sometime tomorrow, but if he kept up the attitude he was exhibiting so far today, she'd go ahead and do it tonight. If it went badly, Jay was twenty-five and had a credit card. She was fairly sure she could talk him into renting them a car and driving back tonight. It was only four hours or so, after all, and not getting home until after midnight was a small price to pay for her potential freedom. It also had the advantage of keeping her from spending one more night sharing a bed with Benny if she didn't have to.

She glanced over and found him hunched over the steering wheel, scowling at the truck in front of them. From what she could tell, Rob was being a considerate driver—putting on his turn signal well in advance of actually making the turns, not fully accelerating after turning until he was sure Benny was close enough behind him to see if he had to make another turn relatively quickly, and never going faster than he thought Benny would be comfortable with. Benny, on the other hand, seemed increasingly irate as they made their way deeper into the woods on the mountainside, though she was hard-pressed to say why. She knew he'd taken an almost instant disliking to their new friend, but so far, Rob had done absolutely nothing to warrant such hostility. She only hoped Benny kept his temper in check until they were finished with this run. If he flew off the handle before they even got started, she wouldn't be able to blame Rob for just getting back in his truck and leaving them all to their fates, potential guilt be damned.

Teddy snickered again from the back seat. When Ami turned her head to look at him, she found him staring intently at her, his smile so broad his teeth were showing.

"What's with you today?" she asked. "You've been giggly all morning."

"Not a thing," he replied, still smiling as he shook his head. "Just in a *great* mood."

Christy rolled her eyes and said nothing, only continued staring out the window at the passing scenery. Ami couldn't help but notice the hint of a smile on her face as well, but restrained herself from asking why. She didn't think the two of them cared for each other at all, but she supposed it was possible Teddy had convinced her to go along with one of his bullshit pranks somehow, and they were waiting for the chance to spring it on them.

Benny mumbled something into the steering wheel. Ami turned to face him again, her forehead crinkling.

"What was that?" she asked.

After a few moments of wondering whether he was even paying attention, he finally shook his head. "Nothing."

"Fine," she said, knowing how irritated her voice sounded but no longer able to hold it in. She turned to look out the windshield at the dust trails kicked up by Rob's back tires. "Don't talk to me then."

This time she caught what he said, mumbling or not.

"Maybe *that'll* make you happy."

She cut her eyes toward him again briefly, but he did not elaborate or even look her way, so she chose to ignore it. There would be plenty of time for them to get into it back at the hotel tonight. She'd made up her mind. She wasn't going to wait until they got home. She'd had all of the shit she was going to take from him in this lifetime, and their break-up was long past due. She'd make sure to ride back with Rob and Jay, and *dared* Benny to say anything about it when they got back.

Rob's truck slowed and she saw Eric's window go down on the passenger side an instant before his head popped out to look at the area along the side of the road. Curious, Ami looked as well. They were riding next to a fairly wide stretch of river. She hit the button and lowered her own window so she could get a better look.

They were practically surrounded by trees, making it shady enough to feel considerably cooler than it had when they set out this morning. The branches overlapped far above them, creating a natural canopy that felt like a tunnel with a very tall ceiling from the confines of the truck. When she tried to look through them to see the sky above, she found it was an impossible task. The foliage was much too dense for even the slightest sliver of sunlight to penetrate.

When she looked out across the river, though, she was able to see what a gorgeous day this had turned out to be, in spite of the storm clouds brewing inside the vehicle. The sunlight reflected off the surface of the water, glinting and shimmering with what looked to be a peaceful current. The sounds proved otherwise, however, as the rumbling of the water striking against the banks and rolling over the myriad rocks lining the river bottom was nearly loud enough to drown out the trucks' engines. If she focused hard enough, she could make out the sound of the tires crunching across the gravel and fallen branches that lined the road.

If the entire route they intended to take was like this, it wouldn't be nearly as bad as she feared. Then again, Rob had told her and Jay where they needed to put in was relatively calm compared to what awaited them farther along the run. Knowing this sent a chill racing along her back. It was almost as though the river itself were a living thing, a predator luring them with complacency before it struck and tried to claim them as its victims.

"Get the fuck off me," Christy said from the seat behind her.

Ami turned around to see Teddy leaning across the girl, his face pressed close to the window so he could see the river for himself. His smile was gone, a scowl firmly in its place.

"Oh, come on," he whined. "That doesn't look like shit. I thought this guy was supposed to be taking us somewhere *good.*"

"Roll down the window and listen," Ami told him. "It just looks like it's nothing."

"Better yet," Christy said. "*Get the fuck off of me!*"

Teddy ignored her and Ami briefly heard the whine of the window lowering before it, too, was lost in the roar of the water. Teddy's smile slowly began to return.

"Okay, okay," he said, nodding. "That's better. That sounds promising."

"What the hell is this shit now?" Benny asked.

When Ami looked back to the front, she saw Rob had turned on his hazard lights and had his door opened. While she watched, he stepped out, stretched, and then started walking back toward Benny's truck. Benny scowled as he slowed to a stop behind him and rolled down his window.

"Right in here somewhere is probably the best place to put in," Rob said, coming up alongside them. "There's not really anywhere to park other than on the side of the road, but there's usually no traffic, so we should be relatively safe. Did you see anyplace you can turn around once we come back this way so you can park on this side? Probably easier to unload that way, if we don't have to haul the raft across the road."

For a moment, Ami thought Benny was going to start arguing with him, but then he sighed and turned to look at what the conditions were on the side of the road. Finally, his eyes settled on a large open area in the trees maybe a hundred yards or so in front of Rob's truck. He pointed to it and turned back to Rob.

"I can turn around anywhere," he said. His voice was clipped and tight, but at least it wasn't outright hostile. "But that looks like the best place to get the raft to the water."

Rob looked where Benny was pointing and nodded. "Sounds good to me. Only other question is whether you want to do a six-, eight-, or ten-mile run on it. Six or eight would be best, and probably give you guys a good run without putting your lives at too much unneeded risk, but your friend Eric's pushing for the ten. It'll take longer, and it'll be harder on those last couple miles, but it's still doable."

"Then we do the ten-mile," Benny said without even bothering to consider it. "Unless you don't think you can hack it for ten miles."

To Rob's credit, the jab didn't even seem to rattle him in the slightest. He only shrugged and nodded. "Like I said, totally up to you. We'll go on ahead about ten miles and see if we can't find a good spot to get the raft back out. You want to go ahead and unload everyone here while we go on ahead, or . . .?"

"No sense dicking around too much," Benny said, cutting him off. "Let's park your heap and then get back here so we can get to it."

Again, Rob refused to rise to the bait. "You got it."

He turned and headed back to his truck, climbed in, and shut the door. There was no way to really tell, but Ami didn't think he slammed the door or anything, just closed it like he'd had the most pleasant conversation of the day instead of having to face down a near pissing match.

"Arrogant fucking prick," Benny muttered, his eyes locked on the other truck's front door.

Ami frowned. "What is wrong with you? He didn't do anything to come off that way."

Benny shot her a sneering look, shook his head, and shifted the truck back into gear. "You *would* take his side. In case you didn't notice, your new boyfriend there's been trying to set the terms of this whole excursion. I don't think he remembers that *we're* the ones paying *him*, so we set the rules."

Teddy snickered again from the back. Ami fought the urge to turn around and slap him. She considered pointing out if they'd gone to one of the places that offered guide services, they'd also be setting the terms of how the runs would go, but she bit her tongue. After all, she was here now, and even though she was still nervous about what they were planning to do, she might as well try to have fun while she was here. Starting a prequel to the argument they'd be having later was about as opposed to that as anything she could think of.

As they followed Rob deeper down the remote mountainside road, she wondered if there would be a way she might be able to "accidentally" bump into Benny on the raft and send him tumbling into the river. She didn't want him to get hurt, but the thought of him soaking wet in the cold water was enough to raise her spirits considerably. Maybe in the rescue attempt, Teddy and Christy could have similar mishaps as well. She could almost see them, shivering and turning blue while they tried to warm up the entire ride back to the hotel.

It was enough to make her smile for the first time all day.

FIVE

IN RETROSPECT, THINGS BEGAN TO go downhill right after Benny's antagonistic discussion about where to put the raft in, well before they were even underway. Ami wished she could somehow go back and warn herself about what was going to happen, but she knew that wasn't possible. For that matter, would she have even believed it if such a warning were possible? Looking back on it, she'd had some idea something would go wrong, but said or did nothing different from what she was already planning to do. She wouldn't ever come to think it couldn't have been avoided, but she could at least content herself with the knowledge nothing *she* could have done would have prevented it.

Things went pretty smoothly when dropping off Rob's truck and heading back to their planned starting point. The only real hiccup had come when Benny couldn't find it again. Luckily, Rob had marked down the GPS coordinates on one of his maps, so he was able to guide them right to it. Benny followed the instructions without comment or complaint, but Ami had not been able to ignore how his lips were pressed together so hard they were turning white. On the outside, he remained silent. On the inside, however, he was ready to explode.

After a quick U-turn in the middle of the road that made Ami's breath catch in her throat when she saw the front end of the truck barely whisper past a massive tree trunk, Benny pulled off onto the shoulder on the opposite side and slammed the gearshift into park. Ami wanted to tell him to act his age, but she bit her tongue. She glanced into the back seat briefly before opening her door to get out and saw Rob staring at the back of Benny's head with a perfectly calm, tranquil expression on his face. She had no idea what he might be thinking, but she was fairly certain he'd picked up on the aggression radiating from the other man. Thankfully, he chose to ignore it rather than comment or act on it.

Eric and Christy were already working on the ropes securing the raft to the luggage rack by the time she stepped out, shutting the door gently behind her. She heard the soft crunch of gravel behind her and turned to see Jay standing almost directly at her back. She jumped a bit in spite of herself, and then laughed.

"I'm getting you a bell," she said. "Maybe then you won't be able to sneak up on me like that."

He smiled back. "Wouldn't work. I'd hold onto it and muffle the sound. Besides, I don't think I'd look good in bells."

"Really?" Teddy asked. Ami looked over her shoulder and found him paused in the midst of getting out of the truck as well, one foot on the ground, his eyes sparkling. "I know of this club downtown where you could find out for sure. I bet they'd all be shaved and smooth, too."

Ami rolled her eyes as Jay sighed.

"*Bells*," he said, making sure to enunciate the word carefully. "Not balls, *bells*. Wouldn't want to intrude on your private life any."

"Weak," Teddy said, chuckling to himself as he climbed the rest of the way out of the truck. "Work on your comebacks, then we'll try again."

Jay shook his head and stepped onto the truck's running board so he could start untying the front of the raft. "I'm not trying to match wits with you, Teddy. I never fight someone at that much of a disadvantage to me."

"Better," Teddy replied, heading in the direction of the thick tree line along the riverbank. "Still weak, but better."

"Where do you think you're going?" Ami asked. "We've got a raft and supplies to unload, remember?"

He didn't bother to turn back around. "In case you didn't notice, that road was bumpy as a corn-eater's shit, and I've been holding it since we hit North Carolina. So unless you want me to whip it out and let it fly right here by the truck, I'm going over here for a minute."

"Classy motherfucker, isn't he?" Jay muttered. "Just think: that's what I get to share a room with while we're on this trip."

"I can see why you were avoiding your room last night, then," Ami said. "I'm going to unload the supplies since it looks like you guys have a handle on the raft."

Jay nodded and went back to working on the tangle of a knot at his corner. As she passed Eric on her way to the back of the truck, Ami couldn't help but notice how precariously he was balanced on the back tire, one knee pressed against the side of the truck for support while he undid the loops of cord holding the raft down. She thought about poking him in the side gently to see if he would fall, but that would be mean. Eric hadn't ever done anything to her, not even anything to make her dislike him nearly as much as she had grown to dislike Benny. She briefly wondered if things might've worked out differently had he been the one to ask her out instead of Benny, but she pushed the thoughts away. Done was done, and the last thing she wanted was to end up asking "what-if" questions about her asshole soon-to-be-ex-boyfriend's best friend.

When she got to the back, she found Rob already there, unloading his assorted supplies and organizing them so they could be carried along on the raft with minimal space. He glanced up as she approached and offered her the hint of a smile.

"Hey, I'm sorry about that earlier," she said, glancing around to make sure Benny was nowhere he could easily overhear her. "I don't know what got into him, he's just . . ."

"He's jealous," Rob said. There was no anger, no accusation in his voice, only the simple statement of a fact he believed was self-evident. "I get it. No harm, no foul. It's cool."

"No, it really isn't," Ami replied. "He should know better than to think I'm going to do anything with anybody while he and I are together."

"That sentence is so loaded with things I could comment on," Rob said, his smile growing wider. "But moving past all that, usually when a guy gets as jealous as he acts, it has more to do with him than it does the person he's feeling the jealousy over. I might say more, but it's really not any of my business. Besides, you seem like a smart chick. I'm willing to bet you already knew what I just told you, and you can probably think of everything else I'd have to say on the matter, so let's just let it go and have fun. Deal?"

While it wasn't enough to make her forget how Benny acted and forgive him for it, at least the mature way Rob was handling being on the receiving end of it made her willing to relax.

"Deal," she said. She reached past him and started pulling their travel bags out and stacking them neatly alongside the truck. She looked around, her forehead scrunching up. "So, strange question: there wouldn't happen to be any place around here for us to change, would there?"

"Afraid not," Rob said. "I'd say your best bet is to find a secluded stretch of trees and hope the wind doesn't pick up."

She frowned at him. "The trees part I get, but why worry about the wind?"

At that moment, a strong breeze gusted down the enclosed roadway, causing goose bumps to rise along her exposed arms as the chill from it enveloped her. The weather said the temperatures today were supposed to be in the mid-sixties, but it obviously had not taken their altitude into consideration, nor did it factor in the temperature of the wind itself. She shuddered and rubbed at her arms until they felt somewhat warmer again. Rob laughed.

"My advice?" he asked. "Change fast."

"No kidding," she replied. "So much for this being a good weekend for this."

"Ah, it's not so bad," Rob said, looking out toward the river. "It's always cooler near the water than it is on it. The sun'll end up reflecting off it, so you'll get it from two directions. Plus, we're in the shade here, remember? And pretty far up into the mountains, not to mention enclosed on all sides by more rocks and trees. Once we're on the water and moving, it won't be so bad."

"Unless somebody falls in," Christy said. She circled around them on her way to the other side of the truck. When Ami looked up, she saw the raft was undone on the side she'd been on, and had canted to the other side at a sharp angle. "That water probably feels like it's been in the deep freeze for a while."

"There is that," Rob agreed. "In the spring or the fall it probably wouldn't be so bad, but right now, when the current's faster because of runoff from melting snow and ice? Yeah, it's about fifteen to twenty degrees colder than average."

Ami frowned. "So what happens if we fall in? Isn't that the perfect setup for hypothermia?"

Rob shrugged. "It can be. Just get to shore as quick as you can and stay in the sunlight until we can get to the bank and come back for you. I've got one of those foil blankets that fold up to damn near wallet-sized in my pack. As long as we can get you covered up with that pretty soon, it'll help keep the cold from getting to you. You'd mostly be okay without it, since the only thing that's really cold right now is that wind. About the worst you can expect is a bad sinus infection or something like that. Might not be pleasant, but at least it won't kill you."

The loud thump of the raft hitting the ground cut off any response Ami might have come up with. Eric stepped back, brushing dust off his hands as he ambled over to them.

"Okay, mister guide, sir," he said, smiling to show he wasn't trying to be overtly offensive. "What say we get this thing in the water while the gals get changed, then they can watch it while we do?"

"I'd rather change with the 'gals'," Teddy said, snickering. Ami hadn't even noticed him returning. She wondered briefly if he'd urinated into the river where they were planning to put the raft in. "Probably a much better view than changing with you fags."

"Dream on, shit-for-brains," Benny said as he joined the group. "That is, unless you've been hiding it, you've got the same equipment as they do."

"Oh, my equipment's so much more impressive," Teddy replied, still smiling. "But yeah, might be a bad idea. I'd hate to drive them both so mad with lust they couldn't concentrate on anything else for the rest of the day."

"I don't think you've got anything to worry about," Christy said, her mouth twisted into a disgusted sneer. "I'm not into bestiality."

"Oh, right!" Teddy exclaimed, turning to her. "That's every guy you've ever been with!"

Christy rolled her eyes, picked up her pack from the pile Ami made, and headed for the other side of the truck. "I catch you peeping, Teddy, and you're not going to like the result."

"He won't," Eric assured her. "He's going to be too busy carrying a raft."

Teddy turned toward him, more than likely with a witty retort on his lips, but when Benny dropped a stack of oars and life jackets into his arms, his smile faded quickly.

"Little warning would be nice," he mumbled.

"So would knowing when to stop," Benny replied. He fixed Teddy with a pointed stare and moved to pick up his corner of the raft. "Grab on, let's give them some privacy."

Eric already had his corner propped on his shoulder as he waited for the rest. Jay took the corner on the opposite side, diagonal from Eric. Rob stepped in behind him, leaving Benny to catch the other corner on the same side as Eric. Once they were all in position, they started down the gentle slope to the river. Teddy rushed to catch up with them. Ami frowned when she saw him pass Eric by so he could walk next to Benny, that mischievous smile back on his face.

From the way Benny leaned toward him as they walked, it was obvious Teddy was telling him something. They were already too far away for Ami to hear what exactly was said, especially with the overwhelming sound of the river rushing by them, so she grabbed her own pack and opened the front door so she could climb in and get changed.

She could not help but look at Christy as she did, and paused when she saw what the other girl was changing into.

Ami had done some research online and packed an outfit she thought most appropriate for what they were doing. She wore sturdy sandals that fastened both across the top of her feet and around her ankles so they wouldn't come off. Her pack contained a pair of spandex yoga pants, a thick wool shirt long enough to hang over them, and a wool cap to keep her head warm. She would've preferred to have a waterproof nylon suit to wear over it, but since they weren't going through one of the established agencies like they planned, she didn't have one. It wasn't ideal, but at least it would help keep her relatively warm during the ride.

Christy had not thought ahead, it appeared. If she had, she elected to go for fashion over function. She had changed into a pair of shorts that hugged her thighs like a second skin and a white t-shirt that would end up being translucent after only a couple of minutes on the water. Ami didn't see a hat or anything else that would keep her head warm. In truth, there was nothing about her outfit that made any sense.

"What?" Christy asked. Ami felt her face grow warm when she realized the girl had caught her staring. "See something you like?"

"I'm sorry," Ami said as she turned away, shaking her head. "It's just . . . aren't you going to be cold in that?"

"I've got my swimsuit on underneath it," Christy replied. Her tone was a little snotty, but Ami tried to ignore it. "Besides, I normally run hot. I've been roasting on all the other runs we did."

Either she didn't stop to consider those runs were in either spring or summer, or she had considered it and didn't see much difference. Whichever it was, Ami saw nothing to gain by arguing with her about it now. Christy wasn't her responsibility. If she wanted to go out as she was, Ami had no right to question her about it.

"Okay," she said. "Wear what you're going to be comfortable in, I guess."

"Thanks for the permission," Christy said, throwing open her door and climbing out. "I think I will."

Ami shook her head and changed as quickly as she could, wondering for what felt like the hundredth time this trip why she'd bothered coming along with a group of people that obviously didn't care much for her. She knew the answer, of course. She was here because Benny was here, and since the trip was planned and the rooms reserved before she realized she didn't want to be with him anymore, she stood to lose a lot of money if she backed out. Besides, Jay had wanted to come since he knew Christy would be here, and if she backed out, he wouldn't have been very welcome either.

At least she had him to talk to, and Eric when he wasn't being molested by Christy. It didn't hurt they'd picked up Rob along the way, either. He seemed nice enough and could carry on an intelligent conversation. Things could be much, much worse.

When she finally made it down to the riverbank along with the rest of the group, it was immediately clear something in the dynamic had changed, even if she couldn't place exactly what it was. Eric was talking to Rob, both of them looking off down the river in the direction they'd be heading shortly. Jay was standing with his hands in his pockets, frowning as he watched Teddy whispering furtively to Christy about something. The girl was smiling, her face animated and excited. Benny was sitting on the ground with his knees up, forearms resting casually atop them, looking at nothing in particular.

That caught her attention more than the others, even more than the strange sight of Teddy and Christy appearing to get along. Normally when she walked up on them without Benny, his gaze immediately shot to her, as though he wanted to verify how fast she was walking, how far away she was compared to everyone else, and whether or not she was looking at anyone other than him. That he wasn't doing that this time was different, and that made her wonder again what Teddy said to him as they carried the raft down to the river. It was likely more of his smart-assery, and Benny was still moping about the confrontation with Rob earlier. She considered asking him, but actually found his silence and lack of attention to her refreshing, so she kept quiet.

When Eric turned and saw her, he smiled. "All right! Now the rest of us can change, grab some munchies, and get on the water!"

He started up the incline toward the truck, his smile widening as he passed her. She could not help but smile back at him. He was always in such a cheery mood, and that managed to improve the disposition of anybody around him. She only wished it would work on Christy and Benny more.

Benny got to his feet, brushed off the seat of his pants, and slowly started after Eric. Not once during that process did he ever look in Ami's direction. She frowned, some part of her that once cared about him was concerned something serious was wrong with him. As he passed, she put a gentle hand on his arm and stopped him.

"Are you okay?" she asked. "You're not acting like yourself."

"Fine," he grumbled. He didn't yank his arm away, but he did shift so she wasn't touching him anymore. "Everything's wonderful."

He opened his mouth as if he was about to say something else, closed it, shook his head, and followed Eric up to the truck. Ami frowned as she watched him go.

"Something very weird is going on," Jay said as he came up alongside her. "You feel it?"

"Yeah," she replied, her eyes still on Benny's retreating back. "You know what that's all about?"

"Not a clue, but keep your eyes open. I think Teddy's planning some bullshit."

No sooner than the words left his mouth, Teddy jogged past them. He didn't seem to have overheard them, and the goofy grin was still firmly in place on his lips. Jay gave her a look as if to prove his point, then headed up as well.

Ami shook her head and turned to head down to the raft. Christy was leaning against it, stretching out so her belly was smaller but her boobs looked bigger and her legs longer. It was a model's pose from someone that had no business modeling. Ami sighed and turned to see Rob sitting on the riverbank, tucking his jeans into what she could only assume was a dry bag. She wasn't the least bit surprised to see he appeared to be wearing a neoprene wetsuit underneath.

"Looks like you thought ahead," she said.

He smiled. "Always do. Picked one of these up after the second or third run I did with my friends. Thing's been a lifesaver. If you plan on doing this often, I highly recommend one."

He pulled off his hoodie and traded it for a warm-looking fleece jacket. He capped the ensemble by planting a wool beanie atop his head and fastening a rubber cord to the ends of his sunglasses before putting them back on and tightening the cord down. Ami couldn't help it—she burst out laughing.

He smiled wider and spread his arms, twisting from side to side at the waist. "Sexy, huh? May not look like much, but it keeps me warm on the water, and that's all I care about."

"You look like you stepped out of an outdoor sports catalog," Ami said, still giggling.

"See?" he replied. "I *told* Dad I'd be a good model one day."

Even Christy snickered at that. Ami turned to see her looking at Rob askance over her shoulder. "I wouldn't quit your day job."

He sighed and nodded. "Yeah, best not."

He went back to tucking his things away into the dry bag and fastening it to one of the plastic loops on the top edge of the raft, up near the front. Something about that simple act sent a chill down Ami's back. It was concrete evidence they really were about to do this. They were about to take a run down the river on a raft, in the middle of winter, on what for all but one of them would be their first attempt without an experienced guide at the helm. Even with Rob's reassurances of taking the easier route, she felt her nervousness coming back stronger than before. When she added in whatever else was going on, she ended up with a very bad feeling about this entire idea.

It was too late to back out now, though. If she did, she was going to be stuck here all alone for God only knew how long until they all made it back. Even discounting that, Rob was counting on her and Jay to help him keep everyone on the safest path to the other truck. She couldn't leave now and let him down.

When the others arrived, it was definitely too late. It took no time at all for them to get the raft on the water and load up into it. Rob fastened his life jacket and turned around to give them all one final look before they set off.

"Everybody ready?" he called.

The answer was a resounding "yes" from everyone but Ami and Jay, who only gave each other nearly identical looks of apprehension. Rob smiled, nodded, and turned to face the front of the raft.

"Then let's do this! Oars on my left, push us off."

He led by example, putting the flat of his own oar against the shallow bottom and leaning against it. Teddy, Benny, and Christy all followed suit. In seconds, they were off. A moment or so later, the current picked them up and they gained speed until they were nearly racing down the river at what felt to Ami like breakneck speed.

Deep down, she thought it felt like they were racing to their deaths.

SIX

AFTER SHE MANAGED TO GET over the initial burst of fear, Ami actually managed to calm down and start to enjoy herself. The rapids were nowhere near as bad as she expected them to be from the sound of the river back at their starting point. They were tough enough they had to exert themselves some, but it wasn't even as constant a fight as the class four rapids they'd done during the summer. She knew, based on what Rob told her last night, things would get harder, but for now, she was actually having fun.

Even Rob seemed to lose some of his apprehension as the run went on, no longer spending most of his time overseeing what they were doing, but actually turning to face the front and simply calling out commands or warnings over his shoulder when needed. Even Benny seemed relaxed and followed direction without argument, dipping his oar into the water along with Christy and Teddy to help steer them.

By her estimation, they'd gone about a mile downstream by the time Rob turned around to address them.

"Okay, folks," he called, "here's the deal. About a half a mile further down, we're going to come to a fork in the river. We need to stay left or we're going to overshoot our end point and have a hell of a time getting back to it. About the same time we hit that, the run's going to get rougher, so keep doing what you've been doing and we'll be through it safely in no time.

Sound good?"

"Let's do it," Eric said, smiling. Jay nodded his agreement, a rare smile on his face as well.

"You're the boss," Ami replied. Rob smiled at her enthusiasm.

She looked over to the other three and felt her smile fade. Teddy had that sly grin back on his face as he nodded, which was nothing too surprising. Christy was smiling, too, but something about it felt utterly and completely fake to Ami. But they were nothing compared to Benny. He was starting straight at Rob, his face impassive other than a tight grin. It was his eyes that bothered her. They were filled with so much hatred that, for a moment, Ami thought he was going to crack Rob over the head with the oar and knock him out of the raft. It was only when Rob nodded and turned to face the front she realized Benny wouldn't actually do something so malicious, but the way he kept staring at the back of Rob's head cut deeply into the good mood she'd begun to foster.

Something was up, something she was not going to be able to prevent, and they had no way to back out now. All she could do was hope whenever this plan went into motion, she would be able to mitigate some of the ensuing damage. She fought back the urge to sigh, not wanting to catch a lungful of the spray buffeting them from the raft's rocking motion across the river.

It didn't take long before that spray picked up, as did the bouncing motions of the raft. Ami leaned to the side, not enough to unbalance her, but enough that she could see past Eric to where the fork was coming into view ahead of them. As she watched, it seemed to be drifting more and more toward the center of the raft, then past the centerline. They were drifting off-course.

"Steer slight left," Rob called out.

Ami dropped her oar into the water and began pushing against it as hard as she could, trying to adjust their course a bit. She could see Eric doing the same and knew Jay must be matching them from behind her, but they were still drifting toward the wrong fork. Her heartbeat sped up as she realized the potential danger in store for them if Rob's warnings last night had been accurate and they couldn't change course.

"Hard left!" Rob yelled. He turned, and Ami thought she saw his face go slightly pale as his eyes came to rest on the three on the opposite side of the raft. "What the hell are you doing?"

She felt her breath catch in her throat when she looked over and saw Benny, Christy, and Teddy paddling for all they were worth, pushing so hard with their oars their muscles stood out in cords. She couldn't tell if the moisture on Benny's face was from the spray or sweat from how hard he was exerting himself to push them into the wrong fork.

This was their plan all along, she realized. Get out here far enough no one could stop them, and then do exactly the opposite of what Rob told them to do. It was a show of defiance, a way to try and soothe the anger and frustration Benny was feeling toward the older man. Ami had no idea why Teddy and Christy were going along with it, though. As far as she knew, Rob had done nothing to offend either of them.

Benny glanced over at her. When their eyes locked, his smile grew wider, and he gave one more massive push against the water with his oar. Ami thought she could hear it creak even over the increasing noise from the river rolling across rocks and other flotsam sticking up from the bottom.

It must have been enough. The raft gave a massive lurch and suddenly they were moving much faster than they already had been. They'd passed the crosscurrent; they were heading down the wrong fork. The more dangerous one.

The one Rob said he didn't think they could survive.

If she'd ever needed validation Benny was an idiot, she had it now. He'd let his jealousy and anger override common sense to the point he might not even live long enough to feel anything from the act. Tragic enough if it were only him at risk, but he'd chosen to take the rest of them with him. That killed any chance at sympathy he might've had. If they died now, he was the one responsible for it.

"*Fuck!*" Rob screamed, scrambling to grab an oar from beside his feet to try and fight right along with them.

Ami looked up and saw nothing ahead of her but roiling white froth as the river fought to rush over massive rocks and changes in contour and elevation. Her mind railed at the sight, trying to convince her she needed to curl up into a ball and pray for this to be nothing but a bad dream. She knew that wouldn't help and fought the urge, gritting her teeth and gripping her oar tightly in both hands, preparing to fight for her life against a force powered by nature itself and intent on resisting any attempts to control it.

The raft hit the first of those turbulent pools and leapt out of the water, shoved by the force of the current and the unyielding hardness of the rock ahead of them. She tried not to tense, the way she'd been taught way back on the first run she'd ever been on, but it was hard to make her body cooperate. Adrenaline was the only thing keeping her going, but it also made her muscles tight and refused to let go.

She had no idea how long they were airborne, but it couldn't have been very long. Things had started to slow in her mind, her brain's response to the imminent danger. Finally, they landed with a massive splash that threw water over the edge of the raft and drenched both her and Eric. She felt something slap her across the arm hard enough to make her fingers tingle. She spared a glance to the side and saw the cords they'd used to lash the bags to the bottom of the raft had snapped and were flapping wildly between them.

No sooner than she looked back, the raft slammed sideways as the back end collided with another submerged boulder. She heard someone behind her cry out and thought it sounded like Teddy. She didn't bother to look—she couldn't afford to.

The raft went airborne again as it crossed over a drop-off nearly hidden by the froth all the displaced water generated. It seemed to take even longer for them to land this time, and the impact was considerably more forceful than the first had been. She felt herself shoved against the side of the raft as the center bulged from the massive boulder they found themselves atop. Had the current been slower, surely they would have stopped, but instead they were shoved relentlessly onward.

The impact threw the bags in every direction. One flew between her and Eric, missing the side of her face by inches and slamming against the back of Eric's head before it spun off into the waves. Instinctively, Eric dropped his oar to reach up and grab his head. The wooden paddle did not sink when it hit the water, nor did it merely float away. Their momentum was too great for that. Instead, it *bounced* off the surface of the river and spun away over the top of her head. She heard a sick thud followed by a heavy splash and the sound of Christy screaming.

This time, Ami did spare a glance behind her. Christy was

twisted at the waist, her own oar missing as she held onto Teddy's legs for dear life. Teddy appeared to have been the one to take the brunt of Eric's oar and was hanging over the back of the raft. From this angle, Ami could not see his head and, for a moment, thought it had been knocked clean off his shoulders. There was no bright red spray in their wake, so she knew this wasn't true, but the illusion was almost enough to send her into a screaming fit right alongside Christy.

As she turned back to the front again, her eyes fell on Benny. His smile was gone, his face grave as he struggled to keep the raft oriented. She hoped he was getting everything from this prank he'd hoped for, and then some. If they lived, she was going to kill him for this.

"Rob!" she screamed. She had no way to know if he'd heard her or not, since he never looked around, only kept fighting against the rapids with his oar. "Down two on the left, one on the right!"

Apparently, he did hear her, for he immediately shifted himself to the left and rammed his oar down on that side. It didn't last long, however, as moments later he threw himself to the right hard enough to nearly send himself head-first into the river. Ami saw part of an oar spinning out in front of them like a stone someone had skipped across the surface of a pond. It was the strangest thing she'd ever seen and managed to be one of the most terrifying as well. Once Rob recovered, she saw his oar was intact.

Her eyes went back to Benny, staring at the broken shaft of his oar, the look on his face one of utter bewilderment. Had the circumstances been different, it would have been comical. As it was, it was only one more thing to add to her list of horrifying developments.

She noticed the trees on that side were no longer the blur of brown and green they had been, but were starting to look more like rapids themselves. At first, she thought they were finally coming out of the fork and into a wider river where they might be able to navigate somewhat, even being down four people, but then she understood what was happening and felt her blood turn to ice.

With no one on the left side to orient them, the raft was being driven sideways. That meant there was more surface area to try and resist the obstacles before them. There were many times where this would be a good thing; running whitewater rapids was not one of them. More resistance with all that force behind them meant an exceptionally higher risk of capsizing. If that happened, they were dead.

She acted without thinking, throwing herself into the space between Christy and Benny. She shoved her oar in and turned it backward, trying to stop their momentum. She was dimly aware of Rob in her peripheral vision, fighting the same battle from the front of the raft. Jay had managed to stay in place behind her original spot, his eyes wide, fighting for everything he was worth. She hadn't been to church since she left home for college, but she still believed, and found herself praying more fervently than any time she could remember for God to not punish her and Eric and Jay and even Rob because three of their friends had decided to act foolishly.

Either He heard her or the three of them had managed to get some semblance of balance back to this insane course they were on because the raft began angling back toward center again. She could also see they were oriented toward the bank on their right side now. That had to be Rob's doing, acting as their guide to the last, trying to get them to the safety of the shore before they ended up dead. She could hear the increased roar ahead of them and knew what it meant. Their time was exceptionally short now. If they hit the upcoming drop with only three of them to try and control things, they would capsize at the very least and probably end up with their bodies shattered against the rocks at the bottom.

That would be even worse than she cared to imagine since the impact stood every chance of not killing them outright but merely forcing them to feel the agony of their bones being pulverized before the current pulled them under and forced water down their lungs. She could not conceive of a worse way to go.

But the bank was in sight, and it slowly, inexorably, grew closer with each passing second. She finally allowed herself to feel the first sparks of hope, and then they hit another rock.

Similar to the first one they'd encountered, this one sent them airborne yet again. This time, however, she was not braced when they landed. The raft hit, and she felt a massive hand pushing at her bottom and the small of her back, driving her up, up, out of the raft. She felt the sensation of flight and wondered if it was the same for birds before tumbling and seeing the back of the raft ahead of her. That she did not appear to be the only one who was in such a predicament was little consolation.

Her butt hit the water first, sending a blast of nearly ice-cold water shooting through her tights. Thankfully, it hadn't given her a full-scale enema, but she was certain when her body was eventually found, the coroner would be rather amused by the immense bruise sure to form there. She tried to prepare herself for what was about to happen by taking as deep a breath as her short time would allow, but the force of the impact when her back hit the water drove it right out of her lungs. She tried to draw another one but found it nearly impossible at first. By the time she was able to successfully inhale, her head was already drifting beneath the surface.

The water felt cold when she first hit, but that hadn't prepared her for the feeling of it on her bare skin. She remembered being a kid, maybe no older than six or seven. The pond behind their house had frozen over during the winter, and she and her brother had decided to go ice skating before school one morning. Neither of them was old enough to realize the pond hadn't frozen solid, that it was only a relatively thin layer on the top of the water. Naturally, it had given way under their combined weight and sent them both splashing into the freezing depths. Luckily for them, it had only been about three feet at its deepest point, so only their legs and feet suffered any real damage. Unlucky for her, she was wearing a skirt that day, so her legs were bare when they were submerged. She remembered how red they'd turned and how badly they'd ached for the rest of the day and part of the next. She remembered how upset her mother had been. Not that they'd ruined their school clothes, but at the risk they'd taken of permanent damage to themselves from potential frostbite.

The water that closed over her face felt much the same as what had been in that pond so many years ago, only this time it was so much worse because she could feel it forcing itself up her nose and into her ears. Then the back of her head slammed against one of the rocks hidden by the rapids, and her thoughts went hazy and indistinct. She briefly felt a hand around her wrist, heard liquid voices, and saw motion and brightness. Then all sensations ceased and the world went black for a while.

SEVEN

HER HEAD WAS POUNDING. ON the one hand, that was a very good thing; a sign she was not dead and had somehow managed to survive whatever happened once she went airborne. On the other hand, her head was *pounding*. Over the course of her life, Ami had experienced headaches from hangovers, lack of food, lack of sleep, allergies and sinus issues, and about anything else that could possibly cause her head to hurt. Thanks to a bizarre incident involving her brother and the mantle over the fireplace in her parents' house, she even knew what it felt like to have a full-blown concussion. But somehow, the pain she now experienced made all those other times feel like they'd been nothing more than practice runs for the main event.

She kept her eyes closed, hoping the pain would subside before she opened them and risked a blast of bright sunlight that would only make matters worse, and took stock of the situation. She was cold, not quite freezing but not too terribly far off from it. She was still wet, though she could feel dry ground beneath her, which was a good sign. Aside from the pain emanating from the back of her head, she didn't really feel anything else that seemed to be a cause for worry—a few deep aches and sharp twinges, reflective of areas that had either already developed bruises or were about to, and assorted scrapes and scratches. No bones felt broken, and when she tried, she could wiggle all her fingers and toes, so there was no spinal cord injury as far as she could tell. All in all, she felt she was pretty damned lucky to have survived with nothing more severe than a seriously aching head.

Of course, the way her luck had been running, there was every possibility her skull was fractured and slowly but surely allowing her brain to become more and more damaged. She didn't think so, but without being checked out at a hospital, there was no real way to be sure.

Satisfied her list of injuries wasn't very extensive, she focused her attention to the world around her, still not opening her eyes, and relying on her other senses to paint a picture of what she would see when she finally did open them. A breeze was blowing, but it wasn't strong. She heard other people not far away, too. No voices, as it didn't sound like anyone was speaking, but assorted quiet groans and heavy breathing surrounded her. She wasn't the only one who made it. Again, a very good sign.

Unable to put it off any longer, Ami turned her head to the side and opened her eyes. Through the tall grass and bare patches of dirt, she was able to make out the edge of the river maybe ten yards away. The sound of its mad rush was muted, though from distance or something she hadn't immediately identified as being wrong with her, she didn't know. She saw something move closer to her and focused on it.

It was a bare foot with bright red toenails covered with drying mud. She didn't need to look up any farther to know it was Christy, the only other person in their group she could imagine painting their nails at all, much less in such a garish shade. She felt a small rush of relief run through her. As much as she disliked the other girl, and as sure as she was the feeling was mutual, she didn't want any real harm to come to her.

Curious who else might have made it, Ami propped herself up on her elbows, wincing as the movement sent new waves of agony coursing through her head. Her vision swam and she closed her eyes again tightly, hoping to stave off any potential nausea that might result from dizziness. She focused on her breathing, drawing in as deeply as she could through her nose, holding it for a ten-count, and releasing it slowly through her clenched teeth. Finally, the pain subsided back to its previous level and she opened her eyes again.

Jay lay on the ground at her feet, one arm thrown up to cover his eyes. Blood caked the side of his face, but Ami had no way to tell whether or not it was from an injury he'd sustained himself or from someone else. She focused her gaze on his chest and was rewarded with the sight of it rising and falling regularly. He was alive, and she hoped he wasn't hurt too badly.

Another sharp blast of pain radiated from the back of her head, making her wince. That only made it intensify, of course. She shifted her weight to one arm, lifting the other and placing a hand gingerly against the spot the pain seemed to be coming from. She hissed out a breath as her probing fingers touched the massive knot raised on the back of her head and made the pain so bad, for a moment, she thought she was about to pass out again. She jerked her hand away, then forced herself to touch it again, even more gently, before bringing her fingers around where she could see them. There was a little blood but nowhere near as much as she expected to find. She hoped that meant her skull *wasn't* fractured. A goose egg she could deal with, potential brain damage was something else entirely.

She heard the sound of footsteps approaching rapidly and fought the urge to turn and look, knowing it would only make the pain worse. Finally, she saw Rob's face appear in front of hers, filled with concern.

"Hey, take it easy," he said, hands held out toward her, ready to grab her if she looked like she was about to collapse again. "Go slow. You had one of the nastier landings out of all of us."

She offered him what she hoped was a reassuring smile, but his expression never changed. "What happened?"

"To you, or to all of us?"

"Let's start with me," she said, not liking the tone of his voice when he made the distinction.

"That last drop," he explained. "You went overboard. When you went under, your head hit a rock. Big son of a bitch, maybe three feet across. If you hadn't hit butt-first and slowed your momentum, I think you'd be having this conversation with Saint Peter right about now."

"You saw me hit?"

He nodded. "Right before I went under, too. With the weight all shifted around, the raft capsized right after it landed. Didn't even make it another five feet down the river. Everybody went in. Me and your friend Jay managed to grab hold of some rocks and get those of you we could to the bank. Thank Christ we got thrown closer when we hit that last drop. If we hadn't, I doubt we'd have had the strength to make it."

Her blood went cold at part of what he'd said. She forced herself to look up and meet his eyes.

"Those of us you could," she repeated. "Meaning you couldn't get everyone."

His face went grim, his lips tightening so much they began to turn white. Finally, he nodded.

"Who?" she asked, heart racing. "Who didn't make it?"

"Just rest for now," he said. "We can talk about everything once you've recovered a little more."

"Who?" she insisted, holding his eyes with her own. "Tell me!"

Rob sighed and closed his eyes, unable to keep looking at her.

"Your boyfriend," he said at last. "The other one, the one who couldn't stop talking. Teddy, I think."

"Oh my God," she whispered. The pain returned when she dropped her head into her hands, but she was so numb from the shock of what Rob said she barely even noticed. She'd been pissed at Benny, ready to break up with him for sure, but he didn't deserve this. She tried to tell herself he'd been the one who had put their lives at risk in the first place, but even considering that, he didn't deserve to die when so many of the rest of them lived. "I can't believe they're dead."

"We don't know that," Rob said, his hands held up as if to ward off the thought. "There's every possibility they made it to shore somewhere else downriver of us."

She forced herself to look back up at him.

"Is that really likely though? You're the one who said the fork we went down was almost certain death."

She heard a long, racking sob and looked over to see Christy watching them, her face contorted into a look of utter misery. Ami had forgotten she was there, but was suddenly reminded she wasn't the only one here who was facing the possibility two of her friends were dead. Ami never realized Christy cared that much about any of them, and it warmed her heart some to see she was wrong about that. Of course, it could be the other girl was merely terrified for herself, at how close she'd come to dying, but for now Ami decided to give her the benefit of the doubt.

Rob sighed. "I really don't know. I think things were starting to ease up after that last hit, but it's not like I had the chance to scope it out before I was scrambling for anything I could get ahold of. If it did ease up, then yes, there's a chance they're still alive, too."

Ami nodded and immediately regretted it as it sent more pain crashing through her. She bit her lip until it subsided, then let out a long breath. "Some chance is better than no chance, I guess."

"Exactly," Rob agreed.

"Tell her the rest of it," Jay said. He still hadn't moved from where he lay at her feet, but it was obvious he was awake and listening to the entire conversation. "Tell them both. They need to hear it."

Rob shot an annoyed look at Jay. "I thought we agreed to wait until everyone was awake. Eric's still unconscious."

"And might never wake up," Jay added. "You didn't see that oar hit him. I did. Combine that with whatever he might've hit when he went in the water, and there's a good chance he's not just unconscious, but actually in a fucking *coma*, so I don't think he's going to mind too much that everyone else knows what's going on before he does."

"Jay!" Ami cried, shocked at how callous he sounded. "That's one of your friends you're talking about!"

He sat up then, his arm dropping to his side as he turned to look at her, his face incredulous. "One of *my* friends? No he wasn't. He was *your* friend. I barely ever spoke more than ten words to him since I met him. I'll admit he was the least annoying of the group, not counting you, but I wouldn't go so far as to say he was my *friend*. No, my only friend here is you. And if you think that's being cruel, I'd like to point out that *my friend* is the one who invited me along on this godforsaken trip in the first place, and without whom, I'd be safe and sound on my couch at home instead of lost in the fucking woods in the middle of the goddamned mountains!"

Ami's mouth dropped open, stunned at the outburst. In all the years she'd known Jay, he had never acted like this. She had no idea what could be so bad that it would make him do so now.

She heard Christy make a sound like a teakettle reaching the boiling point and looked over. The girl had her hands balled up into fists and was pushing them into the sides of her mouth, stretching her lips into a rictus of agonized terror. Ami had no idea if she knew what Rob was talking about or not, but if she did, it was obviously not good to react like that at the mere mention of it.

Rob jumped to his feet and rounded on Jay. "That's enough! We've got enough shit to worry about without trying to lay blame for anything right now, wouldn't you say? So how about instead of lying there bitching about everything, why don't you shut the hell up unless you've got something constructive to add to the situation."

Jay was on his own feet so fast Ami couldn't be sure she even saw him move.

"And exactly who the fuck died and made you the fucking general?" he asked, not quite nose-to-nose with Rob, but not that far from it, either. "You're the asshat that said we'd be fine, if I recall. 'It'll be safe enough,' you said. 'As long as I've got you two to help me, we can do this,' you said. All a bunch of fucking horseshit. We listened to you, now we're fucked, and you think we're going to *keep* listening to you? Smoke another one if that makes sense, you fucking washed up hippie."

"Since I was supposed to know half your group was suicidal," Rob said, nodding. "Yeah, that makes sense. But fine. It's all my fault. I can agree with that, since I knew better than to do this in the first damned place, but we're here now, aren't we? So tell me, smart guy, how much time have you spent in the woods? Not just camping in your daddy's back yard or something, but actually out in the wilderness, no one else around for miles and miles. Have you *ever* done that? No? Well I have, so maybe I'm thinking experience might be useful here. God forbid that insults your precious sensibilities, though. Wouldn't want that, would we?"

During Rob's entire response, Ami had been watching Jay's eyes going more and more narrow, his face growing more and more flushed. Finally, instead of saying anything in reply, he drew back his fist and punched Rob in the face hard enough to spin himself around and knock the other man onto his ass in the dirt next to her.

No sooner than the punch landed, Jay loosened his fist and grabbed his knuckles with his other hand, bending at the waist and biting his lip as he pulled both hands close to his stomach.

"Fuck!" he cried at last, bouncing as he flexed his hand.

"Feel better?" Rob asked. He was sitting on the ground near Ami's feet, using his index finger to wipe away the blood dripping down his chin from his split lip.

"No," Jay replied, still favoring his hand. "That fucking hurt!"

"Usually what happens when you punch someone in the mouth," Rob said. "It's a lot harder to knock someone's teeth out than people make it sound. I'm giving you that one since I understand you're scared and pissed off, but you try it again and you'll find out exactly what this 'washed up hippie' is made of, are we clear?"

Jay studied Rob's face silently, his eyes still angry but no longer as furious as they had been. Finally, he lowered them and nodded.

"Good," Rob said. He didn't bother standing back up, only spit a mouthful of pinkish saliva to the side and draped his wrists over his knees before turning to look back to Ami. "In case you didn't figure it out from that, we're not in a great spot here."

"Okay," she said. She cast a glance at Jay, then Christy, then to Eric's unconscious body nestled against a nearby tree before looking back to Rob. "So how bad is it?"

"Where should I even start?" Rob asked in reply. He began ticking points off on his fingers. "We went down the wrong fork and washed up on the opposite bank from where we wanted to be, which means we have to figure out a way across before we can even *think* about getting to either of the trucks. In addition to being on the wrong side, I'm pretty sure we overshot our planned stopping point. Because I was too busy trying to stay alive, I wasn't paying close enough attention to even guess at how far we overshot by, but if I had to guess, I'd say at least a mile, maybe even as many as three. Because of that, I can't be sure where we even *are* anymore. My maps were in my dry bag, and I have no idea where that might have ended up, so there's no help there. The raft capsized, but it kept going even after all of us were thrown out of it, so consider it gone, too. It's not too bad out right now, but it's the middle of the day still. If we're out here after dark, it's going to get cold fast. We don't have any supplies or changes of clothes, since all of it was in the raft and lost along with it.

"All of which means," he said, standing and brushing the dirt off his pants, "we're lost in the mountains in the winter with no supplies and no idea how to get back to something resembling civilization again. Two of our group are missing, and one is badly injured and in no condition to walk, even if we knew which direction to go. And now you're caught up. Kind of makes you wish you stayed asleep, doesn't it?"

Christy let out another wail of despair. Jay stood staring at his feet, his face unreadable. Even Rob, who seemed to always be able to take things in stride, looked gloomy. Ami did the only thing she could think to do: she buried her face in her hands and wept.

EIGHT

HE WASN'T EXACTLY SURE WHAT had happened, but when Benny awoke to find himself half-submerged in the river, the current tugging at his legs and hips, he thought he could put the pieces together fairly well. The last thing he remembered clearly was being thrown from the raft when it hit a drop that felt like it was at least a hundred feet down, but was—in all reality—probably no more than two or three. He had a vague recollection of splashing into the river, the frigid water engulfing him and trying to force its way down into his lungs. He was fairly sure the raft had flipped shortly after that, his memory dissolving into a jumble of screams and frightened voices before everything kind of faded away for a while. He must have washed up here—wherever *here* was—and managed to crawl far enough onto the bank to keep the current from pulling him away again.

In a way, he almost hoped he didn't eventually remember how it happened. Knowing he was partly to blame was bad enough. He didn't need to relive anything more from the accident than he already did.

It was disturbing how much effort it cost him to roll over onto his back so he could breathe easier and not inhale mud and dirt with every intake of air. His entire body felt like a field of aches and pains that rivaled his freshman year in high school after playing his first football game. No, that wasn't entirely accurate. This was a thousand times worse. Then, he had the thrill of the game to distract him, but now he only had the reminder he was paying for his stupidity.

His legs felt numb from the knees down. Panic started to creep in until he realized they were still in the water, the icy flow deadening his nerves. He sat up and scooted backward until they were on dry land and hoped he wouldn't develop frostbite or anything like that. Stupidly, he'd worn shorts on the raft, so he was able to see how pale they were beneath the streaks of red crisscrossing his shins like he'd been whipped with a branch. His grandmother had done that when he misbehaved, as had been done to her when she acted up as a kid—or so she claimed, at least. He'd thought it was much too aggressive a punishment back then but found it to be strangely fitting now.

There was no way to know how long he'd been lying here, but it was long enough his shirt had dried considerably. He pulled it off over his head and used it to wipe the water from his legs. Thankfully, he felt the blood start flowing through them again as he massaged them, sending pinpricks of sensation racing through them. A couple of his toes still felt dead and wooden inside the soggy confines of his shoes and socks, but he supposed it would be better in the long run to end up losing them instead of both his legs.

It was what he deserved, at any rate. He was so focused on showing up that hippie asshole he'd never once stopped to consider that maybe, just *maybe*, the man actually knew what he was doing. His plan had been to make them drift too far into the middle of the river where the current would be strongest, maybe overshoot their stopping point by a bit, and then blame Rob for not giving good enough direction for them to succeed. When he saw the fork looming ahead of them, it had been too good an opportunity to pass up.

His plan for pointless revenge had nearly killed him. He didn't want to think about the possibility it might have killed everyone else, too.

He wanted to blame it on Rob for not being clear about the route they needed to take, or even Teddy, who had been the one to tell him about Ami and Jay coming out of Rob's room last night, but he couldn't. Not and make himself believe it. The plan had been his, Teddy and Christy had followed his lead, and now they were all paying for it. Some small, angry part of his brain wanted him to blame Ami, too, since she had been the one who ditched him at the party and went to some strange guy's room in the first place, but that wasn't fair either. She'd done nothing over the course of their relationship to make him think she would cheat on him, and besides, taking a male friend along to meet your lover was pretty silly, in retrospect.

Again, something else that was his fault. She'd been growing more and more distant since he'd gotten drunk and accused her of wanting to fuck Jay. She'd ignored him that night, was silent most of the next day, and blasted into him before dinner the next evening. He remembered nothing until she reminded him about it, and he immediately felt terrible. No matter how much he'd apologized to her, no matter how much he tried to pamper her, she'd kept pulling away from him. Eric's advice had been to give her space, the chance to cool off, but Benny was too afraid she'd take it as him ignoring her and leave him. He got desperate, and before he knew it, was seeing everything she did as a way to distance herself from him more and more.

He hated himself for it, but he couldn't stop it, either. Ami wasn't like most of the girls he'd dated through high school and college. She actually had a brain, for one thing. He never thought smart girls could also be hot until he met her, and once he realized how easily she could see through his bullshit, he'd been forced to step up his game. The end result was that she actually made him change for the better. Jay was a prime example. He was exactly the kind of person Benny belittled in school, but because he was Ami's best friend, Benny tried to give him a chance. Much to his surprise, the guy wasn't as bad as he thought he would be and actually shared a couple of interests with Benny. Not enough to forge any real bond or anything but enough Benny could actually tolerate being in his company for extended periods of time.

Through it all, though, there'd been some small part of him waiting for the day Ami realized she was wasting her time with him and left. He was sure that was how the drunken accusations had come about in the first place. Booze lowered his inhibitions and removed his internal filter. If he'd had so much he couldn't even remember what he'd said or done the next day, there was little doubt both had been gone completely by the time he said what he did to Ami. He thought maybe it had been an attempt to confess the insecurities he'd developed while dating her, but the alcohol and the presence of his friends had forced his temper to the surface instead. He'd tried to let her know he hadn't been angry with her, but angry with himself for not being as strong as he thought he should be. He'd fucked it up royally in the attempt.

It was ironic, really. He thought he was slowly winning her back by all the attention he laid on her after, but that was what was driving her away instead. Looking back on it, it was easy to see.

And now she was probably dead, and he'd never get the chance to apologize and give her space and win her back and it was all his fault.

Unless she *wasn't* dead. After all, *he'd* survived the accident. There was every possibility she had too. She'd gone into the water not long before he did. Seconds apart, maybe. Hell, for that matter, *all* of them might've made it. The only ones who had seemed injured before the last drop were Teddy and Eric, both smacked in the head by oars. Eric had only really looked dazed when Benny spared a glance at him. It hadn't been a thorough look, true. There hadn't been the time for that. But Benny thought his eyes were open. If so, it was entirely within the realm of possibility he was still alive out there somewhere, washed up on the bank like Benny was. Teddy, too, though admittedly, Benny had no idea how severe his injuries might've been before the drop.

If they were still alive, and if Benny could find them and show some real effort at getting them out of the mess he'd put them in, maybe Ami could see how sorry he was for how he'd acted. He'd save them, and then apologize to all of them for what happened. He'd apologize again to Ami for everything else separately, and then ask her what he could do to earn back her trust. After that, he would give her the space she needed to sit back and see how hard he tried to prove himself. There was every chance it wouldn't work, that it would be too little, too late, but it *might*. No matter how small the chance was, it existed, and for right now, it was enough.

Benny forced himself to his feet, thankful he had a reason to keep going for a while longer now. He looked up and down the bank on both sides of the river, shaking his head at how calm and peaceful it looked. Back up a ways, he could see the traces of whitewater, which at least helped him orient himself as to the direction they'd come. The bank in that direction was layered with brush and brambles, twisted and tangled roots from nearby trees making a treacherous path to try and follow. The other direction, however, was somewhat less hazardous-looking. It would be much easier to search, but he had no way of knowing how far the others might have been pulled down the river from where they were thrown out of the raft.

It was a coin-toss. If he took too much time looking in the wrong place, any potential survivors would have their chances diminished by the time he got to them. If he took the easy path and didn't find them, he was going to have to backtrack. The overgrown path would be the most likely, since there was more debris sticking out over the water to have caught them or allowed them to grab ahold of, but it would take much longer to traverse and look through. If he had to double back over, it would be nightfall or after by the time he made it back here again. Without any source of light other than the stars and the moon, that would mean another day before he could possibly find them.

He sighed and turned toward the clearer path, deciding he would give it about an hour. If he hadn't found them by then, he'd run back here and start searching the other way. If luck was on his side, he'd find them in time to keep them alive through what would probably be a long, cold night ahead.

He waited until he saw the boy walk away before emerging from his hiding place deep in the trees and ambling over to the spot the boy had vacated. Otis had been watching for what felt like an hour or more, debating whether or not he was alive or dead. If he was dead, did he have anything worth scavenging in his pockets? He'd made up his mind to check, and then the boy started moving and scared Otis nearly out of his own pants.

At least the one question was answered. While he should probably feel relieved the boy was alive, he didn't. It would be different if he stayed along the riverbank and didn't venture deeper into the surrounding woods, but things wouldn't work out that way. They never did. And someone wandering around the woods could only mean trouble was coming. Bad trouble, the kind that could get Otis tossed *under* the jail, as his daddy used to say. Otis was never really sure exactly what that meant, but he figured if being put *in* jail was bad, being *under* it had to be much worse.

Of course, it was winter now, had actually snowed last week. That was when it was supposed to be the safest out here. Eugene said so, and he was maybe the smartest person Otis ever met. Maybe that meant the boy wouldn't go where he wasn't supposed to. If that happened, then everything would be fine as pie again. Maybe if Otis watched him, made sure he stayed away, that would be good enough.

He frowned, remembering the screams that had drawn him down to the river in the first place. Despite what his daddy thought, Otis wasn't a complete dummy, and he thought he'd heard more than one person raising such a ruckus. A couple of the voices even sounded like they'd come from girls, and that meant there had to be other people out here, too. Just 'cause he hadn't seen them yet, didn't mean they weren't out here somewhere. After all, there was a lot of woods to hide in around here. It was why Eugene had picked this place for their job. Only if someone else was hiding out here, they might be looking for Eugene, or Clint, or even Otis himself. And that wouldn't be good at all.

Otis sighed, suddenly feeling sadder than he'd been in a long time. He let himself get excited at the idea he could be the one to make sure the boy didn't go where he shouldn't be and that it would be the end of that, but it really wasn't a possibility anymore. He was going to have to go back and tell Clint and Eugene there were people here. He didn't want to tell them. They would end up making him do bad things, things he didn't like to do. He'd said no before, but they always talked him around. If he tried to say no again, they'd remind him about how it was either do this stuff that wasn't nice to keep them safe, or get himself arrested, just like his daddy said would happen one day.

As much as he didn't want to do the bad stuff, he wanted to get arrested even less. He didn't want to prove his daddy right. He had to tell them, but he didn't have to *like* telling them.

Otis turned and pushed his way back into the brush, heading toward the trail that led to their camp. He forced himself to walk slower than normal, hoping it might give the people a chance to run away before Eugene and Clint found out they were there. He could always hope, but he knew things probably would not go the way he wanted. They never did.

NINE

IT TOOK A WHILE FOR Ami to get herself back under control. Under the circumstances, it was probably to be expected. What she wanted to do more than anything else was to close her eyes, lie back down, and pretend everything that happened so far was nothing more than an exceptionally vivid nightmare. The problem with that—aside from the fact she was more of a realist than she liked to admit—was she would eventually be confronted with the truth when she woke up again. Anything else would amount to lying down and dying, and while that might be the outcome anyway, she refused to submit to it. If she had any say in the matter, she was going to go down swinging.

When she finally looked back up and wiped an arm across her face to clear her vision, she saw Rob, Jay, Christy, and Eric all in the same basic places and poses they had been when she had her breakdown. Jay was sulking, Christy looked like she was still fighting down the aftereffects of a breakdown herself, and Rob seemed to be simply biding his time and waiting for her to collect herself before doing anything else.

She thought about asking him what he was doing to try and get them out of the mess they were in, but that wouldn't be fair. He was stuck in this mess like the rest of them. And what could he really have done? She'd read all the brochures and warnings online about being away from the established trails up here in the Smokies. Wandering off alone was a good way to get yourself attacked by a bear, or God only knew what other kind of wildlife might take offense to your intruding on its territory. It was probably safest for them to stay together as a group, for now.

Rob finally looked over to her and smiled when he saw she was no longer bawling her eyes out. She figured she looked like hell, but thankfully there was no judgment in his eyes.

"Feel any better?" he asked.

"Not really," she replied. "My head hurts worse than ever."

He gave her a sympathetic grimace and nodded. "Sorry. I didn't have anything for a headache in my bags, if that helps."

She heard Jay snort but chose to ignore him. "It doesn't, but thanks for trying."

"Anytime," he said.

He glanced up at the sky and then closed his eyes. Ami could see his lips moving slightly, as though he were calculating something in his mind. Finally, he nodded, and then stood.

"Okay then," he began. "We got started a little before noon, so I put it at nearly three now. That means we only have a couple hours of daylight left to do anything worthwhile. Unfortunately, that also means we're probably not going to make it out of here tonight."

Christy made another of those high-pitched whining sounds, but otherwise didn't respond. Ami glanced at Jay and saw he'd already come to the same realization she had: the likelihood was they weren't going to get out of this *at all*, much less tonight, but he chose to keep that opinion to himself. It was better to try and be optimistic if at all possible. If nothing else, they might be able to fake it long enough to hold out an extra day or two.

"I don't know about the rest of you," Rob continued. "But I don't care to just wait for the weather to kill me off. So, in the interest of trying to better our chances from non-existent to slim, we need to try and do a few things. I'm sure all of you have some ideas, so let's all throw them out there for ten minutes or so and then figure out what's most do-able in the short time we've got before the sun goes down. I'll start by suggesting we figure out how to get a fire going. I don't know about this night, but I know the past few have been pretty cold after dark, so I don't think we should assume any different."

"I don't suppose anybody can pull matches out of their ass,

can they?" Jay asked. He looked at each of them in turn, from Christy's terrified face to Rob and Ami's annoyed ones, and then leaned back on his elbows with his legs stretched out before him. "Didn't think so. And stop looking at me like that. Maybe it was crude, but it was a legitimate question. I know I've heard about rubbing two sticks together to start a fire, but I've never seen it done, nor have I done it myself. So yes, we need a fire. I'll agree, especially since I'm already cold from being in that ice chest of a river and sitting in the shade all day. But how do we start one?"

The annoyance left Rob's face as he seemed to realize the truth in Jay's words. He sighed and shook his head.

"We made it to shore," Ami said. "Is it possible our stuff did too?"

Rob shrugged. "It's possible, I guess. But it got thrown out before we did, so we might have to go back a ways to search for it. I could always *try* the two-stick-trick. I've at least seen it done before, even if I haven't done it myself."

"What about the others?" Christy said. Her voice was still wavering and tight with fear, but at least she seemed to be coming out of her fugue somewhat. "Shouldn't we be trying to find them? I mean, they could be hurt, like Eric, or fine and wondering about us, too."

Rob nodded. "We could always look for them at the same time we look for the packs. The only problem is they'd probably be further downstream, while the packs might be more upstream, since that's where they got thrown free."

"Why don't we split up then?" Christy asked.

"We can't!" Ami said, maybe *too* quickly. She couldn't help herself, though. Her heart had suddenly begun to hammer away at the very idea. "What about bears?"

Christy shot her a dirty look, but Rob spoke up first.

"She's right," he said, looking to Christy as he spoke. "Well, mostly. We *are* going to have to split up to do the searching, but we can't split far enough to search both ways."

"And why not?" Christy asked, turning her venomous stare on him.

"Because of Eric," Jay said, pointing a thumb at the unconscious man. "We would each need at least one partner, right? So two of us go downstream for the others, two go upstream for the packs, and who's here with Eric? Nobody. Unless you plan on leaving him behind as bear food, we can't search both ways at once, and there's no time to do both today before dark."

"I didn't think about that," Christy said, deflated.

"No shit, Captain Obvious," Jay muttered. Ami didn't think Christy heard it, but she gave him a look of warning just the same. He held up his hands, indicating he'd be good.

"Any other suggestions?" Rob asked.

"Food," Jay replied. "If we find the packs, great. But what are we going to do about food? We won't be able to help ourselves much if we've got no energy because we're hungry."

Rob considered this. "It's a valid concern. Quick question: is there anyone here who didn't eat anything for breakfast this morning?"

Ami looked around, but no one had a hand raised. She knew she'd had a bowl of cereal and some yogurt, and Jay had eggs and sausage from the hot bar at the hotel. She didn't know what Christy or Rob ate, but if it had been nothing, neither said so.

"That's a plus," Rob said. "What about one of those sandwiches before we headed out? Anyone choose against it?"

Rob raised his own hand. Christy apparently was emboldened by that a little because her hand slowly slid upwards as well.

"Just us two, then," Rob said. "Fair enough. We've all at least had *something* today. Maybe it was a while ago, and maybe it wasn't enough to do a lot of good, but it's better than nothing. We can survive for a while without food, longer since the river water is drinkable. It won't taste great, but it'll be enough to sustain us for a bit. That buys us time, but food absolutely will become a concern pretty fast. Maybe we don't deal with it right now, but it's definitely something to think about if we don't find a way out of here by tomorrow. You okay tabling that one for now?"

Jay shrugged and nodded.

"Could we build a shelter of some sort?" Ami asked. "In case we can't do a fire, maybe it'll at least cut down on the wind."

Rob glanced around at the trees and undergrowth around them, and then nodded slowly. "It might not be much, but we should be able to cobble something together. I suppose anything's got to be better than nothing. Any more suggestions?"

No one spoke up. After a couple of moments of silence, Rob nodded again. "Then we've gotta build a fire somehow, look for our packs, look for the others, and build a shelter. So what do we focus on right now?"

"Finding the others," Christy said, as though the very concept of doing otherwise was so unbelievably unthinkable it shouldn't be considered. "They need us the most, right?"

Rob sighed and crossed over to her before squatting down on his haunches. "I know it seems that way, but we need to put some cold, hard facts on the table. You're not going to want to hear them, but you *do* need to listen to them and think about them, okay?"

"You're not going to convince me we shouldn't look for them," Christy insisted. "So don't waste your breath."

"I'm not going to try convincing you not to look," Rob said, shaking his head. "But the reality is we don't even know for sure they're alive. The jock, Ami's boyfriend? Based on nothing but the fact we made it, I'd say there's a decent chance he did, too. But we got lucky, and he didn't. Me and Jay were able to help you and Ami. We never saw him do the same. He probably got swept further downstream, and may or may not have been con-scious enough to try and fight his way to shore. You add all that up, and his chances decrease significantly."

Christy's face crumpled, and for a moment, Ami thought she was about to burst into tears. Ami frowned. She never realized Christy cared so much about Benny. She'd certainly never been someone he'd hung out with very much before. Besides, she was with Eric, and he was here, alive. Whether that lasted through the night or not was yet to be seen, but at least he'd made it through the accident. Why wasn't she showing more concern about that? There were answers there, easy ones, but Ami didn't care to think about them right now. No matter what she felt about Christy before this happened, they were in this together now. She didn't need anything creeping into her mind that might damage that forced partnership.

"As for Teddy," Rob said. "You were barely holding him in the raft before it flipped. I didn't see it happen, but I'm willing to bet he took a pretty good shot from that broken oar. There's a very real possibility he was already dead before the raft flipped, not to mention his chances of survival after it did. But for the sake of argument, let's assume he did live through it all, and washed up on shore somewhere. Let's even say he washed up on shore with the jock—"

"*His fucking name is Benny!*" Christy roared. Rob jerked back hard enough to lose his balance and land hard on his butt amongst the scattered sticks and mud. Even Jay seemed surprised by the outburst.

Ami wasn't so much shocked by it as annoyed. She was almost positive her initial thoughts on why Christy cared were true. Some part of her wanted to tell the other girl "good luck, you'll need it", but there was another, smaller, more primal part of her that wanted to snatch the bitch up by her badly dyed roots and slap the living shit out of her.

"Sorry," Rob said, obviously taken aback by the ferocity the girl had displayed. "Let's say Teddy and Benny washed up together. Don't you think if they were able, they'd have headed out looking for us, too? And if they weren't able, how would you propose we get them back here? We haven't even figured out how we're going to move Eric yet, and we know he's alive. We have to focus on our own survival right now. To me, that means we need to find a way to stay warm tonight so we can live long enough to find them. If they're out there, and if they're alive, and if they're unconscious, that might actually be better for them and increase their chances for survival in the long run. I won't whitewash it: any injuries they have might be made worse by spending a night in the elements, but we stand a better chance of keeping them alive and getting them to safety by looking for them when we have more time. I'm not saying we don't look for them; I'm suggesting that looking for them shouldn't be our top priority, the situation being what it is."

Rob was right. What he said was cold, it was calculating, and as much as Ami hated to admit it, it was sound and logical. The urge to find Benny and Teddy was emotional thinking, but emotions would only put them more at risk right now. They had to look at things with that cold and calculating eye.

"If we're taking a vote," she said, unable to meet anyone's gaze for fear she'd feel more ashamed than she already did. "I say we go look for the packs. If we can get ahold of matches, everything becomes much easier."

"You would say that," Christy said. Ami looked over to find the girl staring at her with undisguised hate blazing in her eyes. "You never gave a shit about Teddy, or Benny for that matter. I bet you're fucking *thrilled* to finally be rid of him."

"Think what you want," Ami replied, unable to meet the girl's eyes. "I didn't want to date him anymore, that's true, but that doesn't mean I want him dead."

"I vote packs, too," Jay said. "It sucks, but it does make the most sense."

"You would agree with *her*," Christy shot back, turning her anger on him. "You're so far up her fucking ass it's pathetic. And you wonder why I wouldn't ever fuck you."

Jay flinched as if she'd hit him, but kept his mouth closed. Ami saw him staring at something that must have been rather interesting on the ground beside him.

"I'm sorry," Rob said softly. "But you already heard my decision."

"Well fuck you all!"

Christy scrambled to her feet, her cheeks bright red, all signs of her previous distress gone. Ami thought the change was incredible, especially since all it took was telling her the truth.

"I don't give a flying *fuck* what you three do!" she screamed. "I'm going to find my *friends*! Remember them? The people we came here with?"

"You mean the people who tried to kill us, you included?" Ami asked. She was surprised at how calm her voice was. She was shaking like a leaf on the inside. "Oh, that's right. You were part of that, too, or did you forget?"

Christy stood staring at her, fury in her eyes, her mouth moving soundlessly. Finally, she spun on her heel and stormed off in the direction of the shoreline. In moments, disappeared behind the thick brush that looped and tangled its way around the small clearing they were in. No one made any move to follow her.

"You two go look for the packs," Jay said quietly. "I'll stay here with Eric. She might come back, and maybe I can talk her down if she does."

Rob didn't look at him, only continued staring off in the direction she'd gone with a troubled look on his face. "She should be relatively safe as long as she stays close to the river. At least until dark, that is."

He turned to look at Jay. "We'll take about a half an hour looking upstream for the packs. If we can't find them, we'll come back here and then go after her. While we're gone, you see if you can think of a way to move Eric without making things worse. We'll go until nearly dark, and then try to find another place to set up camp for the night if we don't find her. We were planning on searching that direction come morning anyway, right? We get a head start on it, I guess."

Jay nodded.

Rob turned to look at Ami. "You ready?"

She stood, wincing at the stiffness that built up in her legs and back from staying in one spot, in relatively the same position. After stretching her legs out as best she could, she gave Rob a nod.

"Ready," she said.

"If a bear shows up," Rob said, looking to Jay. "Make a lot of noise. Yell, scream, whatever. Act bigger than you are. Raise your hands, spread your legs, that kind of thing. Just don't rush it or try to run away. Back away slowly and stay calm. It should be enough. They don't like humans as it is, and they tend to shy away from us if possible. We don't have food, so we shouldn't draw their attention. Above all, be careful."

"I will," Jay replied. "You guys watch your asses out there."

"Deal," Rob said before turning and leading the way back up the shoreline.

Ami offered Jay a final smile of encouragement, and then followed him.

TEN

THE ONLY THING OTIS FELT as he hunkered in the brush next to Eugene was how itchy he was. It seemed like nearly every bramble was finding its way onto the bare skin of his arms, the back of his neck, and his face. He wanted nothing more than to scratch at them until every speck of itchiness was gone, but he knew better. If he started scratching, it would make the leaves and things jump around him and give away where they were. If that happened, Eugene would be mad at him. That wouldn't be so bad, but he might get Clint involved. If Eugene was mad, he didn't lash out at you. He just lectured you, the way Otis's mama used to do, until you felt so bad about screwing things up you nearly wanted to cry. Clint didn't stop with words. Clint liked to hit and slap and scream and call you names. Not that any of it really hurt Otis, other than the name-calling, but he'd rather not have to deal with that in addition to everything else going on.

He hadn't expected to run into them out on the trail, but there they were, walking toward him as he turned the corner and started up the gentle rise to their camp. Eugene was checking the rubber piping that fed their crop in the warmer months, to make sure it hadn't cracked during the last freeze. Otis knew he was planning to drive out to Knoxville in a few days to start picking up supplies so they'd be ready when spring hit. He'd been putting his list together for weeks, the way mama always used to make her grocery list every Thursday morning.

Clint had been standing on the other side of the trail, pissing into the bushes alongside it. He'd been the one who noticed Otis skulking about, trying to decide whether or not to slip back down the trail and kill more time or go ahead and get it over with. The decision was out of his hands the second Clint laid eyes on him, though.

"The fuck you doin', dummy?" Clint asked. "See somethin' you like here?"

He'd waggled his penis at Otis then, drawing a scowl in return that he seemed to find hilarious. He'd tucked himself away about the time Eugene looked over at Otis. Before he knew it, Otis had told them everything, from hearing the screams to seeing the boy sleeping, to wondering if there were more like him around somewhere. Eugene listened with a calm look on his face, then tucked his notebook away underneath the rubber pipeline and patted Otis on the back. That made Otis feel good, like he'd managed one of the rare occasions when he did something right without being asked to. It made him glad he didn't take longer to get there.

"I guess you'd better show us where you found him," Eugene had said.

And now here they were, hiding in the bushes and staring at the empty spot where the boy had been a while ago. Otis hoped they did something soon. If he had to sit here quiet and unmoving much longer, he thought he might go insane.

"There ain't shit here, Gene," Clint hissed, his voice barely audible over the sound of the river not far away from them. "The dummy's makin' shit up again. Prob'ly thought it was a fuckin' alien or some shit again."

Otis felt his face burn with shame. It had been dark that time, and he hadn't ever seen a mountain lion before. Daddy always told him none lived natural around here. The idea of somebody owning one as a pet and dropping it off when they realized how foolish that was had never occurred to him. Eugene had been gentle when he explained all that to Otis, but Clint had never let him live it down.

"Somebody was here," Eugene replied, just as quietly. "Look how the bank's all tore up, like they clawed their way out of the water. And there's footprints in the mud leading downriver. Too small to be Otis's, and I don't see a heel, so it's not boots like we wear. That means somebody's been out here messin' around pretty recently."

Clint was quiet for a bit, maybe considering what Eugene said.

"You think we oughta go after 'em?" he finally asked. "Catch the little fucker 'fore he sees somethin' he shouldn't?"

"I'm not worried about one person," Eugene replied. "I'm more concerned with the friends he's probably got out here with him. Besides, he's heading away from us. Only starts being an issue if he's coming *toward* us."

"Well, then, whatcha thinkin'?" Clint asked. "Go upriver some and see . . .?"

"Would you shut your damn yap for a minute?" Eugene said. Otis flinched at the harshness in his voice. "I'm trying to think over here."

"Well excuse the fuck out of me," Clint muttered, then went silent.

Otis felt a bead of sweat break loose on the back of his neck and make a slow trail down his back before settling into the spot above the crack of his ass. For some reason, it itched worse than any of the other places. He ached to scratch it, but forced himself not to. The more he fought it, though, the worse the itch grew. It would almost be worth the lecture to have a little relief.

"One person, clawing their way out of the river," Eugene whispered. "What's that sound like to you, Clint?"

"Hell, how should I know?" Clint replied. "Maybe a raft went tits up, or one'a them fucking kay-acks or somethin'."

Eugene made a soft grunting sound deep in his throat. "Nobody's fool enough to try a kayak on those rapids. Raft seems more likely. But I ain't never heard of nobody rafting by their lonesome, have you?"

"Since I'm all into that kinda gay-ass shit," Clint replied. "Think I'm some fuckin' expert or somethin'?"

"I think you're a loud-mouthed cocksucker who better be glad he knows how to keep an area secure," Eugene said. "Else you'd already be fertilizer, and don't you forget that."

"You know," Clint said, his voice getting loud enough Otis felt himself wanting to shush the other man for fear they might be heard. "I still ain't figured out why the fuck you're the one in charge any-fuckin'-way. I could do the piss-ass shit you do, and probably do it a damn sight better, too."

Eugene moved so fast Otis never saw him so much as flinch. One second he was hunched down, watching the clearing where Otis found the boy earlier, the next he was turned slightly toward Clint, a pistol in his hand with the barrel shoved against Clint's forehead. Otis noted with some amazement he didn't seem to have disturbed their cover at all.

"Time and a fucking place," he said. "This ain't either. I'm the one in charge because it's my fucking show to run. You don't like that, I can put one in your skull right now and get on with my life. If you'll recall, I've made you a metric shit-ton of money since we started this, and ain't said boo when you deal with folks who stumble in too close, no matter what I thought of your methods. So unless you want me to give you something to complain to Old Scratch about, I'd keep my fucking yap closed unless asked to open it. We clear?"

Otis couldn't see him, but he could hear Clint swallow hard. "Yeah. We clear."

Eugene lowered the pistol and went back to looking at the clearing again. "Stupid-ass shit-for-brains."

His voice was pitched so low Otis wasn't sure if Clint heard him or not, but then he realized Eugene hadn't cared either way. He was grumblin', as he said he sometimes did. A part of Otis sort of hoped Clint *had* heard it. It was nice to think he was the one being called bad names for a change.

"Look," Clint said, his voice back to barely more than a whisper. "You want me to, I'll go scope out a bit upriver of us, see if I can find a raft or the guy's friends, or . . ."

"Hush!" Eugene said, holding up a hand. His head was cocked to the side like a dog's that heard a strange noise. "Listen!"

Otis strained to hear whatever it was that caught Eugene's attention. Finally, he was able to make out what sounded like branches breaking somewhere in the other direction from where the boy had gone. He started to wonder how he could've circled around without any of them seeing him, and then realized it had to be the friends they all thought must be around somewhere, too. They must be coming this way. If it was a group, Eugene would want to go back to camp and make plans for how to deal with them. But if it was just one, or even two, he'd want to deal with them right now.

Otis felt a weight in the pit of his stomach. Either way, the fact somebody was coming meant the bad stuff was about to start.

Christy swore to herself as she felt another stick scrape more flesh away from the bottoms of her bare feet. It was her own fault—after all, she was the one who was stupid enough to wear flip-flops on one of these whitewater rafting expeditions, even though she knew the odds were pretty high she'd end up barefoot if the shit hit the fan—but knowing this did absolutely nothing to alleviate her irritation at how torn up her poor feet were getting. It might not have happened at all, had those three assholes agreed with her about going to look for Benny instead of some stupid packs that were probably long gone anyway.

She felt a momentary flash of guilt when she realized she'd forgotten Teddy was missing somewhere, too, but Rob had probably been right when he said it was unlikely Teddy was even still alive. He hadn't seen it when the oar hit him, but Christy had. She'd barely managed to jerk herself out of the way and saw it slam hard into Teddy's face before flipping over him and disappearing somewhere behind them. When he started to fall backward over the edge of the raft, she'd had enough presence of mind to reach out and grab him by the ankles. Because of that, she'd felt the jolt in her arms when his head collided with something she hadn't been able to see not long before they were all thrown out of the raft.

That, combined with the blood that had covered the lower half of his face before he fell out of sight, had been enough for her to go ahead and say he was gone and never coming back.

Benny, though, stood a chance, and no matter what mister smarty-pants Rob thought, *she* thought it was a damn good one. Benny was strong, stronger than any of those pussies, for sure. If they'd managed to get themselves to shore, there was no way he wouldn't have been able to as well. He was probably sitting on the shore, a fire already built from the scrap wood nearby, waiting to see if they were going to come meet up with him or not. It would be a test of sorts, a way to see which of them actually cared and which ones didn't.

She could imagine it when she finally stumbled across him. He'd look up, that questioning look on his face, lips curled into a slight, knowing smile.

"Where's everybody else?" he'd ask. "Where's Ami?"

"She wouldn't come," she'd reply. "It's just me. I'm the only one who believed in you. I'm the only one who ever did."

His smile would grow wider as he stood and came around the fire to her. "Somehow I knew this is how it would happen."

He'd look down and see how banged up her feet were. His face would get all concerned, and he'd rush over to her.

"You're hurt!" he'd say. "You hurt yourself trying to find me. Let me carry you."

He wouldn't wait for her to answer, would pick her up like she weighed nothing at all and put her down gently next to the fire.

"It's okay," she'd tell him. "You're worth the pain."

He'd look into her eyes, no longer smiling, and no longer needing to. She'd be able to see all she needed in those eyes. Their faces would get closer and closer until they were finally kissing, softly, tentatively at first. The kiss would grow more passionate, their tongues getting involved. He'd put a hand on her breast and rub a thumb over her swollen nipple. She'd gasp into his mouth and reach down between his legs to massage his
. . .

A branch gave way under her next step, pitching her off-balance and scraping its way up her leg to nearly mid-shin. She jerked her leg back without thinking and winced as she felt skin tear from the sudden reverse motion. The heel of her other foot struck a jutting rock behind her, and the next thing she knew, her ass was slamming painfully against a jumble of roots clawing their way toward the river. She managed to reach out and grab one at the last second, regaining her balance and preventing herself from going back into the frigid water again.

"Shit!" she said, her arms trembling as she leaned back against a tree trunk and fought to catch her breath. Her heart had sped up more than could be accounted for by her fantasy. She'd avoided another near-accident, at least, which made up for the loss of her daydream but still left her feeling light-headed.

Her entire body felt like electric current was racing through it, making her twitchy and ill-at-ease. Her thoughts of Benny had been a good distraction, but now that they were gone, her fear had returned full-force. She was still hoping—no, *expect-*

ing—to find him somewhere up ahead of her, but the reality was she was alone in the woods, with danger all around her, cold, damp, terrified, and facing the real possibility she would never see her warm bed again.

She wanted to sit here and cry until someone, be it Benny or the asshole trio, found her and brought her back to some semblance of safety, but she refused to let herself. It would accomplish nothing and would make her appear as little more than a burden to whoever found her. Not such a big deal if it was one of the assholes, but the thought of Benny thinking such a thing was enough to get her moving again.

When her legs no longer felt like they were made of jelly, she pushed herself back to her feet. She looked down, grimacing at the amount of blood she saw along her left shin and foot. She'd really managed to do a number on it, it seemed. At least it still held her weight, although with no small amount of stinging pain when she applied pressure to it. It was tolerable, so she pressed on.

Relief flooded her as she stepped out into what looked like another small clearing, similar to the one she and the others had ended up in before. The cool mud felt wonderful on her scraped and bruised feet, a welcome relief from the harshness of the path she'd taken. Ahead of her, the shoreline looked much easier to traverse. She had no idea how far it went, but she would certainly enjoy it while she could.

She'd made it almost halfway across when rustling in the bushes to her side made her freeze in place. She was too terrified to look around, certain she'd see a bear standing there, looking at her like she was a candy bar and he had a serious sweet tooth. She closed her eyes tightly and hoped when it struck it would kill her quickly enough she wouldn't feel anything.

"Well, would you look what we got here?"

Her eyes snapped open at the unfamiliar voice. She turned and found herself facing three men who must have emerged from the bushes. One was grinning at her lasciviously, a hand tugging at the crotch of his camouflage pants that looked ready to slip off his skinny hips at any second. The one on the opposite side from him had a look of what she could almost think of as pity on his broad, plain face. He was quite possibly the largest man Christy had ever seen, easily six and a half feet tall and broad as the side of a house in his sweat-stained t-shirt and filthy jeans.

Those two were bad enough, but it was the one in the center that frightened her the most. Taken on his own, he wasn't so bad. He was wearing jeans as well, though his were considerably cleaner than those of his companions. They still had spots of dirt and filth on them, but that could have happened as he pushed his way through the bushes. Instead of a grimy t-shirt like the others, he was wearing a short-sleeved polo-type shirt with the three collar buttons undone so she could see the faint wisps of curled chest hair that peeked into the narrow slit from the neck of the shirt to just below his collarbone. Even his eyes looked somewhat sympathetic, a look that was directly contrasted by the massive gun he was pointing at her face.

"In case it needs sayin'," the man in the center told her. "You scream, I scatter your brains all over that river behind you. Understood?"

She tried to come up with words, but her throat felt too thick and constricted to allow her much more than wheezing breaths, so she simply nodded.

"Good. So, get thrown out of your raft?"

Another nod.

"Got friends with you?"

She felt her lips trembling as she nodded again.

"Where are they?"

She shook her head, still unable to find the ability to speak. Against her will, she had begun to cry again, further making speech impossible.

The man with the gun sighed. "Well, darlin', this ain't your day. Otis, grab her."

When the huge man started toward her, she felt her legs give out. She crumpled to the ground, trying to weep silently for fear she'd make the man with the gun mad enough to shoot her if she made too much noise. When the big man picked her up with no effort whatsoever, she remembered how Benny had picked her up in that fantasy she'd been having moments ago. As he slung her over his shoulder and started back through the bushes with her, she tried to make it come back, to escape into it so she wouldn't have to focus on what was about to happen to her.

She couldn't do it, couldn't concentrate enough to make the images reappear. To her dismay, she was too terrified to remember what Benny even looked like anymore.

She cried against the big man's back and wished she'd stayed with the others. It might not have stopped any of this from happening, but at least she could have had the comfort of knowing she wouldn't be dying alone.

ELEVEN

SHE NEVER SAW THE TANGLE of roots until it was too late. Ami felt her foot sink into the mud, her ankle struck unyielding wood, and then she was falling. Had she been alone, she would have been lucky to escape with nothing more than a broken ankle. Luckily, Rob caught her before she was fully off-balance and held her steady as she worked her leg out of the trap nature had improvised for her. At first, it didn't want to come free, but after one last jerk of her leg, she was released. She grimaced as she felt layers of skin peeling away as her foot scraped across the rough bark. She looked down, expecting to see rivulets of blood pooling around her, and was pleasantly surprised to only find a series of nasty, barely oozing scratches instead.

"Thanks," she said, tentatively putting her weight down on that foot. There was a slight sting of pain that reminded her of the scraped knees she sometimes got as a child, and her ankle did not feel like it wanted to buckle when she applied pressure to it. "That could've been bad."

"Tell me about it," Rob replied. "If we find those packs, there's no way I'd be able to carry them *and* you back. Well, I guess I could float you in the river and guide you along, but that's a lot of work, you know?"

She turned to face him, shocked at how callous he sounded, but immediately noticed the grin he was fighting to hide. She tried to look serious but couldn't hold back a smile of her own.

"Is that how we're handling injuries now?" she asked. "Let the river do the hard work?"

He shrugged, still grinning. "It's how I got you to shore the first time. Figured it would work just as well now, too."

It hadn't crossed her mind until now to wonder whether it had been Rob or Jay that hauled her to shore after the raft flipped, but for some strange reason she found it a relief it had been Rob. It didn't make much sense that she would prefer someone she didn't know saving her life over her oldest friend, but that was the case. Maybe Benny had seen something she hadn't realized herself. Maybe she really did have something of a crush on Rob. Nothing she was consciously aware of, but she supposed it was possible. Not that it mattered. The situation they were in was more important than her emotional issues.

She could feel her cheeks starting to redden from thinking about it. If she looked at him any longer, she knew they would explode into a full-blown blush, so she looked up at the sky instead. The sun was still out, but it didn't look like it would be for very much longer. They'd made it a good distance up the shore, but they weren't going to be able to go much farther if they wanted to be back at the clearing before nightfall. So far, their search had been fruitless. She had a sinking feeling it would remain so.

The temperature was dropping steadily, but so far it was still tolerable. The stiff breeze that had been there when they set out this morning had faded to barely more than a whisper against her bare skin, which probably helped. If it was still as strong as it had been, she was sure she'd be chilled to the bone. Without a fire, there was no way she'd be able to get rid of that chill, either.

Of course, if they didn't find the packs, there was a very good chance she'd get to experience that anyway.

She looked back to Rob and found him holding onto a hanging branch for balance as he leaned over the river and poked at something with a large stick he'd picked up somewhere. His face was a mask of intense concentration that lent an air of rugged handsomeness to him she'd never noticed before now. Not that he was bad-looking to start with. It was just that seriousness changed his features in some indefinable way she found appealing.

She shook her head, wondering what was wrong with her

that she was thinking about such things while they were trying to find a way to stay warm during the cold night ahead. Some way to stay alive. Beyond that, she was still technically in a relationship with Benny, even if she was planning on ending it when the day started.

"Find something?" she asked, hoping to distract herself by focusing on the task at hand.

"Maybe," he replied through clenched teeth as he leaned out farther over the river. "If I can just . . . there!"

He carefully and methodically dragged whatever it was he'd caught on the end of that stick toward the shore. With what appeared to be considerable effort to maintain his grip on both the stick and the branch, and still maintain control of whatever he found, he flipped the object up onto the muddy bank nearby.

It was a scrap of blue rubber no bigger than a washcloth. Ami noted duly it was the same shade as their raft had been. But they had flipped farther down the river. If they were finding parts of it all the way back here, they had been in more danger than they'd known.

From the look on Rob's face, he'd come to the same conclusion. He shook his head and let out a low whistle. He stepped down off the root he'd balanced on and studied the edges of the scrap. Finally he looked over at her, his face drawn.

"I knew we got lucky," he said, gesturing to the piece of raft. "But I didn't know we got that lucky."

"What's it from?" she asked. "I mean, I can guess it's part of the raft, but I don't remember any holes."

He flipped the piece over and studied the other side. "If I had to guess, I'd say it's from the bottom. There's some pretty deep gouges in it that probably came from all the rocks it's gone over during its lifetime. At a glance, I'd wager that first drop punctured it, and the continued abuse tore it loose before it finally caught on those rocks over there and came off completely. No wonder it got so hard to steer the thing at the end, even discounting all the power we lost as people lost their oars or got hurt or whatever."

Ami shivered and rubbed her hands across her arms to try and stop the goose bumps that suddenly broke out across them. "So there was no way we would've made it to the other side of the river, back to the side where the trucks were, was there?"

Rob shook his head. "It's possible, but it would've been a bigger miracle than us surviving getting thrown out of the thing. The only reason we hadn't already sunk was because so many rocks were so close to the surface, and the current was strong enough to keep pushing us along. As soon as we'd hit smoother waters, we'd have gone under."

"At least we know we're in the right spot," she said, no longer wanting to think about how close they'd come to death. "Think we'll find the bags around here anywhere?"

"We found this," he said. "That *is* a good sign. Let's go further upriver. I kind of lost track of distance and time once things got crazy, but I think we're close to where we lost the bags."

She nodded. He stood up and brushed off his knees, then picked up the scrap of rubber and tucked it under his arm. She frowned at him, but he smiled and shrugged.

"You never know what you might need," he said.

She expected him to take the lead as they continued onward, but instead he walked alongside her. She hadn't even noticed how the pathway had widened the farther they went, with only the occasional tree along the side of the river to break it up. A part of her wanted to keep glancing over at him as they walked, but she restrained herself. She remembered reading somewhere that people who find themselves in life-threatening situations sometimes develop an attraction to one another as a sort of defense mechanism, a way to bond so they could be a more efficient team to survive whatever came at them. Maybe what she was feeling was that instinct coming out and not anything that would survive beyond the amount of time they found themselves stuck in the woods. If it wasn't, well, she would deal with that when the time came.

They continued on in silence, and while it wasn't at all uncomfortable, Ami found her mind wandering in directions she didn't want it to go. Fears about how they were going to survive not just tonight but however many nights there were yet to come. She was sure they'd try to look for a road or some other sign of civilization or safety tomorrow, but that was no guarantee they'd be rescued.

"So, what were you and your friends from Boulder doing all the way out here?" she asked. She tried to tell herself she was doing it to drown out all those negative thoughts, but she knew there was more to it than that.

"Vacation," Rob replied, stopping to help her across a particularly nasty tangle of underbrush. "We were trying to think of a place to do what you guys were, and none of us had been this far east in a while, so we decided to give it a whirl."

"Where'd you guys end up going?"

"Nowhere exotic or crazy, if that's what you're thinking," he said. "Just a basic run down the Upper Pigeon. Honestly, I think we spent more time hitting the normal tourist stuff than we did actually on the river."

She nodded. "Your group been doing this a long time, then?"

He laughed softly. "Too long, maybe, at least in my case. The group's changed over the years, but there's always been a few of us in it for the long haul."

"You guys all go to school together, or something like that?"

"Actually, the core group's been together since *high* school."

"That long?"

He laughed again. "I look old enough for you to be that surprised?"

"I didn't mean that," she said, her cheeks starting to burn again. "I just . . ."

"I know what you meant," Rob said, still chuckling. "I'm busting your chops. And I guess when I stop to think about it, it really *has* been a long time. I'm facing down my twenty-year reunion next year, so to you I probably *am* old."

"Not that old," she said, trying to steer this conversation back into less embarrassing territory. For her, anyway. "And I'm not *that* young. I've got a reunion coming up in a couple of years myself."

"Oh, yeah? Which one?"

Instead of making things better, she was only making them worse. "Tenth. In three years."

Luckily she was saved from whatever response he might have when he stopped and leaned out over the river's edge again, his eyes locked on something beneath the surface. He studied it for a few minutes then shook his head and resumed walking.

"Found part of an oar," he said. "Wedged between a couple of rocks. Wonder whose it was."

She had no idea, only a faint recollection of extreme fear followed by her hitting the water. She knew who was hurt before that, but could not for the life of her remember the order it happened in. Since she didn't know, she didn't bother replying.

Instead she said, "So, you ever bring your girlfriend along on your runs?"

She immediately wanted to kick herself for asking. It was the least subtle thing she could've done, and for that matter she wasn't really sure why she was so curious about his relationship status in the first place. She thought she'd moved past that. Obviously, she hadn't.

"When I had one, sure," he replied. Thankfully, he didn't sound amused or offended by the question. Ami hoped he took it as idle conversation and not an attempt to pry. "A couple of them even liked it. But this time, all of us found ourselves single and bored, so it was a kind of guys' weekend that lasted a little longer."

She jumped at the chance to get back onto a safer topic. "How long did it last?"

Rob chuckled. "Two weeks."

"Seriously? You must have a super understanding boss to let you off for two weeks."

"Nope," he said, shrugging. "I got laid off. That's sort of what prompted it, actually. Since I had no job and no prospects yet, the guys decided we should do this to take my mind off it. I had a decent chunk in savings, so I pulled some of it, we loaded up a couple of our vehicles, and off we went to see the country."

"That's why you agreed to be our guide even though you thought it was a bad idea," she said. "You needed the money."

"No, like I told you back at the hotel: I did it so I could rest easy knowing someone had tried to keep you guys from killing yourselves."

He was silent for a moment, then let out a long sigh. "The money didn't hurt, though."

"Good."

He stopped and turned to face her, a bemused look on his face. "Good? How so? Especially considering what a *wonderful* job I did."

"You did do a wonderful job," she told him. "None of this is your fault. You tried, but you can't overcome stupid. And it's good, because for a while there, you didn't seem real. I mean, nobody's that altruistic, especially with people they don't know."

"Happy to see the perfect man actually has a raging zit on his nose?"

"Was that a thinly veiled shot at my age?"

A crooked smile formed on his lips. "Maybe."

She swatted him playfully on the arm, then froze. Just beyond him, she could see something red floating in the river. She ignored the curious look he gave her and stepped to the edge of the bank, straining to make it out. Finally she recognized it: Eric's bag. From here, it looked like the strap was looped around a branch sticking up out of the water, the current pulling the nylon taut as it tried to rip the bag away from the obstruction.

"Well I'll be damned," Rob said, finally noticing it as well. "Not mine, but it's progress."

"It's Eric's," she told him. "He took this stuff seriously. There's a good chance he might have something useful in there."

Rob looked around and found one of the trees that sat along the edge of the riverbank before moving over to it. Using the root to keep himself somewhat secure against the raging current, he stepped into the water, wincing at the sudden change in temperature, and began easing his way toward the spot where the bag was. Ami could see him set his legs firmly and reach as far as he could. His fingertips came within inches of the strap, but it wasn't enough. He couldn't reach without letting go of the tree keeping him from being pulled into the current.

It took obvious effort, but he finally managed to pull himself back onto shore.

"Damn it all," he said, struggling to catch his breath. "Any ideas?"

She did have an idea, but it wasn't one she particularly liked. Even considering it caused her stomach to feel like it was turning somersaults. She didn't want to mention it, but they needed that pack. They needed matches or something they could use to start a fire, and she was fairly certain they would find them in there. She had to try.

"What if I went out?" she asked, her voice barely audible over the noise of the rushing water. "You hang onto me so I don't get pulled in, and I grab it."

Rob's head snapped up to look at her, all traces of humor gone from his face. "No way. No way in hell you're doing that."

"We need that bag, Rob," she said. Her voice came out rough, which made sense to her since she felt like her heart was in her throat. "Even if there's no matches in it, I know he's got a first aid kit. You can't honestly tell me we don't need it."

She could tell her words were having an effect on him, but he still shook his head. "It's too dangerous. Maybe if I tried again, go out further this time . . ."

"You'd be able to touch it, not grab it," she finished for him. "I was watching. I saw how close you got and how hard it was to keep yourself upright. I can't hold you so you can try. I'm not strong enough. You have to hold me and let me go for it."

He dropped his head and stared at the ground, nodding slightly. She knew what he must be thinking. He wanted to tell her to forget about it, they'd make do. He also knew how right she was about needing a first aid kit and a fire tonight. Finally, he looked up, his face unhappy, but resigned.

"We try it once," he said. "And when I tell you to stop and come back, you do it. No heroic efforts here. If you can't get it, we forget about it and go back. I will *not* let you kill yourself on a maybe, understood?"

Ami took a long, shuddering breath and nodded. "Understood."

"Can't believe I'm doing this," he muttered. "Come here."

He took hold of the tree again and stepped back into the river. He nodded to the spot directly in front of him. "I'll block the current as much as I can until we're situated. And it's *strong* out there. It was all I could do to stay on my feet. I have no idea whether I'll be able to keep you up, too. But I promise you I won't let go of you until you're back on shore and safe, you hear me? And don't you even *think* about letting go of me."

She nodded and took hold of his shoulders before stepping off the bank and back into the water. She remembered it being cold when she was thrown from the raft, but it had dropped several degrees since then. Her feet were exposed through her open sandals, and felt like she'd dipped them into a pool filled with ice cubes. They started to go numb almost immediately, so she knew she wouldn't have any time to waste.

Using Rob as a brace, Ami worked her way across his chest with her hands, grabbing onto his shirt for purchase until she reached his other arm. When she got to his wrist, she felt his hand close around her arm almost tight enough to hurt. She was sure she was going to have a handprint there when this was all over, but if it kept her safe, she'd wear it like a badge of honor. She turned her hand enough to clamp onto his forearm as well and began easing past him toward the bag.

As soon as she was past the shield of his body, the current snatched at her legs, threatening to rip them out from under her and send her splashing into the river. Rob hadn't been kidding about how strong the current was here. Taking even the smallest step and trying to not be knocked off course was like fighting the momentum of a car pushing against her. She tried to not let herself focus on it, to concentrate on taking small but productive steps, on the elation she'd feel once she grabbed that bag, on the iron grip of Rob's hand keeping her safe.

When she got to the spot she thought he had been earlier, she felt him hook his ankle around her leg for added support. Crazily, she wondered if he could feel the bristles of new hair the cold had raised on her legs through her tights. She felt no embarrassment from the thought, only relief. It was something else to think about other than the insane danger she was putting herself in.

She reached out and felt her fingers brush against wet wood before transitioning to tight, smooth fabric. She reached again but was unable to get her fingers between the branch and the strap. She changed her angle and tried to get in front of the branch, where the sides of the strap trailed out in nearly parallel lines to the bag itself. She could manage it—just—but she still couldn't get her fingers under the strap enough to snag it. She tried to take another step forward, but Rob had given her all the ground he was willing to. She could feel his hand trembling as he fought to hold onto her.

Ami refused to come so close and yet fail. She unhooked her leg from his and made one final lunge. The second she did, it was like the car that had been pushing against her had suddenly floored the gas pedal. The current hit her full force, throwing her severely off-balance. She fought to regain her footing, but every time she tried to get her legs beneath her again, the current renewed its efforts to thwart her attempt. Her foot came down on a submerged rock and went out from under her, the soles of her sandals unable to find any purchase on the slick surface.

She hit the water face first and suddenly realized the freezing pain in her feet hadn't been so bad. She floundered for air, struggling to keep her mouth and nose above the water with only minimal success. She realized this was it—she was going to die. She'd come this far, but she'd ignored Rob's warning, and now she'd managed to kill herself. She hoped he wouldn't blame himself too much for it.

She wondered if her body would ever be found, so her parents could have a decent funeral for her.

She felt as though she were being pulled in two, her shoulder screaming in agony as the current tore at her. Her eyes had been closed since she first hit the water, and she kept them that way, praying for her death to be fast in spite of the knowledge that drowning–especially when she could still get *some* air—was apt to be a long and agonizing affair.

Inexplicably, she felt herself moving sideways in the current and decided she didn't want to die. She wanted to fight, to live, to somehow make it out of this, to cheat death for a second time in a single day. She scrambled to regain her footing and found the current seemed to be releasing her. She didn't question it, only continued struggling to remain upright.

She felt the pressure in her shoulder relent as a pair of arms encircled her and dragged her to the side. She wanted to fight against it, but a voice kept whispering in her ear, telling her it was all right, she was okay, it was all over. She stopped fighting and felt exhaustion try to overtake her. Her legs felt rubbery and weak, barely able to support her weight. She felt the pressure of the water slide farther and farther down her legs, until finally her feet reemerged into the cool air and began to burn furiously, expressing anger at how they had been mistreated.

She felt herself being laid gently on her back and opened her eyes. The sky was above her, beyond the outstretched tree branches. Suddenly, it was replaced by a face—Rob's face, filled with terror and concern. Hands wiped at her forehead, pulling errant strands of hair out of her eyes with a jerky quickness that bordered on frantic. She was still breathless, but after a furious coughing fit that left her legs and stomach muscles aching, she was able to breathe somewhat normally again.

The full impact of her failure and near death crashed down on her. She felt hot tears well up in her eyes and begin to stream down her cheeks, warming them and stinging when the salt came into contact with nicks she didn't even know she had.

"I'm sorry," she wailed when she was finally able to form coherent words again. "I was so close and I didn't want to give up and I almost had it but I couldn't get it and I should've listened and I almost died because I didn't listen and I messed up and I'm so *sorry.*"

"It's okay," Rob said, his voice gentle and soothing. He stroked her hair, trying to calm her. "You're safe. It's okay."

"*No it's not!*" she cried. "I was *so close!* I couldn't reach!"

"Ami," Rob said. "Look at your hand."

The strange request actually managed to cut through her anguish enough to raise her curiosity. She lifted her head and let her gaze trail down her shaking arm, past what looked like a nasty bruise forming on her forearm, finally coming to rest on the tangle of red nylon twisted around her wrist. She raised it and felt the weight behind it, the soft patter of water drops hitting the ground sounding like an angel's chorus to her ears. She let her gaze travel farther, to the red nylon bag suspended above the muddy riverbank.

TWELVE

HIS WATCH HAD BEEN BROKEN at some point along the line, probably when he was thrown mercilessly from the raft, so Benny had no idea how long he had been walking when he made his discovery. It wasn't the raft, or the remains of the raft, or his friends. Instead, he found himself staring at a wooden dock someone had built on the riverbank. It looked old and weathered, splinters sticking up in various spots from wood that wasn't quite gray from exposure, but was far from the normal tan of relatively new timber.

Visions of backwoods, shotgun-toting hillbillies raced through his head as he quickly crouched behind the brush. He hoped wildly he hadn't stumbled across someone's shack in the wilderness, where they lived off the land and probably had never seen another living soul in roughly ten years or so. He hadn't survived this long only to wind up with an ass full of buckshot or a slug ripping the top of his head off. If he was lucky enough to die fast. He'd seen *Deliverance*. He wasn't squealing like a pig for no-fucking-body.

After several tense moments while he waited for someone to yell out an alarm, fire a weapon into the air to try and draw him out, or something else like they did in the movies or on TV, Benny forced himself to peek out at the dock again. There was no one there, and from what he could see, there wasn't even a boat tied up alongside the dock. If this was the landing port for someone's property, they must not be home at the moment.

He stepped slowly out of his hiding place, ready to take off running in the opposite direction should anyone accost him. Once standing beside the dock, he turned, scanned the area around him, and realized his fears were all for nothing. He was as alone as he could be.

A trail led from the end of the dock up through the trees before curving slightly and disappearing behind them. It looked well-traveled, the dirt packed so hard that stepping onto the mud didn't even leave a hint of a footprint behind. Faint tread marks were visible along the trail, reminding him of the massive tires on his cousin's ATV back home. Taking that into consideration, it wasn't very likely he'd stumbled onto a hillbilly's home out here, but more likely a hunting camp of some sort. People probably took the road he and the others came in on to a point opposite this, ferried over to this side, and then rode the rest of the way to the camp for a weekend to try and bag some big game. These woods were probably full of all kinds of wildlife that would make a hunter piss his pants with joy.

Benny turned and squinted against the glare of the sun reflecting off the river. It was much wider here, probably the result of the two forks joining back up somewhere behind him. He probably passed it without noticing, focused as he was on the shoreline he was walking along.

He could make out what appeared to be another dock on the far side of the river as well, helping to confirm his suspicions. A wider river also meant it was probably deeper—and obviously calmer—than it had been farther upstream, so crossing on a raft or ferry or whatever would only take moderate effort. He frowned and shaded his eyes with his hand, trying to get a better look at the far dock. Best he could tell, there was nothing tied to it either; no way for anyone to actually get across the river. It was entirely possible the raft or whatever they used had been pulled in for the winter and would come back in the spring once all the major thaws were done, but it seemed like a lot of trouble for something only a handful of people might ever stumble across in the first place.

He looked back at the clearing surrounding the dock on his side and felt more confusion set in. If his theory was correct about people ferrying over from the other side and then riding into the camp, where was the storage area for the ATVs on this side? Even if they were kept at the camp during the off-season, there should still be some kind of shelter around for when they were left out here while everything was running.

Maybe it was a work in progress and they hadn't built the shelter yet. Not likely, considering the amount of weathering on the dock itself, but it was the only thing that made any sense. The craft they used for passage was pulled up for the winter so it didn't break loose and wash away. The ATVs were stored at the camp itself, probably locked in a garage or heavy-duty shed or something. Benny could imagine the first person across every year having to walk up the trail to the camp, grab an ATV, and drive it back down to start shuttling his group up with all their shit. Maybe they stayed up there until someone called and asked for a lift down at the dock.

His eyes widened as he realized the implication there. If someone called for a ride, it would mean there was cell phone service up here. His hand flew to his pocket and patted at it frantically until he remembered he hadn't brought his phone with him. It was locked up in the center console of his truck, all the way on the other side of the river and several miles back up the road. In all reality, it probably wasn't that far, but with the river as a barrier, it might as well be on the other side of the Atlantic.

Still, if there was a hunting camp somewhere along that trail, there was a slim chance they might have a landline or something. He could call for help, get some park rangers out here to get him and help find any other possible survivors. He knew it was probably a false hope. He also knew that even if the camp had a landline, it was unlikely he'd run across anyone there to let him use it at this time of year. Still, it was better than wandering around aimlessly along the river, searching in what was, for all he knew, the wrong direction. For that matter, he had no way of knowing if his friends were even still alive. Having help would simplify things immensely and would also serve to shelter him from the possibility of discovering all his friends lying dead and broken along the river. There really wasn't any choice to make.

He turned and started up the trail.

He felt the muscles in his calves grow tight and then begin to burn. He shouldn't have been surprised. They were in the mountains, after all. It was only natural to think he would have to start walking uphill at some point. And if he thought about it, it made perfect sense. He'd been walking in the direction the river flowed. This far up, that meant he was walking on a decline the entire time. A gentle one, to be sure, but a decline all the same. Now that he'd switched directions and was walking away from the river, and curving back upstream to boot, he was on an incline. His legs weren't used to it, that was all. He'd deal with it. Hell, he'd already dealt with worse.

He wished he knew something about tracking, but he'd never been a Boy Scout, didn't have the patience for hunting, and never saw any reason to learn it. If he had, though, he might have some idea of how old those tracks embedded in the trail were. It might tell him if there *was* a chance of running into someone at whatever lay at the end of this trail. It wouldn't really matter all that much either way, but it would be nice to be prepared so he didn't startle anyone unintentionally and get himself shot for his trouble.

The trail led him beneath a thick canopy of branches, not too dissimilar to the road they'd been driving on when they first arrived this morning. Then, however, the sun was still high in the sky and penetrated enough to keep the road visible, even without headlights. Now that it was creeping behind the mountains, the trail ahead filled him with a sense of foreboding. It was quiet, empty, and desolate, with not even the sounds of birds to break the tension he felt building within him. It was ridiculous; he knew that. Still, the view made him remember every horror movie he'd ever seen, only this was in real life.

His bladder suddenly clenched, alerting him that, despite the abuse his body had taken over the course of the day, he was still alive and relatively healthy. Even with nothing going in, waste needed to go out. He veered off the trail into the trees, facing the river, freed himself from his shorts, and let fly. It burned at first and was a dark color when he glanced down at it. A sure sign he was dehydrated. His coach drilled him over and over back in school about the dangers of not taking in enough water when you were exerting yourself. Benny wondered what Coach Richards would say to him now he that didn't *have* any water to keep himself hydrated.

Once he was finished and had everything tucked away again, he looked up and saw another, smaller trail branching off the main one in the direction he was facing. He started down it, making sure to throw his leg way out on the first step so he'd miss the puddle he'd made. It didn't take long for him to find himself staring out at the river again, partially hidden by the thick foliage, but easily visible. The trampled brush continued on in that direction, apparently all the way to the bank itself, but that wouldn't help him. He was positive he'd already searched there. For all he knew, it was the place he'd awakened after the accident.

He turned to go back to the main trail and paused. There was a lot of damage to the brush here, mainly in one large grouping as if an animal had rolled over it a few times trying to make a nest for itself. He'd always thought bears lived in caves or something like that, but that was the only animal he could think of big enough to create an area that size. If it hadn't been a bear, he wasn't sure what it could have been, unless . . .

Benny shivered as he realized it could have been a person hiding there, watching the area near the river. He was almost positive now it *was* the place where he'd washed ashore, and the thought of someone watching him as he lay there unconscious was more than unnerving. Of course, judging from the size of that trampled-down brush, it had probably been more than one person hiding there, but he didn't want to even consider the implications of that.

It could have been his "friends" watching him. He could imagine that asshole Rob sitting on his ass and not doing anything to help him. Considering the way things were going, it wouldn't be too much of a surprise to picture Ami and Jay right there next to him. But even if he ignored the fact that Ami wouldn't have let him lie there, no matter what she was currently feeling about him, it still didn't add up. What about the others? What about Eric and Christy and Teddy? They wouldn't have allowed it.

Assuming they were still alive themselves, of course.

He shook his head, trying to force the paranoia away as he turned and headed back to the main trail again. He was jumping at shadows, his admittedly prejudiced views of backwoods rednecks out for human blood becoming too Eli Roth for his taste. His friends hadn't sat and watched him without trying to help.

Unless it was someone else.

His first assumption was correct, had to be. It had been an animal nesting there. It had probably happened long before he ever washed up on shore. For that matter, that might've been what scared it off. Maybe it even came out from cover, sniffed him a few times to see if he seemed like an appetizing meal, then scampered off to find something more tantalizing for breakfast. Looking at it that way, it was even a little cute.

So why was he more nervous than ever?

He felt the texture of the ground change under his feet and knew he was back on the main trail again. He didn't think he'd been gone that long, but it was considerably darker than it had been before he stopped to piss. The trail was barely visible, continuing forward for another hundred feet or so before curving sharply to the left. Hopefully he would come out of this shaded area pretty soon and find the camp on the other side of that curve. He seriously wanted to get there before he lost the light. The idea of creeping up on a strange place after dark was beyond unappealing.

Luckily, the cover provided by the overlapping branches did fade somewhat after he made the curve. The bad news was the trail continued in an obvious upward slope. This incline would be even steeper than what he'd made it up so far. His legs screamed in protest as he planted one foot in front of the other and forced himself onward.

He was panting by the time he made it to the top of the rise, sweat plastering his hair to his forehead. He wasn't this out of shape; he knew he wasn't. It had to be the combination of everything else he'd endured today piling up on him. He stopped, bent at the waist with his hands holding onto his legs above the knees, and fought to regain his breath.

There was enough light left when he straightened again to make out the shapes of buildings in the hollow below him. None of them seemed overly large, and for a moment, the layout made him think of his initial concept of someone living up here completely off the grid. He could make out what looked like a barn, another smaller structure next to it that could serve as a storage shed or something along those lines. Opposite them on the other side of a large clearing was another building that looked suspiciously like a house. Smoke eased its way from a chimney along one side and lights burned in the windows on what he thought must be the front.

He didn't see any buildings that could serve as barracks or sleeping quarters for a bunch of hunters, but that didn't really mean anything. He supposed they could always haul some sleeping bags or cots or something up here and sleep in the main house or cabin or whatever it was. It hardly mattered at this point. It was obvious there were other people down there. Even if they didn't have a landline, they might have working cell phones. Barring that, they might have a way out of the woods where they could get him some help. It was what he'd been hoping to find, even if it wasn't exactly what he was *expecting* to find.

Going down the hill again was considerably easier than coming up it. He even found himself nearly running in spots where the slope got steeper than he anticipated. At least it was never steep enough to send him tumbling forward. It would be just his luck today to go rolling ankles over ass down the hill and break his neck at the bottom when he was so close to potential salvation. He forced himself to take it easy and not let his excitement get the better of him.

As he neared the camp or whatever, he was able to make out more details about it. Poles were set up at apparently random intervals along the central clearing. When he glanced up, Benny could see massive lights mounted atop them, angled so they pointed at the ground. He felt hope: lights meant electricity. It was possible—even likely—they were powered by a generator, but either way, it meant civilization. If those things were powered by a generator, they had to have a way of getting a substantial amount of gas in here. Ferrying it across the river wouldn't be practical, not in large amounts, which meant a road. A way out of here. Safety.

He could also make out the vague shape of another large, barn-shaped building along the back of the property. He wasn't sure why he hadn't seen it from the top of the hill, but it could've been almost anything. Angle, trick of the fading light, who knew? And ultimately, who cared?

Inside what he thought was a storage shed, he could see the shapes of two massive four-wheeled ATVs resting in the shadows. A long trailer sat nearby, its tongue resting on a chunk of wood so it wouldn't be hard to attach when needed. Just beyond that, he thought he could see a fairly good-sized boat of some sort, a canoe or Johnboat or something. He had no idea why it would be on *this* side of the river instead of stored near the opposite dock he'd seen, but that was a riddle for more comfortable surroundings.

As he made his way into the compound, he saw the door to the other barn he'd seen was slightly ajar, flickering light outlining its edges. He thought he saw a shadow pass across it and realized someone was in there. Maybe that would be better. He could tell them what happened and ask them for help without disturbing them in their home or whatever. He angled toward it and picked up his step. Not too much, he didn't want to scare them, but enough to let his excitement feel he was giving in a little.

He forced himself to stop before the doors rather than swing them open and race inside. He knocked, three hard but respectful raps with his knuckles, then eased the door open wide enough to stick his head in.

"Hello?" he called. "Anyone in here? Me and my friends need some help pretty desperately. Our raft flipped down on the river. Hello?"

He thought he heard scurrying sounds, but no other answer came. That shadow briefly blocked the light again and then moved away. He felt a flash of fear, sure someone had heard him but didn't want to let on they had, but he ignored it. He wasn't in a position to even look threatening right now, nor had his words sounded so. Why wouldn't they answer him if they were in there?

"Hey, I don't want to hurt you or anything," he said, stepping tentatively into the barn. "I need your help. Wouldn't even be here, otherwise."

The scurrying sounds were not repeated, only that strange blockage of the light that went away as soon as it appeared. He frowned and took another couple of cautious steps inside. He could see whatever was casting the light was coming from deeper in and around the side of a partition of some sort. He started toward it.

"Look, you help me out and I'll make sure you're rewarded for it. I don't have much, but I'm sure my parents will chip in. You'll make out pretty good, and all I need is to either use your phone or catch a ride to a ranger station or something."

Still no answer. Benny realized he was starting to sweat

again but couldn't figure out why. The air had gotten distinctly cooler as the sun started to set. He wasn't the least bit warm, nor was he exerting himself, so why the sweat?

He finally made it to the partition and stepped around it. He froze, unable to comprehend the sight before him.

A girl hung from the crossbeam under the second floor, a thick length of chain looped around her wrists, leading upward. She was swaying, the motion carrying her back and forth in front of the candle resting on a table behind her. Her head lolled to one side, hair covering her face. She was obviously unconscious. She was also obviously naked, the long shadows from the candle wrapping her even as they highlighted bare breasts and the space between her thighs.

Benny found his gaze wandering across her body, lingering on her breasts, the nipples barely detectable in the dim light; down her stomach, drawn tight by her weight against the chain that bound her; across the shadowed cleft between her legs that made him think she kept her pubic hair trimmed—if she had any at all; all the way down to the painted toenails that were a deep shade of red the candlelight seemed to enhance.

Benny drew in a sharp breath: he knew those toenails. He'd watched her paint them last night, after their dip in the hot tub back at the hotel.

"Christy?"

He took a tentative step closer, his breath going ragged as he began to make out the dark stripes across her torso not caused by some trick of the light. He reached out with a shaking hand and brushed the hair out of her face, wincing as he saw the massive bruise forming along one entire side of it.

"Well I be dipped in shit," a voice said behind him. "The dummy was right about somebody else bein' there."

Benny spun and saw a man standing out of arm's reach. The man was thin, but his bare chest and arms were crisscrossed with wiry ropes of muscle that looked hard as marble. He was smiling, one hand behind his back, the other holding onto the side of his camouflage pants. His belt and the top two buttons were undone, sending a sick realization through Benny of the cause for all the scurrying when he knocked.

He glanced back at Christy, forcing himself to focus on her lower body, and finally noticed the trail of liquid running down the inside of her thigh as she turned into the light. Anger raced through him, anger on behalf of his friend and the violation she apparently endured before he arrived. He spun back around, his hands balling into fists, ready to beat the life from this little shit who seemed so nonchalant about raping someone, much less someone Benny knew and cared about. He took a single step and then scrambled backward, shocked by the appearance of a large pistol in the man's hand. Even with only shadows to work with, Benny could see the hammer was cocked and the gun was ready to fire.

"I don't think so, dipshit," the man said, his smile going wider at Benny's reaction. "Only reason I don't plug you right now is on account of you havin' use to us. That bitch there didn't know shit about shit, but I'm thinkin' you might."

"I'm not telling you anything," Benny said, his heart pounding. "I don't even know what you're talking about. I've never seen this girl before in my life."

"That so?" the man asked. The way he said it told Benny he didn't believe a word Benny was saying. The man closed the distance between them, the gun never wavering from Benny's face. "Well I know lotsa shit. For example, did you know torturin' somebody don't usually tell you nothin' useful? They tell what you want to hear, so's the pain'll stop."

It seemed like a question, so Benny answered, too afraid of what might happen if he didn't. "No, I didn't know that."

"It's the God's honest truth," the man said, his eyebrows raising. "Course, that only really works if you been trained to resist it some, which I'm bettin' you ain't."

"Clint!" another man's voice called out from the doorway. "Otis saw somebody up on the hill, that him?"

"Yeah!" the first man—Clint, apparently—called back. "Back here, Gene."

Benny felt his heart drop. If they weren't taking precautions about using their names, there was little chance he was going to make it out of this alive.

"Here's the thing, though," Clint said, addressing Benny again. "I don't much like torturin' guys. Seems kinda faggish to me, you know? But there's this other trick I know. You want somebody to tell you somethin', you do the torture on somebody they care about. Then, unless they're a cold-blooded prick or somethin', they tell you damn near anything. Takes longer 'fore you get the real shit, not bein' them feelin' the pain directly, you understand. But they end up talkin'."

The man was almost nose-to-nose with Benny now. He ached to punch him, but the gun was right between his eyes, blocking his vision. It would be a wild punch, and if he missed, he doubted he'd get another chance. Not to mention Clint might decide to do something with the gun other than kill him.

"So, best you settle in, shithead," Clint said, his breath redolent with stale cigarettes, whiskey, and what to Benny smelled like a sewer. "We got us a long night ahead." The gun disappeared. Benny started to let out a relieved breath, and then he felt the handle smash against his temple. The world went hazy as he drifted toward the earthen floor of the barn. He saw he was about to land in a puddle of what looked like blood, and wondered briefly if it belonged to Christy before the darkness overtook him for the second time that day.

THIRTEEN

THUNDER RUMBLED OVERHEAD, MAKING Ami pause while pulling the things out of the bag she and Rob recovered. She glanced upward, a worried look on her face. There didn't appear to be any threatening clouds overhead, but it could still be blowing in from somewhere. She didn't remember anything on the weather reports about storms, but weathermen had been known to be wrong before. Besides, after the day they'd already had, it would be their luck to get caught in the middle of a freak thunderstorm while they were in the process of trying to survive the night without freezing to death.

No one else seemed to have noticed. If they had, they didn't react to the thunder in any way she could see. Rob was placing stones in a circle to create a pit, and Jay was collecting scraps of wood from farther inland so they'd have a better chance of it being dry enough to burn easily. Eric was sitting nearby, holding his own folded and now soaking wet shirt to his head to try and keep the swelling down. From what Jay said, he'd awakened not long before she and Rob returned from their search, confused and with a headache that apparently rivaled her own. At least hers had faded somewhat the longer she was awake—provided she didn't touch the nasty bump on the back of it, that was—but his held on despite their best efforts to help him get rid of it.

He'd also complained of difficulty getting his vision to focus at times, but whether that was a normal side effect of the trauma he'd endured or a sign of something far worse developing, was something none of them had been able to answer. As far as Ami knew, Eric had only been hit by one of the bags as it was thrown from the raft, but there was no telling what other things he might have hit after he was thrown out. And he had been unconscious for the better part of the day, while she had awakened relatively quickly after her own injury. Food for thought, perhaps, but not something she needed to focus on immediately.

"You're sure you had matches in here?" she asked, still digging through the bag and spreading its contents on the ground around her. So far, she'd managed to find the first aid kit, a towel, and the clothes he'd been wearing when they started out today, but there was so much other apparently useless crap stuffed down inside the duffel she felt like she was looking for a needle in a haystack.

"They were in there last time," he replied, not raising his head to look at her. "The bag's waterproof, so except for the towels and wet clothes, I usually don't bother with unpacking it."

She pulled out a wad of papers that on closer inspection appeared to be receipts from fast-food places and sporting goods stores and raised an eyebrow at him. "Yeah, I can tell."

Finally, she felt her fingers close around something that seemed like it was the right size. She pulled it out and let out a laugh when she saw the box of kitchen matches resting in her palm. Her hand trembled slightly as she pushed the cardboard drawer out, but the laughter died on her lips as she saw the contents.

"There's only two left in here," she said, looking over to Eric. "Did you know there was only two matches left in here?"

"No," he said. He winced as he looked up at her, his face apologetic. "I told you, I don't unpack anything I don't have to out of there, so I hadn't noticed."

"When have you used them?" she asked, unable to remember any occasion where he'd pulled them out while they were together.

"I don't remember," he said. "I think the last time was when we rafted over to that little island and camped out for the night."

It took her a few moments to remember the occasion he was referring to. Once she did, she found herself giving him an even more incredulous look than before. "That was, like, three years ago."

He winced again. This time Ami didn't think it was from the pain in his head so much as from the shame she was unintentionally making him feel. "Yeah, sorry."

"It's fine," Rob said, mercifully saving her from putting her foot any farther into her mouth. "Two should be plenty if we're careful. One for a fire tonight, and one for another fire tomorrow if things don't go well trying to find a way out of here. If we're stuck out here in these woods any longer, we've got bigger issues to deal with than running out of matches."

She nodded, closed the matches back up and tossed them to him. He caught them one-handed, almost snatching them out of the air in a swift downward motion. He held them in his cupped hand as he dropped some of the dry leaves they'd gathered into a pile before stacking several of the smaller sticks on top of them. Once that was done, he began arranging some of the bigger sticks in a pyramid above that.

"Looks like you know how to do that part of it at least," Jay said as he knelt beside Rob and dropped the armload of potential firewood he'd gathered. He glanced up at the darkening sky. "Not a moment too soon, either. I think we're officially out of light."

"Looks like," Rob murmured. He took out one of the matches, checked for the direction of the wind, and turned his back to it before leaning over the makings for a fire and striking the match. Nothing happened. Ami felt a moment of fear that dissipated when he managed to get it alight on the second attempt. He cupped his other hand around it to further shield it from any errant breeze and leaned even closer to the dry leaves. There was a moment of worry as the flame dropped from a healthy bright orange to a small, pale blue, but it flamed back up after only the briefest of heart-attack-inducing threats.

He touched the flame to several spots around the pile of leaves. Ami heard him hiss in a breath as the match burned down to his fingers, but she could see the thin tendrils of smoke beginning to rise from the kindling. Rob held on as long as he could before dropping the spent match into the middle of the pile, shaking his hand to try and alleviate some of the sting he must be feeling in his fingers, and then began gently prodding at the smoldering leaves with another stick.

Just as Ami was beginning to think the embers weren't going to catch, she saw a flickering glow begin to emanate from the smaller branches atop the leaves. A minute or so later, the flames grew as the pyramid of sticks began to catch as well. It wasn't perfect, and it was still in danger of going out easily, but at least they finally had something resembling a fire.

Rob and Jay both worked carefully, adding, moving, and adjusting the burning sticks until they had a nice blaze. Rob let out a long, shaky breath and leaned back on his heels, admiring it before turning to Ami and giving her a relieved smile.

"Whatta ya think?" he asked.

"It's the most beautiful thing I've ever seen," she said, smiling back at him. She scooted herself closer and nearly sighed when the warmth of the fire began to caress her outstretched hands. "All we need now are some marshmallows."

"Oh, God," Jay said. "Don't mention f-o-o-d right now. We're going to end up all Donner party if we don't watch it."

Rob chuckled. "I doubt it'll get that bad. If it helps, I'm probably pretty stringy. Wouldn't be very appetizing."

Eric barked a laugh that he appeared to immediately regret because of how it made his head move. He quieted and scooted closer to the fire himself.

The four of them sat in silence, hands outstretched to the growing flames. Ami was almost positive she was going to turn into a cloud of steam if it got any warmer. At the moment, she couldn't care less. She was shivering already. If she'd had to go any longer without a chance to warm up, she was positive she would turn into an icicle. She inched closer, hoping to warm the rest of her body the way her hands were. After several more minutes of silently trying to warm up, she frowned. Her shivers weren't going away.

She was starting to think about getting on all fours with the fire beneath her like a pig on a spit to try and get warm when she felt a hand on her thigh. It was on the side where Rob was, and she felt a flash of excitement at his boldness. It faded quickly into puzzlement at why he would make such an overt move in front of the other two. He didn't seem the type, not to mention he hadn't shown any interest in her so far. She knew she should tell him to stop, but she also didn't want to. It actually felt kind of good there.

The hand squeezed gently and moved down to above her knee before returning to a spot above where it began. Rob pulled his hand away and put it on her stomach.

"Um," she said, thankful no one would be able to see how red her face was becoming in the glow of the fire. "Rob, you're kind of in my personal space here."

She smiled over at him, but he was not smiling in return. His face bore a look of concern instead.

"You're freezing still," he said. "Do you feel cold?"

"A little," she admitted. "Not bad, though, thanks for asking."

"Shit," he said, jumping to his feet and rushing over to the pile of clothes and junk she'd pulled from Eric's bag. "Can't believe it never occurred to me before now."

"What never occurred to you?" Jay asked. Ami saw a look of confusion and concern on his face that made her nervous.

"Hypothermia," Rob said. He grabbed the two towels and Eric's jeans from the pile. "When you went in that last time, you got soaked all over. The sun was going down, so it didn't have time to dry you out again. The temperature's been dropping steadily since then, and you've been out in it in soaking wet clothes."

Ami started to argue she wasn't catching hypothermia, but another round of shivers racked her body and made her reconsider. She frowned, realizing those bouts were coming further and further apart, but she didn't really feel any warmer. "How is that possible? I've been sitting next to this fire just like you have."

"It dried the outside," Rob said, handing her the bundle of clothes he'd collected. "But you were soaked to the skin. It's lowered your body temperature, and now all the moisture is absorbing the heat before it gets to you. You need to get those wet clothes off, dry off, and put on dry ones. And you need to do it fast."

Her face felt as hot as the fire again. "With the three of you sitting right here? Somebody have a dollar they're going to throw at me or something?"

"We'll go over there," Rob said. Jay immediately leapt to his feet and started toward Eric. "We'll keep our backs turned. You let us know when it's safe to come back."

"But Eric's pants won't fit me," she replied. "We're not exactly the same size, in case you didn't notice."

"You're not trying to make a fashion statement," Rob shot back as he moved to the other side of Eric and helped Jay get the man to his feet. "You're trying to stay alive. Lay your stuff out by the fire. They'll dry, and then you can change back in the morning before we head out."

She got to her feet, the towels and pants clutched to her chest, and watched as the three guys moved off toward the edge of the fire's light and sat Eric down before joining him, all of them looking off at the trees. She was not relishing the idea of changing her clothes with the three of them still within sight of her, but at least she was on the opposite side of the fire from them so there wouldn't even be a shadow play for them to watch and potentially get their kicks from. She knew Rob was right, she needed to be in drier if not precisely warmer clothes, but knowing did nothing to help with her embarrassment.

There was no point in delaying the inevitable, so she took a deep breath and dropped the things she was holding to the ground next to her. She lifted her shirt and reached for the waistband of her yoga pants, then stopped, frowning, as she felt cool wetness on the backs of her hands, too.

"What about my shirt?" she called. "Eric was using his dry one as an icepack."

"Shit," Rob said. "Great thinking on our part, wasn't it? We could've given him one of the towels instead."

He stood and came back to her by the fire, unzipping and peeling off his fleece-lined jacket as he did. Underneath she could see he was wearing a long-sleeved t-shirt, but it looked exceptionally thin in the firelight. It would not be nearly enough to keep him warm if the night got much colder. She shook her head, not taking the jacket.

"No way," she said. "What are you supposed to wear?"

"I'm fine," he said, pushing the jacket toward her.

She took a step away from it. "I'm not making you freeze to death because I did something stupid earlier."

"That stupid thing you did is what makes it okay for you to take it," Rob insisted. "We have a fire now, remember? Since we do, I'll be fine. Don't forget, I've also got my wetsuit on under all this, so that helps even more. If you're still worried about it, give me one of those towels. I'll wrap myself in it if it gets too bad. But *you're* taking the jacket. You need it more than I do right now. That shirt's wet, so you *have* to get out of it. If it dries out enough before we get ready to crash for the night, change back. Until then, take the damn jacket."

Realizing she wasn't accomplishing anything by trying to argue with him, she took the jacket. He offered her a crooked grin as he let go of it. He picked up one of the towels she'd discarded and held it up so she could see he had it, and then returned to the others who were twisted around, watching the argument. Before Jay turned back around, he gave her a knowing grin that made her want to go over there and smack him one.

When they were all facing the other direction again, she dropped the jacket and quickly began unbuttoning her shirt. When she pulled it open, it felt as though she'd pressed herself against the wall of a walk-in cooler at some restaurant. She danced closer to the fire and sighed as she felt its warmth finally caress her skin and break through the chill she'd been fighting since her second fall into the water. She picked up the remaining towel and scrubbed vigorously at her skin, using the friction to assist in the warming process. Her hand brushed against the damp underside of her breast within the cotton of her bra and paused. She knew what Rob would say: if it was wet, don't wear it. After one more furtive glance to make sure no one was watching her, she reached behind her back and unsnapped it, then leaned forward so it fell down her arms.

She knelt next to the fire and spread it out to dry, reminding herself to cover both it and her underpants with the towel before telling them they could come back. She hesitated before rising, enjoying the feel of the fire's heat as it played across her bare breasts. There was something exhilarating about being topless out here in the wilderness with three men barely twenty paces away from her. At first, the concept had embarrassed her, but for some reason, it now felt strangely exciting.

Since she knew there was no way she was going to get her tight pants off over her sandals, she took the time while she was enjoying the fire to unfasten them and pull them off. The ground was actually warm under the soles of her feet as she stood again, the fire doing its job nicely. She hooked her thumbs under the waistband of her pants and panties and pulled them both down her legs at once before quickly stepping out of them and spreading them next to the fire.

As she dried herself, she found herself almost wanting Rob to turn around and see her standing naked in the firelight, her skin red and shimmering from its glow. He would come to her slowly, that crooked grin on his face, and take the towel from her with gentle hands before carefully and reverently rubbing it up and down across her legs, then moving up and in between them . . .

"Can you hurry it up over there?" Jay called. "I'm freezing my ass off."

She shook her head, forcing the vision away and wondering again what the hell had gotten into her. It had to be a result of that knock on the head. She didn't have thoughts like this about people she barely knew, stuck together in a crisis or not. She dropped the towel, turning one last time so the fire could warm her on both sides before pulling on Eric's jeans. As she expected, they were loose enough she could almost pull them back off again without unfastening them, but luckily, there was a belt threaded through the loops she was able to tighten enough to keep from exposing herself unintentionally. That done, she pulled on Rob's jacket and zipped it almost all the way to her neck, sighing as the soft lining caressed her bare skin and whispered across nipples she tried to convince herself were only hardened because of the cold.

She froze in place as she thought she caught a glimpse of something moving in the woods off to one side. She tried to look, moving nothing but her eyes for fear she might alert whatever it was that it had been spotted, but from what she could see, there was nothing there. The wind moving some of the branches or something simple. After another couple of uneventful minutes, she decided she was letting her mind play tricks on her.

"Okay," she called as she covered her underthings with the towel and started putting her sandals back on. "I'm decent again."

The others wasted no time in returning to the fire and huddling in close again. Ami made sure to take up as much space around the spot where her underwear was hidden as she could without being obvious. Luckily, with only four of them to share the fire, it wasn't difficult.

"Feel better?" Rob asked. He was giving her a crooked grin, the same he'd been wearing in her daydream, so she found she could not meet his eyes. She looked below them instead and hoped he wouldn't notice in the limited light they had.

"Much, actually," she said. "Thank you."

"Anytime," he replied.

"So," Eric said. "What next? Find Christy and the others?"

Rob sighed and ran a hand over his face. "I suppose we'd better. Christy at least was mostly fine before she left out of here earlier. I honestly expected she'd be back by now."

Eric nodded and remained silent, but Ami thought she saw the hint of a scowl on his face. Jay had been the one to fill him in on everything that had happened since the accident and had apparently shared Ami's theory about exactly why Christy was so anxious to find Benny again. Unlike Ami, he'd had no thought of keeping that theory to himself and had practically slapped Eric in the face with it at his earliest opportunity. Eric didn't seem to doubt the veracity of it all that much himself. This was the first time he'd mentioned the girl since then.

Rob either hadn't figured it out, or he didn't really care. Ami was betting on the latter.

"Hopefully she ended up finding Benny and Teddy, or even one or the other, and now they're huddled up for the night to try and stay warm, too," he said.

Ami winced as she saw Eric's scowl deepen. He wasn't such a bad guy. Not bad enough to deserve the way Christy treated him, at any rate.

"What if she wanders back to camp on her own?" Ami asked, trying to shift the conversation away from whatever methods Christy and Benny might be using to keep warm before it got there. "She did know where we were, after all. Even as mad as she was, I can't imagine she'd abandon us out here."

"We'll do like we did today," Rob said. "Jay and Eric can go look for her the direction she ran off in, and we can stay here and wait for either her or them to come back. If they come back without her, we can all go looking and try to find some help at the same time."

Ami halfway expected Eric to say he didn't want to go looking for her, or Jay to complain about leaving her and Rob alone at the camp together, but both men merely nodded their agreement. She wondered if there were some ulterior motive involved, but that was silly. After all, she and Rob had been the ones who went out looking for the bags today; it was only right that those two would take their turn together in the morning.

"Should we post watches tonight?" Eric asked, dragging her out of her thoughts. "Or is that being too paranoid?"

Rob considered it. "If it's paranoia, I've got it too. If nothing else, we need to keep the fire going through the night so we don't freeze in our sleep. We do only have one match left, so it's not like we can afford to light a new one in the morning."

"I slept all day," Eric said, the hint of a smile breaking onto his face for the first time since he'd awakened. "I'll take first watch, if that's all right."

"I'll join him," Jay said quickly. Ami saw him giving her that strange, knowing look again and wondered what he was thinking. "Buddy system and all, I guess."

Rob nodded and checked his watch. "It's right at seven now. Figure we'll try to get some sleep starting at about ten or so. We need to be up early, at first light if possible, so that's around six. That makes, what? Eight hours?"

"I'm wiped," Jay said. "Figure sleep at eight, up at six. Ten hours total. Me and Eric'll watch the fire for four hours, you and Ami do four hours, then we'll finish off the last two and wake you guys before we start searching. Sound good?"

"You sure?" Rob asked.

Jay nodded and shrugged. "Unless you've got something better in mind. You guys get a little extra sleep, but you had a rough time getting the pack from what you told us, so it seems fair to me."

"I'm good with it, too," Eric said. "Hell, you could make me keep watch all night and I'd be fine with it, being as how you guys saved my ass today. But that might make doing anything tomorrow pretty hard, so this might be better."

"It's settled then," Rob said. "So, what to do for three hours?"

"Anybody know any ghost stories?" Jay asked, grinning.

Ami's groan was lost amidst both Rob's and Eric's.

FOURTEEN

WAKING UP THIS TIME WAS worse than it had been right after the accident. Then, Benny felt a dull ache, like every muscle in his body had been individually abused with a meat tenderizer, but this time the pain was not as diffuse. It was concentrated, seeming to radiate outward from somewhere on his temple and ending in his ankles with brief detours to his wrists and neck. If not for the cold breeze blowing across his apparently bare chest, he would've been sure he woke up in Hell.

When he opened his eyes, he realized he wasn't far off the mark. The only difference, aside from the temperature, was that the devil apparently didn't have horns and a tail, but he did wear camouflage pants and carry a big-ass gun.

"'Bout fuckin' time you woke up," Clint said. "I was thinkin' about startin' without ya, but it wouldn't have been near as much fun."

The man was seated in a nylon camping chair, his legs stretched lazily out in front of him. The gun in question was balanced on his thigh, within easy reach should he need it. Benny had no desire to die tonight, even if it was looking increasingly like the inevitable outcome, so he did nothing to make his captor point that thing in his direction again. His heart leapt as Clint picked it up anyway and stood, stretching languidly before scratching his crotch with the barrel of the gun.

"Damn," he muttered. "Think that bitch gave me somethin'?

I'm itchin' like fire over here. Ah, that's right! Fuckin' went and bled on me. You comin' along threw me off, so I never thought to clean up 'fore now. Shit done dried and started crackin' loose. Don't ya hate it when that happens?"

Benny couldn't stop the disgusted look that came to his face, but instead of angering Clint it simply made the man laugh out loud.

"Stupid question, right?" he guffawed. "You ain't got the balls to do somethin' like that, do ya?"

"Think what you want," Benny said, his eyes flicking briefly to Christy's nude body behind the man, still swaying gently from the chains around her wrists.

The candle had been replaced with a propane lantern considerably brighter, especially since it had been hung in front of her now rather than behind her. Benny wished it wasn't. Now he had a clear view of the damage done to her before his arrival. Aside from the bruise on her face and the blood he'd seen trickling down her inner thigh, he could see numerous welts and red patches across her torso and legs. Her toes barely touched the ground, but apparently it was enough to scrape the ends of them raw as she swung across the rough dirt. They weren't bleeding—not yet, anyway—but they looked like they were extremely tender.

Her eyes were open, but from what Benny could tell, it didn't seem like she was actually alert and aware of anything. There was a faraway look on her face, as though she were daydreaming. She probably was, for all he knew. He hoped she was anyway. It might help her endure whatever this psychopath still had in store for her.

Clint noticed his staring and glanced at Christy before turning his grinning face back to Benny. "Think I wore her out some, huh? And that was with you interruptin' and shit. Think how she'd be had I got to finish what I started."

He tucked the pistol into the waistband at the back of his pants and circled around behind Benny. A moment later, Benny felt the chair he was sitting on pulled back onto two legs before being shoved forward across the ground. When he was only a couple of feet from Christy, the movement stopped. Clint didn't bother setting him down easily, just shoved once more and let go. The front legs of the chair hit the ground hard enough to make Benny's teeth click together painfully.

"Now, if you remember, I done told you what's comin'," Clint said as he came back around in front of Benny again. "In case that whack to the head scrambled your brains, let me go over it again. You got information I want. You don't tell me what I want, she pays the price for your stubbornness. And just so you know, I don't plan on takin' all fuckin' night playin' around with you, here's the kicker: you're on a counter. I wanted to give you three chances, the whole baseball thing, right? Problem is, I don't much like baseball. Borin' as shit, you ask me. 'Sides, that ain't enough fun for me if you try to hold out on me. So, you get *ten* chances. Ten times to do whatever the fuck you want when I ask somethin'. Ignore me, tell me to go fuck myself, whatever you want to say. Every time you do, she pays for it. I'll start small, seein' as I want this to last a good while. Not all fuckin' night, mind you, but a while. But it'll get worse every time you fuck up. As an example, I ask somethin', you don't say shit. Maybe I tweak her nipples real good for her, get her to squeal. I ask a second time, you still wanna play the tough guy. That's fine by me. This time I knock one of her fuckin' teeth loose. Maybe you think I'm bluffin', or maybe you flat don't like this bitch none, so we get all the way to ten. That last time, I ask you somethin' and you still tell me to fuck myself, she dies slowly, and in great pain, then you sit there starin' at her till I put you in those chains come mornin' and start in on you, too."

Clint's smile went from merely frightening to lascivious in the blink of an eye as he ran his tongue over his lips. "A hole's a hole, far as I'm concerned. You'll be callin' me 'Daddy' come lunchtime. We clear, cowboy?"

Benny swallowed hard and nodded his head slowly. Clint sighed.

"No more of that shit, neither," he said. "I ask you a question, you speak when you answer me or it don't fuckin' count."

"Yes!" Benny cried. "We're clear."

"That's better," Clint said. He stood next to Christy, took a deep breath, and then let it out slowly. "Let's get goin'. We'll start with the easy shit first. How'd you get here?"

"I walked."

Clint smiled. "Smartass, huh? Okay. That's one."

He turned and grabbed Christy's left nipple between his

thumb and index finger and twisted. Just as Clint said, she actually squealed, her eyes flying wide open as her back arched, trying to get away from his grip but unable to find any leverage to do so. Benny could clearly see tears begin to run down her cheeks as she struggled against the pain.

"No!" Benny yelled. "Stop! I didn't understand the question!"

After a slow five count, Clint let go of her nipple and turned back to Benny. Christy panted in relief.

"Maybe you oughta say that instead of runnin' off at the mouth, then," Clint told him. The man didn't seem the least bit angry or frustrated. In fact, he actually seemed amused by the whole affair. "Ignorance ain't no excuse for a bad answer, so it still counts. You best remember that. So I'll ask again and try to speak clear for you: how'd you end up all by your lonesome down at the riverbank?"

Christy's confused and desperate eyes found Benny's and tried to hold them, but he couldn't look at her. Not knowing that his carelessness had caused her pain, and she didn't even understand why.

"Our raft flipped," he said. "We took the wrong fork and it flipped."

Clint nodded as though this was nothing less than the answer he expected all along. "Pretty stupid-ass mistake. How'd you end up doin' that?"

"Taking the wrong fork?" Benny asked, not willing to make the same mistake again. Clint nodded. Apparently, the rule about using voices to answer didn't apply to him. "It was my fault. I convinced everybody on my side of the raft to do it. I didn't know it was going to be that dangerous."

"Your smarts end up runnin' down your mama's leg?" Clint asked, laughing. "That one don't count, by the way. I don't 'xpect you to answer. Didn't your faggot guide try to stop you?"

"We didn't have one."

Clint's eyes narrowed and he started to turn toward Christy again.

"It's the truth!" Benny yelled. Clint paused, listening. "We wanted to go without one, but this guy at the hotel said the runoff from last week's snow would make it too dangerous. He had more experience than us and knew the area better, so we hired him to be our guide."

He let out a relieved sigh as the man turned away from Christy and faced him again.

"You paid him, then fucked him over," Clint said. "Ain't you the nicest fuckin' guy? The fuck you do that for?"

Benny sighed and dropped his head. "I thought he was flirting with my girlfriend. I knew she wanted to leave me, and figured if I could make him look bad, at least she wouldn't leave me for him."

"You are one pathetic son of a bitch, I tell ya," Clint said. "Looks like that plan turned out real good for ya. So you an' your friends go diddly-boppin' down the wrong fuckin' fork in the rapids, and flipped the raft. How many of ya was there?"

"Three," Benny said. He knew he'd messed up as soon as the word left his mouth, but his mind was so jumbled he was having trouble thinking straight.

Clint turned suddenly and slammed a fist into Christy's belly hard enough to swing her backward. Her legs rose toward her stomach as she attempted to double up in pain. The only sound she made was the rush of air as the man drove it from her. Benny was the one who cried out this time.

"You must've been born stupid," Clint said, turning back to him. "You, this bitch, your faggot guide, and your little princess. That's four people you done mentioned already, dipshit. Want to try that one again?"

"I can't think!" Benny screamed. "Not with you hurting her all the time!"

Clint spun and punched Christy in the forehead as she swung toward him again, still caught in the momentum of his previous strike. Her head flew backward and the speed of her swing increased again.

"Better learn to think under pressure, shithead!" Clint called. "'Cause *that's* three right there. How fuckin' many of you was on that raft?"

"Six!" Benny cried. "No! Wait! Seven, I mean seven! Six in the group that came out here, plus the guy we met, that's seven."

"You sure about that?" Clint asked. "Sure it weren't eight, or five, or some other fuckin' lie?"

"It was seven," Benny said, starting to cry now. He felt more ashamed than at any time in recent memory. The last time he could remember himself crying was when he was a kid. He couldn't even remember why he cried then, only that his daddy told him to knock it off since real men didn't cry over bullshit. "I'm sorry I couldn't remember at first, but it was seven. Seven. I swear it was seven."

"Apologizin'," Clint said, nodding appreciatively. "That's good. Shows respect. Name 'em."

"Wha—what?"

"Tell. Me. Their. Fuckin'. Names. Dipshit."

Benny closed his eyes and tried to think, his shame increasing that he couldn't for the life of him remember the names of people he'd been friends with for ten years or more. Finally, they started to come to him.

"Christy," he said, nodding in her direction. "Eric. Ami. Teddy."

His face scrunched up as he concentrated. "Jay? Jay. Me. The guide, fuck! I can't remember his name!"

"Better fuckin' figure it out by the time I get to that table over yonder," Clint said, pointing to a table Benny hadn't noticed before sitting off to one side of the stall Christy was chained up in. It looked like basic tools scattered across its surface, but Benny didn't want to know what Clint would choose to do with them, other than what they were designed for. "You don't, Christy here ain't gonna like it much."

Benny forced a mental image of the man into his head; long, scraggly hair streaked through with gray, a thin face, a friendly smile he'd wanted to punch so badly he could feel the lips squashed beneath his knuckles. He'd introduced himself while they were in the hot tub, he could remember that much. And his name was . . .

"Rob!"

Clint stopped, mere steps from the table. He turned to look at Benny, his face calm.

"You sure?"

"I'm positive," Benny said. His chest felt like it was on fire, every breath a shuddering effort to draw and release. "His name's Rob."

"Good," Clint replied. "That's seven all right. You made one mistake, chief, 'cause I seriously doubt your fuckin' name's 'Me'."

"Benny! My name's Benny!"

Clint shrugged. "Shouldn't have fucked around so long,

might've given it to you. What're we up to now, four? Yep, four sounds right."

"No!" Benny screamed. "No, you can't fucking do anything to her! I fucking answered you!"

"Told you I didn't have all night to play with you," Clint said. He picked up a box cutter from the assorted junk on the table and pushed the blade out of the protective handle. "Don't take so long next time."

He moved around behind Christy, ignoring Benny's pleas for him to stop, and grabbed her legs under one of his arms. Christy began screaming as well, bucking against him, trying to get away, but his grip was like iron and he kept ahold of her legs as he spun her around so Benny could better see what was happening. Her back was worse than her front, the red welts nearly covering her from shoulders to just above her hips. Several of them had broken open and begun to clot already, leaving dark streaks where the blood dried. Benny wanted to look away, but he was too afraid the punishment would be worse for her if he did. Clint forced her legs up, exposing the bottoms of her feet. They were scratched to hell and back, but nothing major that Benny could see.

In one quick motion, Clint dragged the blade across the soles of Christy's feet. Blood welled up immediately and began pattering onto the dirt beneath her. Her screams became incomprehensible as the pain shot through her severed nerves. Clint let go of her legs, allowing them to drop back toward the ground again. Blood landed in crazy patterns across the earthen floor.

Clint tossed the box cutter casually back onto the table and spun Christy around so she was facing Benny again. Her face looked red and swollen, her eyes nearly hidden from crying. At least her screams had dwindled to panting moans of pain now. Benny didn't know how much longer he could have handled them the way they were.

"Now that's done," Clint said. "Maybe you'll remember to not fuck around so long next time, Benny-boy. So how many survived your fuck-up?"

"I don't know," Benny replied. He was too exhausted and his throat hurt too badly for his voice to go much more than a whisper.

Clint shrugged and started for the table again.

"It's the truth!" Benny forced himself to yell. His voice cracked on the last word. "Until I found her in here, I didn't know anybody else lived. I woke up alone!"

"'Bout what Otis said," Clint muttered. "Okay, I believe you, Benny-boy."

He moved around behind Christy again, where Benny couldn't see him. Benny heard the sound of chains rattling, and a moment later Christy dropped a little. Her wounded feet hit the ground and she cried out, not as ferociously as before, but still in obvious pain. She quickly pulled them back up again, trying to take the pressure off them but once more putting all her weight on her wrists and shoulders. Benny winced sympathetically. Sure, she could stand up and relieve some of the unimaginable pressure, but it would be agony to do so. This was even crueler than letting her hang where she was.

A minute or so later, Clint stepped up alongside her again. Benny was alarmed to see at some point the man had removed his pants, leaving him naked save for the gun in his hand. Equally disturbing was the massive erection he was sporting. There was no question the man was aroused, and Benny felt sick to his stomach at the idea that he'd gotten that way from torturing Christy.

Thankfully, she didn't seem to have noticed yet, or if she had, was resigned to whatever else the man had in store for her. Her head hung limply on her shoulders, hair covering her face. The only way Benny knew she was even still conscious was by the sound of her near-constant weeping.

"A couple more questions and we're done," Clint said, stroking himself idly with the hand that wasn't holding the pistol. "What've you seen here?"

"What are you doing?" Benny asked, unable to help himself. "Why are you . . . like that?"

"That your answer?"

"A house," Benny said quickly, before the man thought he was avoiding the question. "A couple of barns. Some four wheelers. A trailer. A boat. You. Her. The inside of this barn."

"That it?" Clint asked as he stepped around behind Christy again. This time, Benny could see him clearly over her exposed back. The man tucked the pistol under his arm, grabbed ahold of her bottom and spread her cheeks wide before spitting into the crack of her ass. He retrieved the gun and began rubbing her with his free hand. Her weeping grew somehow more despondent.

"That's it," Benny said, wishing he could look away but too terrified to do so.

"What do you think's goin' on here?" Clint asked. He stopped rubbing Christy, spat into his hand, and began rubbing himself.

"I don't know," Benny replied.

"Take a guess."

"Something illegal?" Benny offered. He'd already figured out the direction this was going, and was powerless to do anything to stop it. His arms were securely bound to the wooden chair he was sitting on, as were his ankles and chest. The ropes had already torn streaks into his skin from the motions he'd made screaming and struggling earlier. There was a slim chance he could wiggle out of his bonds given enough time, especially if he could make himself bleed to make the ropes more slippery, but there was no way this man would give him the time alone he'd need. "Something you don't want any of us telling anyone about."

"Shoulda used that kinda thinkin' when that stupid-ass idea to fuck with your girl's new lover came up," Clint said.

His hips thrust forward and Christy let out a strange sound that was a combination grunt and scream all in one. From the way she sounded as her crying intensified, and the angles of hers and Clint's bodies, Benny knew exactly where she was being raped. It was a sick reflection of what probably awaited him come morning, no matter what the rules of the sadistic bastard's game had been.

"One last question, hotshot," Clint said, his voice growing rough as his thrusts sped up. Benny could hear the slap of his skin against Christy's.

The man raised the pistol and put the barrel against the back of her head. Her cries slowed as she seemed to realize what was about to happen. Benny thought she might actually be welcoming it. "How's it feel knowin' that even if everybody survived the fuck-up on the river, you still got all your asshole friends killed?"

He smiled as his entire body tensed with the pleasure of his climax, then he pulled the trigger, still inside her. Benny closed his eyes, no longer caring what the man did to him for looking away, but it wasn't fast enough. He saw the top of Christy's head explode outward, blood and hard, pinkish chips he thought had to be part of her skull flying in every direction. Something plopped against his chest, and something larger hit his foot, but he refused to think about what it could've been.

Another first since his childhood, Benny began to pray, but he knew it wouldn't do any good. He doubted God had any desire to watch this, just as he doubted He would listen to anything Benny asked for. Psychopath or not, Clint was right. This was all his fault, and now he was being punished for it.

FIFTEEN

IF HE HAD THOUGHT THINGS through before setting up shop way out here in the middle of nowhere, Eugene was sure he'd have done it differently. The place had its advantages, to be sure. They were easily an hour or more from the nearest spot that could even be called a town, much less a big city, and to get there required careful maneuvering and impeccable timing to find a road. The surrounding trees served as natural camouflage for anyone looking down from an airplane or helicopter—not that either came this way very often. Occasionally, someone from the National Park Service would do a flyover, but all they'd be able to see was what looked like a hard-to-reach vacation home for someone who wasn't interested in an overabundance of frills. Since there was no way to get any vehicle larger than the ATVs into the compound, and no nearby area for park rangers to land the copter, they didn't get visitors very often, except for ones they expected or ones who stumbled upon them by accident—an exceptionally rare occurrence in normal times but happening with increasing regularity of late. He didn't know why. It was something else he'd learned to live with.

While all of these things were beneficial for the work they were doing out here, the disadvantages were tough to overcome at times. No electricity for the main cabin meant they were forced to make do with candles and lanterns after dark and a fire for warmth during the winter months. If there was an emergency, getting help was next to impossible. They had to load the boat up, haul it down to the river, get it in the water, make it across to the other side without having that monstrous current drag you away, then hike to where the truck and the runner car were hidden down the dirt road branching off the main one. Assuming, of course, some dickless piece of shit hadn't found them and decided to play real-life *Grand Theft Auto* with them. It had happened before. Clint still went on and on about what he would do to the person or persons responsible if he ever caught them. Eugene was more practical. He knew they were already beyond reach. He simply put plans in place to discourage or stop it from happening again.

Which created another drawback of being out here in the process: if you forgot the remote that disabled the failsafe on those vehicles, you had to hike back to the boat, go back across the river, hike all the way back up to the camp, get the thing, then repeat your original process all over again. That, or risk those shotguns rigged up underneath them blowing your legs off. He'd set the spread pattern himself. There was no safe place to stand other than far, far away.

All of these things were valid concerns, but to Eugene they were inconsequential. He'd known about them before setting up shop here, so he'd already accepted them as part of the price of doing business. What bothered him the most, more than anything else he had to deal with out here in the boonies, was the boredom. The sheer, uninterrupted, maddening *boredom*.

Clint at least had discovered something of a cure for that boredom, but it had only happened because of the strange increase in uninvited guests that had been arriving as of late. Otis was also easily amused, but his mind was closer to that of a child's, so entertaining him was as easy as telling him to go see if anything had changed in the woods since the last time he checked. But Eugene considered the both of them simple men, in their own ways. Otis was simple of mind, and while the same could be argued for Clint, Eugene saw him more as being simple due to the sheer primal impulses that guided him. Otis was here because he genuinely didn't know any better. Clint was here because he saw it as an opportunity to fuck someone up on occasion without anyone busting his balls over it. And while one might think that being here solely for the money he earned made him as simple as his companions, Eugene liked to think he was somewhat more complex than that.

The money was a motivating factor, true, as was the desire to not be killed for trying to walk away from everything, but the same could be said for the other two as well. Otis had no other marketable skills beyond intimidating people through his sheer size, or using that size in a manner similar to how farmers used oxen long ago. Clint would find himself in jail or dead rather quickly should he try to apply his only skills in whatever it was that passed for civilized society these days. Eugene, however, could have applied his skills anywhere. He simply chose not to. The money here was beyond good, the work was easy, and so long as things happened according to the schedule he'd been given when he started, he could set his own hours.

It would take years of grueling, backbreaking work to accomplish something similar in polite society, and he still would only be making a fraction of what he was here. That the specter of being killed for failure hung over his head the nine months out of the year he had to stay out here was a small trade in exchange. It only became a concern if he failed, and he had no intention of doing so.

It was the goddamn *boredom* that got to him.

The front door of the cabin opened, making him look up from the book he was reading. He saw Clint framed in the open doorway, covered in gore from his hairline all the way down to where his legs disappeared into his untied work boots. Eugene was sure once he took them off, his feet would be likewise adorned by blood. The man was scowling as he entered, his pants clutched in one hand and kept well away from his body. When Eugene glanced at his groin, he could see why. In addition to the thick layer of blood, the man's flaccid penis seemed to be covered in a thick, viscous substance that bore more than a passing resemblance to liquid shit.

"Clint," Eugene said calmly, marking his place with a finger and closing his book around it. "If you take one more step inside this cabin where we eat and sleep, I'm going to flay the skin off your bones and make you eat it. Go outside and wash off before you even *think* of coming in here."

"Fuckin' bitch shit on me," Clint said. To his credit, he didn't come any farther into the cabin, but he was certainly taking his time obeying Eugene's order. "Can you fuckin' believe that? Least that other faggot was cryin' too hard to notice when I left. Thought I was gonna fuckin' puke."

"Clint," Eugene said again, his tone firm.

"Didn't even have nothin' to wipe off with," Clint said, making no motion to go back outside. "Just my fuckin' pants. Fuckin' bitch."

"Last time, Clint," Eugene said. It was hard for him to stay calm. Clint had been challenging his authority at every opportunity this season, and it was rapidly becoming tiresome. He supposed he was going to have to replace the man once this year's stint was done. His boss wouldn't like it, but some things couldn't be helped. "Go wash off."

Clint looked over at him for the first time, his scowl darkening. "I'm gonna grab me a fuckin' towel first, asshole. It's fuckin' cold out there."

Eugene shoved himself out of his chair with a speed and agility that most people who saw it had a hard time believing. He was older than Clint by a good ten years, but he kept himself in impeccable shape, refusing to be complacent when ignorant shitheels challenged him like this. Before Clint had time to react, Eugene had him by the throat, using his momentum to shove the wiry man back out the door and off the low porch before stopping and shoving him onto his ass. The sudden movement displaced the air enough for him to catch a whiff of excrement. Had he not been so angry, he was sure he would have retched.

Clint's pistol fell onto the ground next to him, still half-covered by the man's pants. Eugene kicked it away before landing another kick into Clint's side. The air rushed out of the man as he doubled over. Eugene reached down and grabbed him by the hair before dragging him to the side of the cabin, stopping beside the series of five-gallon buckets they caught rainwater in to fill the irrigation tanks. He let go of Clint's hair, picked one of the buckets up, and dumped its contents onto him.

Barely noticing as Clint's body went rigid from the sudden shock of the cold water on his bare skin, Eugene picked up a second bucket and dumped it on the man as well, feeling a satisfied smile creep onto his face as he saw the jagged layer of surface ice precede the splash. He dropped the bucket, picked up Clint's pants, and tossed them onto the man's crotch before using his foot to scrub at the filth covering his groin.

He didn't bother with being gentle, applying more pressure than was probably needed as he ground his foot into the pants, using them as a makeshift washcloth. When the cords on Clint's neck stood out and his eyes bulged, he knew he'd found the man's genitals. He increased the pressure and scrubbed harder, twisting his foot so he could be sure he'd cleaned Clint's penis on every side.

When he felt the point had been sufficiently made, Eugene stepped back. Clint curled into a ball, his hands dropping immediately to his abused and cold-shrunken prick. Eugene knelt beside him and was pleased the detestable odor had faded somewhat.

"You have no one to blame for this but yourself," Eugene told him in a calm voice. "First, you caused the mess by fucking that girl while you killed her. I'll wager you shot her in the head, not realizing that among the other things a person does when that happens to them, they void their bowels. Your fault. Then, you think you're going to soil a home I'm forced to share with you by dripping her blood and shit across the floor while you 'get a fuckin' towel'. I told you to go clean yourself first, but you chose to insult me for suggesting you keep our house sanitary. Again, your choice, so your fault. Finish cleaning yourself up, then come inside and get dressed. If you try to fuck with me again tonight, I won't flay you like I said I would, I'll castrate you and save you from making the mistake again."

He stood and dunked his hands into a third bucket, rinsing them off. When he was finished, he sat the bucket next to Clint's head and walked back inside, making sure to close the door behind him. He hated wasting three buckets of water to make his point when they would've only used one if Clint had simply done as told, but sometimes you had to break a few eggs to make an omelet.

He was on the last page of the chapter he'd been reading when the door opened again. He glanced up as Clint stepped inside, teeth chattering from the cold, still holding his wounded junk. Cold and in pain didn't concern Eugene. All he cared was that this time the man was clean, save for a few spots where the blood had begun to stain his skin. He didn't say a word as he made his way to the communal sleeping quarters in the back of the cabin to put some clothes on, but Eugene clearly saw the look of utter hatred whenever Clint's eyes shot his way. He sighed. It would probably be a good idea to have Otis stand guard during the night to make sure Clint didn't try to kill him in his sleep.

There was enough time while Clint got dressed to finish his chapter and mark his place with an old candy bar wrapper Otis had left lying around. He was closing the book as Clint returned to the room and collapsed onto the sagging couch across from Eugene's chair. At least he wasn't holding himself any longer; for a while he'd reminded Eugene of a child that needed to relieve himself but wasn't near a bathroom.

"Did you find out anything from the boy?" Eugene asked him.

Clint started to respond, but stopped, glancing about the room. "Where's numbnuts? Shouldn't he be here for this?"

"Otis went out wandering," Eugene replied. "You know he doesn't like being around while you're . . . *entertaining* yourself."

"Chickenshit dummy," Clint said. "Yeah, he told me some stuff. You guessed it right. Him and some other shitheads was out on a raft and flipped the fuckin' thing. I'm bettin' they all washed up different places along the bank. He says he don't know how many of 'em lived other'n him. I know he sure looked surprised to see that shittin' bitch hangin' in the barn when he interrupted me the first time."

Eugene nodded. As strong as the current was right now, it was entirely possible they'd been split up after they went into the water. "How many?"

"Seven, all told," Clint said. "Five left now."

"And no idea where they are," Eugene added, sighing. "I suppose I won't be going to order supplies tomorrow after all."

Clint's face seemed to brighten some as he caught onto what Eugene was saying. "We goin' huntin' for 'em?"

"Do we have a choice?"

"Not really," Clint said, shrugging. "'Less you want 'em to wander in here while we ain't lookin', see some shit they don't need to see, then manage to give us the slip 'fore we can catch 'em."

"That boy found us. It's possible the others will, too. We'll leave a shotgun with Otis when we go out tomorrow. Assuming you can direct your anger at me on our visitors for the time being."

"One of these days, Gene," Clint said, his voice low but subdued. "I'm gonna have all your shit I'm willin' to take, and your ass'll be mine, boss be damned."

"Remember you'll be trading your own life for the pleasure of taking mine," Eugene told him. "I wish I could see what happens to you as a result, but then again, I'll be dead, so why should I care? What did you do with the girl?"

"Left her nasty ass hangin'," Clint replied. A faint smile tugged at the corners of his mouth. Eugene thought it was a genuinely disturbing sight. "Faggot's still tied to the chair so he can see what's in store for him come mornin'. I'll get up early, dump her, then deal with him when we get back."

"Good," Eugene said. "Better get some sleep, then. I'll wait for Otis to get back, fill him in, and then turn in myself. We have a long day ahead of us."

Clint nodded and got to his feet. He stopped at the entrance to the sleeping area and turned to look at Eugene again.

"You fucked up my plans for that faggot, you know," he said. His tone was calm, conversational even, but Eugene could clearly hear the false bravado beneath his words. "We get back and I still ain't able to deal with him how I want to, it's liable to make me think fuckin' you up's the best choice."

"And like I've told you before," Eugene replied, his voice hard as steel. "I don't care what perversions you inflict on unwanted guests, but you will not drag me into them. That includes bringing their bodily fluids into the house we share. There are rules for a reason, Clint. You know that."

"I know I do this 'cause I ain't much of one for rules," Clint replied. "*You* know that."

He continued on into the sleeping area. Eugene waited until he heard the springs on Clint's cot squeak a few times and then settle before picking his book up again and flipping to the page where he'd left off. He hoped Otis got back soon. He was exhausted, and while he was in good shape, there was no way he'd be able to hunt down five people tomorrow if he had to watch for the knife in his back instead of sleeping.

Otis wandered back toward camp on legs that were not entirely steady. He knew what he'd done was a bad thing, a *nasty* thing, but he hadn't been able to help himself. It wasn't anything he'd planned—which would've meant he knew those people were there before he nearly stumbled into their camp—but that didn't change the fact it happened.

But it wasn't just the shame bothering him, it was the guilt over what he was considering now. He found people who weren't supposed to be here, and whenever that happened, he was supposed to tell Eugene about it quick as he could. He was planning on doing exactly that, right up until the pretty blond girl had taken off her clothes and everything he'd been thinking about disappeared from his mind. It wasn't the first time he'd seen a naked woman before. He'd been unfortunate enough to be present while Clint amused himself a couple of times, but this was different somehow. This girl wasn't bruised or screaming or crying, and she was standing upright, giving him a look at her from all angles. The ones he'd seen Clint with were always bent or twisted into strange poses that blocked his view of them to a large extent.

This time he'd seen it all as the blond girl turned and bent and moved through the process of changing her clothes. He'd seen her breasts, nipples hardened from the cold. Her bottom jiggling as she dried her upper body. And when she'd bent over to put something onto the ground, he'd seen the shadowed cleft between her legs. He'd felt himself growing hard as he watched and couldn't stop from freeing his engorged penis and stroking it slowly.

His strength left him as he finished, and for a few minutes, he was sure it was going to get him caught. He'd stumbled forward and rustled some of the branches together before managing to get his balance again. He saw the girl stand stock still, her eyes shifting in his direction. He'd stood there, his deflating penis in hand, trying as hard as he could to not move a muscle. Finally, thankfully, she'd looked away. She called out to her friends, but she hadn't called out in alarm, so Otis knew he was safe.

This time.

It had been a stupid risk to take, but he couldn't help himself. Now he had to figure out what to do about it.

If it had been the first time this had happened, maybe it wouldn't be so bad. The situations were different—last time the girl hadn't been naked, but her boyfriend had spotted Otis in the woods and had been pretty angry at what he was doing. A fight had started, and as ashamed as Otis was, he'd almost lost. If Clint hadn't been close by, things would have ended up very differently. Eugene hadn't been mad when he found out about it, but he'd told Otis he was extremely disappointed in him, which was so much worse. Clint, on the other hand, threatened to cut his pecker off if he ever did anything like that again.

Otis had no desire to have his pecker cut off, but he was supposed to tell Eugene any time he saw people around that weren't supposed to be here. He could always tell that he'd seen people and leave out what he'd done, but he knew Eugene and Clint would come out looking tomorrow and would want to know where he'd been. He didn't know what happened to his *stuff* after he finished. What if one of them found it? What if it was Clint?

There was another reason he didn't want to tell, too. If he told, Eugene and Clint would find them eventually. Once that happened, Clint would take her and do bad things to her. He'd hurt her, just like he did all those other ones he'd gotten ahold of. Then he'd end up killing her and dumping her body somewhere in the woods for the bears and wolves to feast on. Otis couldn't explain why, but he didn't want any of that to happen to her. She'd looked so beautiful standing there in the firelight, just thinking about Clint ruining her was enough to make his heart hurt.

He couldn't tell. It would mean big trouble for him if they found out, but he couldn't say anything about the girl. If she somehow got separated from her friends, he'd tell Eugene about them. But as long as they were together, he wouldn't say anything at all. That would present its own problem, since Eugene was usually good at knowing when Otis was keeping something from him. He would have to say something.

Otis slowed his pace, knowing he only had until he got back to camp to think of something. He only hoped Eugene would believe it.

SIXTEEN

THE ONLY THINGS HE KNEW were that it was dark, it was cold, and his face was stuck to the ground. As awareness grew, he started to feel how badly his face hurt, in addition to everything else. Why that was the case, he couldn't remember. There was a dim recollection of something flying at him, then nothing until now. It was obvious *something* happened, though, and he was positive once he figured out what it had been, he wasn't going to be very happy about it.

Teddy started to get his arms underneath his body so he could push himself upright, but as soon as he shifted his left arm the slightest bit, agonizing pain shot through it, making him feel nauseous and almost driving him back into unconsciousness. Whatever bad thing had occurred while he and his friends had been on the raft this afternoon—and there was absolutely *no* question that whatever it was had been bad—it seemed to have left him with a broken arm in addition to the aching face and long, forced nap.

He gritted his teeth against the coming onslaught of torture and somehow managed to roll himself onto his back without too much difficulty before sitting up and opening his eyes to take in his surroundings. Only one of them opened enough to see, the other felt like it had been glued shut while he slept. He reached up with his good hand to brush the detritus away and nearly screamed when making contact with the swollen mass in the center of his face. What was supposed to be his nose brought another wave of pain that rivaled that of his arm for intensity. He couldn't know for sure without probing further to confirm it—an act nearly dead last on his list of things he wanted to do right now—but he felt it a safe bet his nose had been broken. He upgraded his rating of what must've happened from "bad" to "fucking terrible."

Taking great care not to touch his ruined nose again, he wiped away the layer of silt congealed over his eyes and was finally able to look around properly.

Or at least somewhat properly. The surrounding darkness prevented him from getting too good of a look at anything, but he was able to put a few pieces together. He was on the shore next to the river, the white tops of the rapids glinting in the starlight where they sped across the rocks that broke the surface. He was alone, so there was no way to tell whether he'd been thrown out and forgotten, or whether his friends had been thrown out somewhere else along their route. Considering the number of times his big mouth had gotten him into trouble, the former was actually a distinct possibility, though he didn't think it likely.

It suddenly occurred to him that he couldn't feel his legs. He slapped his hands down quickly onto the spot where he thought they should be and screamed when he realized he'd momentarily forgotten about his broken arm. Once the pain subsided, he felt with his good hand, letting out a sigh of relief that his legs were still there. He couldn't feel them because they were submerged in the icy water. At least he *hoped* that was why he couldn't feel them. It was entirely possible he'd sustained a spinal injury at some point and was now paralyzed from the waist down.

Teddy dragged himself backward until his legs were on dry land with the rest of him. He was wearing old desert-print camo pants his brother had been issued when he was in the Army. Usually they dried pretty quickly, so he hoped they would do so now. Of course, with how cold it was on shore, there was a chance they'd end up freezing and make frostbite set in on his legs. They were probably fine now, but once that happened, he'd end up losing them both anyway. Then again, since he couldn't really feel his dick either, hypothermia would be a more likely cause of death. And if he didn't end up dying but had to have both legs and his dick and balls cut off because the cold killed them, he'd eat a bullet and be done with it.

He closed his eyes and took a deep breath. There was no sense getting all defeatist and maudlin about things. There was a very good chance the feeling would come back to his lower extremities as soon as he dried out some. It was cold, yes, and the water was probably near freezing, but the air out here wasn't. It felt that way because he was wet. If he really did have hypothermia, he doubted he'd have woken up at all. He'd have slept until his body said fuck it and shut down on him. He had to give it time.

That would be harder than it sounded, though. Patience might be a virtue, but as far as he was concerned, he'd lost his virtue a long fucking time ago.

In an effort to try and distract himself for a while, Teddy tried to remember what happened to him. He could remember setting out in the raft clearly and could also remember Benny giving him and Christy the signal to start fucking with Rob. Shortly after that happened, though, things started breaking down and becoming hazy. They'd gone down the opposite fork from where Rob had been guiding them. He remembered a sensation like some giant had kicked the raft as hard as they could, then . . .

His face started to burn as he remembered pissing himself from fear after that first huge drop-off. Their bags had gone flying, and one of them caught Eric in the back of the head. Then something must have hit him in the face and knocked him cold, but he couldn't put together what it was. An oar was the likely culprit, but without anyone else to ask for verification, he had no way to know for sure. The rest he didn't know, but he could guess. Things had been getting steadily worse after taking that fork, so it was easy to conceive, at some point, the raft either got torn to shreds on sharp, exposed rocks, or it flipped entirely and dumped everyone out. That he was alone seemed to indicate perhaps they were thrown out at different times, but he wasn't sure what might've happened.

Either way, he had to downgrade his rating of the situation. This was officially "fucking cataclysmic."

On a more positive note, his lower body was starting to tingle as blood began flowing through it normally again. When the pins-and-needles sensation settled into his groin, Teddy thought he was going to lose what little sanity he had before it finally warmed and returned to something resembling normal again. When he was finally able, he got slowly to his feet and took a couple of leaden steps toward the river so he could see if there was any sign of life to give him hope.

He finally found it in the form of what he hoped was a camp-fire and not some strange trick of the light. It was on the other side of the river and downstream a good three or four hundred yards from where he was, but there was definitely something there. Rob had seemed the outdoorsy sort, so maybe he had a pack of matches or something stowed away in his coat. Teddy wondered if he'd been the only other one to make it. He doubted it. If Rob lived, there was an excellent chance some, if not all, of the others had, too. As to what kind of shape they might be in, that was another argument.

Teddy started to make his way down the shoreline, hoping to at least end up directly across from them. It helped to move his legs, too. The activity seemed to be making the blood flow a lit-tle more, taking away some of the heaviness that settled into his feet. Logic would say the more blood flowing through them, the less the chance he'd end up losing them. He didn't like that they weren't hurting—which in retrospect was one of the stranger thoughts he'd ever had—but at least he was feeling something. That *had* to be a good sign.

Luck hadn't been with him so far, and it held true to form as the shoreline ran out some distance from his hoped destination. The tree cover had given way, leaving him on a sharply sloped plot of land wide enough for him to lie on, should he choose to. If he hadn't been the only one to split from the group, whoever was at that fire would be able to see him come daybreak, provided they searched this direction. He had no idea how long he'd been out. For all he knew, they'd already been this way and were go-ing to move farther away from him once they had some light.

He'd have to keep watch for them himself. As soon as he saw them come to the river, he'd scream his fool head off to try and get their attention. He had no idea how they were supposed to cross over to him, or vice versa, but it would be comforting to know they were alive and to know they knew he was alive, too.

He was fairly certain he was on the island that split the forks in the river, so at least the likelihood there were bears hiding out on here somewhere ready to make a meal out of him was slim. Still, he supposed it was best to keep an eye out on the woods for the rest of the night, just in case. He had no idea what he could do should something large, furry, and hungry emerge and come after him, but it would be better than sitting there hoping for the best and suddenly finding something chewing on him from behind. He sighed and turned his back to the fire and hopped back and forth from one foot to the next. Eventually he was going to tire out and have to sit down, but first he needed to keep his legs active as long as he could.

Whatever ended up happening, he had a feeling it was going to be a very long night.

SEVENTEEN

AMI LOOKED UP AS ROB emerged from the woods nearby and quickly moved to sit beside her near the fire. She smiled at him sympathetically. She'd already made her trip to relieve herself after being awakened for their turn at watch duty and had already dealt with the cold night air making her grateful for the fire's warmth. She had no idea what they would've done if they hadn't managed to find some matches. She supposed they could all curl up together like newborn puppies or something, but she wasn't too keen on the idea of being in the middle of three guys all struggling to stay warm.

"That was rough," Rob said. "If I can keep my bladder from forcing me back out there until the sun's up again, I think I'll be fine."

"Count your blessings there, mister," she said, chuckling. "Some of us had to expose a lot more skin to take care of the same problem, you know."

Her face went immediately crimson as she realized how her comment could remind him she wasn't wearing anything under the jeans or jacket. It was ridiculous when she stopped to think about it. After all, *everybody* was naked beneath their clothes. There was no way he could take her comment as anything even resembling a come-on, but the knowledge did nothing to assuage her embarrassment.

Thankfully, he allowed the moment to pass without further

comment. "Did you manage to get any sleep?"

"Some," she replied. In truth, she'd been shocked at how easily she'd drifted off. She normally had a hard time falling asleep when she was in a strange place, even when it wasn't cold or uncomfortable. No sooner than she settled her head against her folded arm, she'd been sound asleep. When Jay shook her awake for her and Rob to take their turn watching the fire, she'd been astounded four hours had already passed.

"Same here," Rob agreed. "It's not the first time I've slept on the ground, but normally I've at least got a sleeping bag to curl up in, if not a tent over me, too. This 'roughing it' stuff isn't exactly what I'd call a good time."

"Me neither," she said. "We make it out of here, I think I'm about done with this whole rafting, camping, outdoor living thing."

Rob smiled. "I won't say I'm done with it forever, but it'll be a good long while before I do it again. And no offense, but I think the next time someone asks me to be their guide on a run, I'm going to tell them to go fuck themselves."

Ami giggled and before she knew it was outright laughing, struggling to keep quiet so she wouldn't disturb Jay or Eric while they attempted to get some sleep, too. Finally, she managed to get control of herself, and the two of them slipped into a companionable silence.

She looked up at the sky and was relieved to see stars peeking through the low clouds. The thunder she'd heard earlier was a false alarm. With a little luck, the storm she thought was coming would hold off until they either made it back to civilization or found something they could use for shelter to try and survive another night out here.

Thinking of that possibility robbed her of the remaining humor she'd been feeling from Rob's earlier comment. She sighed and tossed a couple more of their larger sticks onto the fire, then looked at him. He was staring off into space, a look of concentration etched onto his features.

"What are you thinking about?" she asked, not entirely sure she wanted to know the answer; at least not if his thoughts had gone down a similar path to her own.

"Trying to remember some things about the map I had of the area," he said. "I studied them for hours before I crashed out last night, wanting to make sure I knew exactly where we were going today. I want to say there was a group of cabins not too far away from here, but I can't remember. I was paying more attention to the river and the access road, not to the other stuff nearby."

"You couldn't have known this would happen," she said, putting a comforting hand on his arm. "I've known these guys for years and *I* wouldn't have ever guessed they'd pull a stunt like this."

"I know," he said, offering her a thin smile. "I don't feel guilty about the accident, not as much as I did at first, anyway. I feel guilty I didn't plan for every contingency. Did you know I was in the Boy Scouts?"

She chuckled. "No, but it doesn't surprise me."

"I was," he said. "Well on my way to Eagle Scout, until life got in the way and I had to drop out. One of my biggest regrets, actually. Anyway, the Boy Scout motto is 'always prepared'. Had it hammered into my head for most of my childhood. What happens when I need to follow it the most? I don't. My old Scoutmaster would kick my ass if he knew about it."

"You plan on telling him?"

"Oh, hell no," Rob said, laughing softly. "I plan on telling him how I single-handedly saved the raft and dragged all of you back into it before surfing it down a waterfall and landing gracefully next to a ranger station."

"Did you get a medal?" Ami asked, laughing along with him. "In this imaginary world where you turned into Superman?"

"I got *two* medals," Rob told her. "And the key to the city and sizeable rewards from your families, of course. Oh! And the book and movie deal, can't forget about those."

"No, don't forget about them," she said. Their laughter subsided, but she couldn't stop thinking about what he said. "You thinking about trying for the cabins, if you can remember where they are?"

"Maybe," he replied. "I think they're on this side of the river, maybe ten, fifteen miles away from it."

"That's not good," she commented.

"It's not bad either," he said. "Think about it. The average walking speed for a human being is around three miles an hour. Considering the terrain and all the other things working against us like no food, tired, sore, all that, and we'll probably make half of it. If we tell Jay and Eric to only search an hour each way, and they start right around daybreak, that puts them getting back to camp with us at around nine or so. We let them rest another hour, and we're moving by ten. It got dark around six, so that's a good ten to twelve miles we could cover tomorrow. If our direction's right, we could end up at the cabins around the time anyone in them would be sitting down to dinner."

"Assuming they're really there," Ami said. "And we go the right direction, and your estimate of how far away they are is right, and there's actually anyone in them this time of year."

"How do you keep up that optimism?"

"It's a talent, what can I say?"

Rob sighed. "You're right, it's some long odds. But it's the best I can come up with. I mean, we obviously can't just sit around here forever and hope to be found. More than likely, no one even knows we're gone yet. The hotel staff's going to figure out something's going on when we miss check-out in the morning, but my friends won't be expecting me back in Colorado for days yet. And your families, if they knew you were coming out here and when you were planning on heading back, won't start worrying until tomorrow night or the morning after. We've got to do something, or we're going to end up dying from exposure out here."

It was Ami's turn to sigh. Everything he said was right. She told her parents she was coming, but not how long she'd be gone. She only said she'd call when she got back home. She took an extra day off from work to recuperate, so they wouldn't even miss her for two more days yet. The access road along the river had been hard to find, and they'd known it was there. Chances were, nobody would stumble across their vehicles for a long time, and then only if a park ranger decided to patrol somewhere he didn't normally go. His plan of looking for the cabins was probably the best idea they were going to have.

"What if we tell Jay and Eric to only look a half hour away, then a half hour back, then we don't rest but start walking right then?" she asked. "That would put us leaving two hours sooner, so we'd cover another three miles, right? That way, if the cabins are fifteen miles out, we still get there tomorrow. And if we don't, we still can do a fire one more night, then search for them all day the next day. If we don't find them by then, though, I think we're pretty well done for. That's as much optimism as I can give you right now."

"I'll take it," he said. "And it sounds like a good plan to me. Do you think those two are going to be willing to only search for half an hour? For that matter, are *you* sure about it? If Christy made it much further, you're pretty well writing her off. The others, too."

"Not really," she replied. "We're going for help, right? We tell them the others are still out here somewhere, and then let the rangers do the searching so we don't have to. Besides, she's the one who chose to leave rather than do things sensibly."

It was cold and calculating and not at all what she really felt, but she was still angry and bitter at how Christy had treated them all and wasn't in a charitable mood toward the other girl right now. Besides, like Rob said, they had to do something, and this was their best hope for the most people to survive.

That didn't mean she had to like the choice she'd made, though.

"And those two?" Rob asked, jerking a thumb toward where Jay and Eric were ostensibly sleeping. "I think both of them are carrying something of a torch for Christy. You really think they're going to be willing to 'abandon' her like that?"

"After what she said to Jay before she left, I think his torch has been dropped," Ami said. "And I'm pretty sure Eric's put two and two together and figured out she was only with him to get to Benny, so I doubt he's going to worry about it too much."

"We'll mention it to them when we wake them up then," Rob said. "If they're on board, then we'll try to find the cabins after a quick search for the others. And since you mentioned Benny, can I ask a personal question?"

For some reason, Ami knew this was coming, but it didn't bother her nearly as much as she thought it would. "I might not answer, but you can ask."

"You and Benny," he began. "What's the deal there? I know you're together, but why is he so jealous?"

"You're the one who said that had more to do with his own issues than it did with me," Ami said.

"I did, and it's true," Rob replied. "But that man was willing to risk killing everyone on the raft to prove a point, it seemed. I don't picture you as the type to put up with something like that."

Ami sighed. "I'm not. Not really. He wasn't like that when we first started hanging out, or even when we first started dating. He was caring and kind and loving and generally anything a girl could want out of a boyfriend. But he liked to drink. He never got physical with me or anything, but he would occasionally say hurtful things he'd apologize for as soon as he woke up the next day and remembered what he'd done. I was able to ignore it for the most part, until we went to a party celebrating Eric getting a promotion at his job.

"Jay and I have been friends since we were kids. We tried the relationship thing, but decided we worked better as just friends, so we gave it up and never looked back. Benny knew that, but I think he sometimes thought *Jay* didn't know. Well, Jay crashed the party that night because his cousin had been killed in a car crash earlier in the day. I wasn't answering my cell, and he really needed a shoulder to cry on, so he came looking for me. Benny was telling drunken stories about his days playing football, so Jay and I went outside to talk where it was quieter.

"Benny came out a while later and found Jay holding onto me with his face pressed against my neck. He was crying and I was comforting him, but I guess Benny thought we were making out. He didn't say anything then, but once Jay calmed down and left and I went back inside, Benny cornered me and tore into me. He accused me of trying to fuck Jay right in front of him, and said we'd probably been doing it since before me and him started dating, and generally made a drunken ass out of himself. If we'd been alone, I might could've dealt with it better. Since he did it in the middle of the party in front of all his asshole friends, it was something else altogether."

"He embarrassed you," Rob said. "Let me guess, he thought apologizing again would make everything better, right?"

"Yep," Ami said. "He called me the next day and left probably twenty voicemails on my phone, each one more panicked than the last, trying to tell me how sorry he was. He found out what really happened from someone—I have no idea who—and knew he'd screwed up. I eventually called him back and told him we needed to talk, which we did. He did seem sorry and even promised to stop drinking since that was when he started acting like an idiot. I told him I needed to see how sorry he was, not just hear it. I told him we weren't broken up, but I needed time to decide how serious he was about our relationship."

"Let me take a stab at how this went from there," Rob said. "He gave you a day, maybe two, then started calling again. You didn't answer every call, so he started freaking out, sure you were about to break up with him. He sent flowers, cards, letters, texts, left voicemails, and did everything else he could think of that, to his mind, showed how much he cared about you. You, on the other hand, were more annoyed he couldn't follow simple directions than you were won over by what probably was for him a heartfelt attempt to win you back. You started to feel like he was suffocating you—which he kind of was—so you kept pulling further and further away from him. Am I close?"

"Sounds like you've been here before yourself," Ami said, nodding.

"I have," Rob confirmed. "Only I was in Benny's shoes, not yours, and it was a long time ago. First serious girlfriend my senior year of high school, actually. I didn't get drunk and accuse her of screwing her best friend or anything, but I still made the stupid mistake that sent me on a downward spiral that ended with her telling me to never speak to or look at her again. Took years for me to realize how badly I'd overreacted, and I'd been the one to drive her away when all I had to do was sit back and be patient and she'd have come around on her own. It's a testament to my overreaction that now I don't even remember what it was I'd done that started the whole thing in the first place."

"You defending him?"

"Not at all," Rob said, shaking his head. "Just because I understand what he's doing doesn't mean I think it's right. Now I can look back and say it happened the way it was supposed to so I could learn a lesson, so maybe that's what's happening with you and Benny, too. Maybe he has a lesson to learn and this is how it happens."

"Everything happens for a reason?" Ami asked, smiling.

"Something like that," Rob replied, returning her smile. "You planning on breaking up with him?"

The question was spoken casually enough, and it was the obvious follow-up to everything she'd already said, but it still set her heart to racing again hearing him ask it. She wanted to reply by asking if he wanted to know because he was interested in picking up where Benny left off, but she knew he was just making conversation. If there was more to it, he seemed like a decent enough person that he wouldn't push for it until the break up was over and done, and he *definitely* wouldn't ask while they were in the dangerous situation they were in.

"I think I am, yes," she finally said. "I was planning on doing it when we got back home from this trip, kind of using it as our last goodbye. I may wait longer, since we've already got enough to cope with when we get back. No sense making him feel worse than he already does, being he's the one who caused all this."

"It could be argued that making him feel worse is exactly what he deserves, but kudos to you for still caring enough to be considerate about his feelings," Rob said. "That tells me you don't hate him, you just can't date him anymore, and that's probably the healthiest response you could have to everything, both before this happened and including it. It's kind of refreshing to know there's still some good people in the world nowadays."

He stood and stretched before tossing another couple of sticks onto the fire. "I need a drink, so I guess I'm going to brave the cold and head down to the river. Care to make sure I don't fall in?"

She didn't really want to leave the relative warmth of the fire, but she wanted to be away from Rob even less right now. She smiled and stood before following him over to the river. She knelt beside him and caught some of the icy water in her cupped palm before taking a drink herself. It didn't taste very good, and she had to force thoughts of what might be swimming around in it out of her mind, but it was refreshing all the same. She realized she hadn't really had a drink since she involuntarily swallowed when she fell into the water while she and Rob retrieved the bag earlier, so she took another couple of drinks while she was here. She didn't want to overdo it, but she did want enough to sustain herself. She remembered reading somewhere a person could survive longer without food if they had water, and since their future meals were not a guarantee, she should probably drink up while she had the chance.

She caught herself sneaking glances at Rob as he drank from the river as well and thought maybe she shouldn't wait to tell Benny they were finished. After all, once they were rescued and the fervor surrounding that died down, Rob would be heading back to Colorado. They might stay in touch online, maybe become friends on Facebook or something, but it wasn't likely she'd get the chance to see him face to face again, at least not for a very long time. And while he probably wouldn't try anything with her—assuming, of course, he wanted to in the first place—while they were lost in the wilderness, or while she was still technically dating someone else, the thought of him asking her out after all of that was said and done wasn't the most terrible thing in the world.

In fact, it gave her something to look forward to.

EIGHTEEN

GIVEN THE TIME TO THINK about it, Benny was fairly certain the gentle weight he felt against the top of his left foot was brain matter, maybe with a few bone fragments mixed into it. He knew he should be experiencing some kind of emotion over the realization, something like revulsion or anger, or even just irritation, but he felt too numb for such things. It wasn't every day you watched one of your friends get anally raped and then have the top of her head blown off right in front of you, and the ordeal had left him with a deep-seated lethargy.

He'd barely noticed when the bastard who'd done it left the barn, mumbling incoherently about something that appeared to have disgusted him. He'd heard the ruckus outside a little later, followed by the strange splashing and the other man's voice, low and chastising, but he hadn't felt even a modicum of curiosity as to what it was all about. Even Clint's haunting words about how Benny would be sharing Christy's fate come morning hadn't penetrated the fog that fell over his mind.

For some reason, though, the feeling of her brain and part of her skull against his foot was registering clear as a bell.

She'd died horribly, there was no question of that. She'd been in pain, humiliated, and then that Clint fucker's gun had taken it all away at the same time it took her life. The scene replayed itself over and over in Benny's mind until he was sure he was going to go insane before it finally took on a hazy, dreamlike quality that allowed him to close his eyes without having to fight back a scream. It didn't go away, he could still see it, but it was like watching a bad movie on the internet. He could almost trick himself into believing it hadn't happened at all, but then he'd noticed the pressure on the top of his foot and knew it had.

And he wasn't being honest with himself to say he felt nothing about what happened, or from that pressure. The only word he could think of to explain how he was feeling was *resigned*. Resigned to his fate, as the old adage went. In psychological terms, he was broken. Clint had broken him so there'd be less chance of a fight when he came back to rape and kill him.

For some strange reason, that glimmer of understanding made him think of the old Vietnam war movie *Full Metal Jacket*. Benny's dad loved the movie, being a former Marine himself, and had exposed Benny to it almost from the time he could sit upright on his own to watch alongside his old man. Benny had watched it in later years, too, but he generally stopped watching shortly after the troops had been sent to the war itself. What Benny liked most—and what began to play over and over in his head—was the beginning where they were in basic training with that dumbass Pyle and that asshole-on-legs drill instructor.

He remembered his dad telling him that R. Lee Ermey, the actor who played the drill instructor, had actually been one on Paris Island at one time, and had initially been hired as a consultant on the movie. It was only after he barked an order for the director to sit up straight when he was talking to him that he landed the role itself. Benny had asked if they really acted that way, yelling and screaming and belittling the recruits, and his dad told him absolutely they did. When Benny asked why, his dad explained they were trying to build Marines, and that meant they had to break down everything you'd been prior to joining the Corps before they could make you better.

He hadn't understood at the time, but during the Psychology class he'd taken his freshman year of college, he'd learned enough to make sense of it. Like how you'd tear down a building that wasn't put together right before erecting a more stable structure in its place, a person's mind had to be torn down before it could be rebuilt stronger than it had been before. The concept was where the old saying of "that which doesn't kill you only makes you stronger" had come from. Things forged in fire were harder and more durable once they'd been tempered in the flames. The mind worked the same way.

Benny forced himself to raise his eyes back to the ruined remains of Christy's head. Clint had left the lantern burning for him, and while it was nearly out of propane, it still cast enough light for him to make out more detail than he cared to. The hole where the bullet exited was massive, nearly big enough for him to stuff a grapefruit in, should he be so morbidly inclined. Her hair had a strange, uneven look he assumed was due to the explosive fracturing of her skull. Strangely, there appeared to be very little blood, only a dark liquid that appeared nearly black in the dim light, dripping from the lower edge of the wound. He couldn't see the entry point, but was sure it was considerably smaller than the exit. He'd been shooting before and knew how bullets mushroomed on impact, forcing everything before them away in whatever direction they could. His dad had used a pumpkin to show him the result, and sickening as it was to consider, this wasn't all that different.

He tore his gaze from the grisly wound and looked down the length of her limp body as she hung from the chains, her shoulders bent back at an impossible angle. If he needed any further proof she was dead, this was it. Any living person who had their shoulders pulled back in such a way would be in sheer agony and would probably be screaming for all they were worth. Christy was silent, head bent as though she were merely sleeping, though her wound broke the illusion.

He felt a pang of regret. He knew she'd liked him, knew she'd wanted to be with him. Not that she'd ever said anything aloud to him, but he'd known. More than once he'd caught her staring at him while they were drinking together, and last night he'd seen how she cut her eyes over to him while practically dry-humping Eric right in front of him. At the time, he'd found her attention disturbing. After all, he was dating Ami, and she was dating his best friend, and that wasn't a road he even wanted to *consider* going down. Now that she was gone, he found himself wishing he'd have at least acknowledged it, even if it was to tell her it was never going to happen. It probably wouldn't have changed anything, but maybe they could have been more relaxed around each other and enjoyed their times together more.

Too late for that now.

His eyes shot back to her head, and he felt himself trying to push the chair away when he saw her head was no longer facing the ground but raised, her cold, bloodshot eyes staring at him. Her lips pulled back into a horrible rictus he thought was supposed to be a grin, but when combined with the blood dried around her mouth and across her chin, made her look like an undead clown from some low-budget horror movie.

"At least you tried to save me," the apparition said. *"You fucked it up big time, but hey, it's the thought that counts, right? Oh, wait! No brain, no thoughts! Guess I don't count for shit anymore, do I?"*

"Nonononono," Benny whispered through gritted teeth. "This isn't happening. You're dead, I watched him shoot you, no *fucking* way are you talking to me right now."

He heard the chains rattle softly and could make out the grating sound of bone rubbing against bone as her shoulders moved in what he thought had to be a shrug. For some reason, that unnerved him more than the fact she was supposed to be dead and was talking to him.

"You might be right," she said. *"You're probably imagining this, or dreaming it, or hallucinating it or something like that. But if you are, what's that say about your mental state right about now, hmm?"*

Benny wanted to scream, not caring if it pissed off his captor and made him come back out here. Better to be shot and killed right now so he wouldn't have to see the grotesque visage any longer.

"This isn't real," he told himself instead, shaking his head. "Not real, not real, not *real*."

"Maybe, maybe not," she said. He nearly groaned as he realized her lips weren't moving when she spoke. *"And does it really matter either way? You're losing your shit, Benny. You can live through this, but you have to get it together. You tell yourself you're so tough, so why turn into a pussy because you saw me die? So that sadistic bastard threatened to pop your anal cherry before doing you in, too. Big deal. Threats are words until he actually does it. And you've got all night before that happens, remember?"*

"I can't," he said, then winced. He was actually taking part in a conversation with a corpse. He knew that had to mean what thread of sanity he had left must have snapped, but he couldn't stop himself. "I tried to get loose. The ropes are too tight. Hell, I can't even tip this chair, how am I supposed to get out of it?"

She gave him that morbid shrug again.

"Why don't you try to focus instead of crying like a little sissy?" she asked. *"Bet you didn't even stop to think what happens when he's done with you, did you? I lived, remember? Pretty good odds the others did, too. Even Ami. She always was better looking than me, way too attractive for the likes of your sorry ass. Can you imagine what ol' Clint's going to do if he catches up with her? Pretty girl like that, bet she won't get the blessing of a semi-quick death like I did. Doesn't seem like he's got much to do up here, so he'll probably hold onto her for a while, at least until he gets some good use out of her. Even if she somehow gets away from him, gets to safety, I'm willing to bet he'll have fucked her up so bad she'll never be able to find a guy that'll even look at her twice. Assuming she'll want to be with a man again. More than likely, she'll escape so she can kill herself and end the torture."*

"No," Benny whispered, feeling his eyes start to tear up again.

"Oh, yes," that leering face went on. *"Most definitely yes. And she probably won't even know you were here, won't even know you died. She'll just think about how you abandoned her to it, let that bastard have her. And you know what? The longer you sit here dicking off waiting to die, the more your fault it'll be. You'll die knowing you had a chance to get loose and stop it before it happens, but didn't. Guess you didn't love her as much as you claimed to, huh?"*

Benny ground his teeth and fought the urge to scream. Not in fear or pain this time, but out of *rage*. Ghost or figment of his imagination, real or not, every word was true. Not once had he stopped to consider the full implication of Clint and his buddies finding the others. The guys would be tortured and killed—of that there was no doubt. But Ami wouldn't be even that lucky. Clint would turn her into his pet for as long as he could keep her alive, assuming she didn't end up getting passed around like a party favor. Either way, the pain and suffering she'd be subjected to would make Christy's final moments pale in comparison. And all he was doing was thinking of himself and the potential fate that awaited him come morning. He had to do something. Even if he failed, at least he could die knowing he'd given it everything he had.

He lurched forward instead of backward in the chair and felt his toes brush the ground before the wooden legs slammed back down and jerked him backward against the seat again. His ankles dragged painfully against the ropes that held them, but when he arched his foot, he thought he could feel dust with his big toe. If so, it was a definite improvement over his earlier, half-hearted attempts. He took a deep breath and repeated the motion a couple more times before he had to stop to let his quavering muscles rest for a moment.

A smile spread across his features as he felt the dirt beneath his feet.

He shoved his legs forward until his thighs trembled and he heard the welcome creak of the chair's wooden back as it began to separate from the seat. Black spots began to swim in his vision but he refused to let up the pressure. His shins felt like they'd been dipped in kerosene and set ablaze as the ropes jerked upward a couple of inches, dragging hair and skin along with them. He tried to ignore it and kept up the pressure.

Finally the back of the chair broke free with a loud, squealing crack. The back legs went with it, unbalancing him and nearly sending him sprawling. He twisted and got one foot underneath him and by some miracle managed to say upright. He was hunched over, and his back and shoulders were screaming at how they were being mistreated, but at least he wasn't on the ground. He leaned forward, wincing as his legs assumed the weight of the broken chair back, and contemplated his next move.

His ankles were still bound to the front legs of the chair, so running or even walking was out of the question. He found if he tried, he could sort of shuffle from side to side and make progress, even if it was slow going. But at least it was something. His eyes landed on the table where Clint kept his "toys" and his heart leapt when he saw the box cutter was still lying on top of the pile. And wonder of wonders, the blade was still pushed out as far as it would go.

Benny looked back to Christy, halfway expecting to see her nodding her approval, but she wasn't. Her head was hanging limply again, her face and eyes hidden from his view. There would be no more motivation offered from there, if there ever had been.

He shuffled toward the table, taking special care to not let the chair legs get tangled on anything and trip him up. It wasn't far away from him, but getting to it was agonizing. The added bulk of the broken chair was like an anchor weighing him down. By the time he finally came abreast of the table, he could feel sweat running off him and he was struggling to catch a breath. He refused to stop now, though, turning slowly and carefully to angle his reaching fingers closer and closer to the box cutter.

As he should have expected, the position he was forced into also changed his center of gravity, causing him to overreach and lose his balance. Before he knew what was happening, he was falling sideways, crashing into the table and flipping it over on top of himself. He cried out as he hit the ground, cringing as the heavy tools bounced off the spots where he was unprotected by the wooden chair. He somehow managed to get rolled over onto his side and breathed heavily until the bulk of the pain subsided into a dull ache he could deal with.

The scant remaining light began to flicker randomly, dimming more each time. He was almost out of time. Once the propane was used up and the lantern went out, he'd be in pitch darkness and unable to see anything that might offer him a way out of this mess. He scrambled back onto his knees, ignoring the chair's seat as it began to dig into the backs of his knees above his calf muscles. He saw the box cutter and dragged himself over to it, clutching it between his index and middle fingers as the lantern went out.

That was okay now. He had what he needed. Working by feel, he got the blade pointed back along his wrist and shoved it between his skin and the ropes, not caring as the sharp tip dug into his forearm. Slowly, he worked the blade back and forth against the rope, stabbing himself with every motion. He hoped it was as sharp as it had appeared to be when Clint sliced into Christy's feet, since there was no way for him to apply any real pressure to it.

After what felt like hours, the rope began to slacken, and then gave way entirely. He nearly moaned at the joyous feeling of blood flowing back into his hand properly again, but rather than waste time celebrating, he turned the cutter around and began sawing furiously at his other wrist. This time the process went much faster, and in only a few minutes, he had himself free and was able to get to his feet again.

He considered feeling around for a better weapon, but anything he could get out here would be nothing next to the gun he knew Clint had. He'd keep the box cutter for now, somehow break into the house across from the barn, find Clint, slit his fucking throat, and steal the gun. He could use that to take care of the other guy, then he could go and find the others.

After catching his breath, and maybe after a short nap. It wasn't like he could do much good wandering around in the dark, was it?

Benny staggered blindly for what he hoped was the exit, his pace quickening when he saw the sliver of starlight at the other end of the building. He grabbed both doors and swung them wide before running out of the barn and in the direction of the house where he slammed into something large and knocked himself on his ass.

At first he thought he must have hit a tree he hadn't noticed on his way in earlier, but when he finally shook his head and looked up, he found a huge face frowning down at him. He dimly remembered the other man mentioning someone named Otis who had seen him up on the hill just before a massive hand easily the size of a country ham wrapped around his throat and jerked him to his feet.

"You ain't s'posed to be here," the giant said. "Eugene's gonna be mad he catches you."

Benny acted without thinking, just swung his arm around and tried to bury the box cutter's blade in the man's throat. His aim was off, and the blade disappeared into the thick knot of muscle where the man's neck met his shoulder instead. The man roared in pain and his grip tightened around Benny's throat. His vision began to tunnel inward as he struggled for air that wouldn't come.

"You hurt me!" the man bellowed. "I was jus' gon' tell Eugene and let him deal with you. I wasn't gonna hurt you!"

Benny felt the crazy urge to apologize, but he couldn't breathe so he couldn't say anything. All he could accomplish was a faint gurgling sound that used up what little air he'd had left in his lungs. His chest started to burn from lack of breath, and red spots danced across his vision. He was able to make out the sight of the door opening on the house and two men emerging onto the porch. He had time to think that he'd somehow managed to fail once again, and then he heard a snapping sound somewhere inside of himself. His arms and legs went limp, and his vision faded to darkness.

NINETEEN

AMI WISHED IT HAD BEEN more of a surprise when Jay and Eric both quickly agreed to cut their search for their friends short in favor of the possibility of finding cabins, and thereby civilization and the chance for rescue. Neither of them had come right out and said it, but she was sure they were thinking exactly what she'd told Rob they'd be thinking: whatever happened to Christy at this point was her own doing, and considering the horrible way she'd treated them, they had no real desire to face her any time soon. If she wanted to consider it, their actions could say something profound about their character, but she chose not to think about it too carefully.

Even suspecting what they'd been thinking, she'd been surprised when they returned from their trip downstream after barely half an hour. They both reported there was another clearing not far from the one they washed up on, but there was no sign Christy had ever been there. Ami had no reason not to believe them, and they had sounded sincere, but their words troubled her more than she was willing to let on. The way they told it, there weren't even any footprints to indicate Christy had passed through the clearing. That didn't make any sense. Even if she didn't stop there and kept going, they should have at least been able to see signs of her passage. It wasn't like they were all on the beach near an ocean where tides came in and out and could've washed away footprints.

Rob seemed more troubled about the report than she was, but he didn't comment on it. He'd merely gathered up the few things from the recovered pack he thought they might need, tried once more to remember where the cabins had been on the map in relation to where he thought they were now, and then started off into the thick trees in what they all hoped was the right direction.

She wasn't completely sure how long they'd been walking, but she knew the sun had come off hot today, even through the heavy canopy of limbs above them that shaded the area as though it was still either just after dawn or just before dusk. Sweat was standing out on her face, and she could feel damp patches under the arms of her shirt and where her tights clung to her. She almost wished she was still wearing Eric's jeans instead of being back in her own clothes again. As loose and baggy as they were, they'd have provided considerably more airflow than her own fitted garments did.

The group finally crested a gentle rise they'd been climbing for the last little while, and Ami breathed a sigh of relief at the sight of several large rocks scattered amongst the fallen tree branches. She was about to ask Rob if they could stop here and take a break for a few minutes when he surprised her by sitting down atop one of the juts of rock and leaning back on his hands. Eric and Jay quickly followed suit, Eric sitting on one of the other rocks while Jay propped his back against it and groaned as he stretched his legs out before him.

"Five minutes," Rob said, and she was thankful to hear the slight edge of breathlessness in his voice. She was starting to think he was a machine that would be able to walk all day and leave them crawling along behind before it was all said and done. "That was a rough climb, and I need to get my bearings again."

Ami smiled as she sat down next to the rock he was resting on and propped her back against it, mimicking Jay's position. Rob obviously wasn't going to come right out and say he needed a break too, but she heard his unspoken addition all the same. The muscles in her thighs immediately began to twitch and tighten, so she rubbed at them with the flats of her hands.

"How far you think we've come?" she asked, turning to look at Rob over her shoulder.

He shrugged. "Two, maybe three miles, tops. We're making

good time, I didn't consider we'd be hiking up the side of a mountain to get where we were going."

"If the cabins are even there," Jay said. "I want to believe they are, but the way my legs feel right now I'm having a hard time with it."

"Oh, I'm sure the cabins are there," Eric added. "As to whether or not we're going in the right direction, that's where I'm having to go on faith alone. You sure you don't remember anything else about that map, Rob?"

"Wish I could say I did," Rob replied. "You know how you're trying to remember something, but the more you try, the harder it is? That's kind of how I'm feeling right now with that stupid map. I've never wished more that I had an eidetic memory."

"You've kept us alive this long," Eric said. "But if we're heading the wrong direction and we don't find those cabins, you're the first one on the menu."

Rob chuckled. "I suppose that's fair."

The four of them settled into an easy silence as a light breeze wafted across them. Ami felt the spots where she was damp from sweat grow slightly cold as the breeze hit them, but instead of being uncomfortable, it actually felt decidedly refreshing, as though she'd run a cool rag across herself to try and break the heat. From the way everyone else's eyes closed and their faces took on contented looks, she figured they were feeling the same way.

"Huh, that's weird," Eric said after another couple of minutes. "If I didn't know any better, I'd swear somebody was smoking a joint not far away."

Ami laughed. "That's called wishful thinking. Unless one of you was holding and never said until now."

"No, he's right," Jay said. Ami looked over to find him sitting up straighter, his nose crinkled up as he sniffed the air. "I smell it too."

They all got to their feet, turning and smelling at the breeze, trying to figure out exactly where it was coming from. After a moment, Ami could make out the distinct odor of marijuana as well, not overly strong or pungent, but still evident alongside the other scents of nature the breeze stirred up as well.

"Is that possible?" she asked. "Could someone else be camping somewhere around here?"

She looked over at Rob, expecting to see his normal bemused expression. Instead, he was wearing a deep frown.

"I'm sure there's trails all over the place through these mountains," he said. He sounded distracted, but he wasn't elaborating on why just yet. "Someone could be burning one while they hiked, I guess. Or fired up while they took a break. But I don't think that's the case. I mean, yeah, that smells like pot, obviously. But it doesn't smell like someone smoking a joint. Smells a little too . . . green for that."

Eric snickered. "How appropriate that you think pot smells green."

"You know what I meant."

"Yeah," Eric said, stopping and staring off into the distance. "Wind's coming from that way, so I bet that's where it is. Come on, let's check it out."

He was moving before anyone else had a chance to respond. Jay looked back to Ami, shrugged, and then followed after him. Rob's frown deepened as he watched them go.

"What's wrong?" Ami asked. "What do you think it is?"

He shook his head. "Probably nothing. I've got a buddy back home that grows for the state. It's legal there, you know? That smells a lot like his place does during harvest season, but it's the wrong time of year for it. Someone *could've* built a greenhouse up here, I guess, but it's not exactly something we want to walk in on, is it?"

"If they got materials up here to build something," Ami said. "They must know how to get out again, too. They could point us in the right direction or something."

"Right," he said, turning to her. Ami thought he actually looked frightened. "And what exactly should we say? 'Hey, we're lost, can you show us how to get home again? Nice illegal grow operation you have here, by the way. Oh, fair warning, a couple more of our group are missing, so we're going to be sending the park rangers up here to look for them, so you might want to lay low for a while.' More than likely we'd end up with bullets in our heads for our trouble."

"So we get to it, hide, look around for the way in and out, then bypass it altogether," Ami said. "Can it really be more dangerous than what we've already had to deal with?"

He winced. "Illegal growers aren't like your normal stoner.

First off, they don't usually partake. Hard to stay alert and watch for cops when you're stoned out of your mind. Also, they're not exactly known for being the welcoming sort. I'd just prefer we avoid it completely if we can."

Ami shrugged. "Still have to know where it is to do that, right?"

Rob sighed. "I suppose. Just take it easy, all right? And watch where you're walking."

"We'd better tell those two," she replied, gesturing to the shrinking forms of Eric and Jay as they began descending the outcropping on the other side. "I think they've already decided what they're doing."

"Shit," Rob said once he realized how far ahead of them the other two were. "Let's go."

They headed off side by side, Rob glancing around nervously every few seconds while Ami tried to figure out how to catch up to their friends without sending themselves tumbling down this ever-steepening slope. Finally the two paused, Eric reaching out to grab Jay's arm as he pointed excitedly at something that, to Ami, was still hidden in the trees. Jay remained where he was, but Eric rushed off ahead, his gait much more boisterous than it had been before.

Finally, Ami was able to see what had him so excited. The trees gave way at the bottom of the slope, and stretching across the clearing were random piles of what she thought were marijuana plants, rotting away in the elements. Even from this distance she could tell they were the dregs of a crop, the leaves tiny and wilted, the stems barely larger than drinking straws. She frowned as she was able to make out blue tubes running across the clearing beyond those piles, neat parallel rows that stretched from one end to the other and back again. There were only rows of dirt between those tubes now, but she could imagine how it would look if there were plants growing there instead. Her breath caught in her throat as she turned her head and saw how the clearing opened up and grew larger, only blue strips breaking the stretch of dirt. The scope of this operation was immense, and she began to feel fear herself at the thought of what the people running this would do if they found four unknown people traipsing around out here.

"Stop!" Rob yelled. "Wait! Don't go in there!"

Her head snapped back to see what had Rob so upset. Eric was running full-tilt now, his course one that would run him straight into one of those refuse piles. At first she couldn't understand why Rob sounded so panicked; after all, Eric looked like he'd be sticking close to the woods and not actually moving far onto open ground. Then the sun came out from behind a cloud and glinted off something stretched between the surrounding trees and she felt her heart drop.

Rob took off at a dead run. Not wanting to be left behind, Ami started running after him, fighting to keep her legs beneath her as they descended the steepest part of the slope. Jay turned and watched them come, confused, but Ami couldn't spare the time to watch his reactions right now. All she could think about was staying upright and how it seemed that Rob wanted to catch up to Eric and stop him, but they weren't closing the distance fast enough. She could no longer see whatever it was the sun had reflected off of, but that only made her more frightened. If she couldn't see it, the odds were Eric couldn't either.

Eric came to the edge of the tree line about the time Ami and Rob came abreast of Jay. His body went straight, his hands flying to his throat at the same time Ami heard a sound like a guitar string being plucked too hard. Eric went flying backward as if shoved by some unseen hand, his momentum throwing his feet out in front of him as he fell. He landed on his back and immediately rolled over onto his stomach. He managed to get his knees under him and started to raise himself slowly to something resembling upright once more.

As soon as Ami was able to see him, she knew it was too late to help him. His hands were clasped over his throat, blood already running through his fingers in rivulets. His mouth worked but no words emerged, only a thick gurgling sound she could hear from ten feet away. One hand reached out then fell away, allowing a stream of blood to spray from his neck and cover Jay from head to waist in gore. The other hand fell to his side as well and his head leaned back, exposing a wound that looked to have been filled with raw, glistening hamburger. Ami swore she could see the opening of his throat where it led up to his mouth, and then mercifully he was toppling onto his side, hiding the sight from her again.

She screamed, barely noticing as her knees hit the ground,

her own hands rising to her cheeks, pulling at the skin below her eyes as if she was involuntarily trying to claw the vision of Eric's death from her eyes. She saw Jay drop to his knees as well, one hand reaching out for Eric and then a pair of strong hands grabbed her by the shoulders and turned her away from the scene. She looked up into Rob's pale face, his eyes locking onto hers the second he had the chance.

"Stop it!" he hissed. "Someone might hear you and come looking!"

Somehow that broke through the fog descending on her mind. If someone was within earshot, there was no way they'd have missed her scream. One might could be written off as just a wild animal, but if she kept it up, there was no way they could mistake it for anything other than a human being screaming in mortal terror. She slammed her mouth closed so hard she felt her teeth click together painfully and forced the screams back down her throat. She couldn't stop completely, but at least now the only noise she made was a whimpering, whining keen that reminded her of how Christy sounded when Rob had first told her about their situation.

Rob sighed heavily and nodded, apparently satisfied she was as under control as she was going to get right now.

"I'm going to . . . make sure," he said. "And see if I can figure out what did it. You don't look, understand? You watch for anyone coming this way, but *do not* look back over there until I say you can."

Ami nodded, unwilling to risk verbal confirmation for fear she might start screaming again. Rob moved away, but she did not watch him go. She forced herself to scan along the edge of the woods, waiting for someone to burst out of them at any moment, gun in hand, demanding to know who they were and what they were doing out here.

She could hear Jay dry-heaving somewhere behind her. Of course it would only be dry heaves; they hadn't eaten anything for him to be puking up since yesterday morning. She heard Rob's footsteps moving away from her, getting closer to where her ears told her Jay was. The footsteps paused, then she heard Rob's moan, low in his throat.

"Jesus *Christ*," he said, his voice strangled. "Oh, sweet fucking *Christ!*"

He let out a thick, wet belch, then went silent. A minute or so later she heard the twanging guitar sound again, only much more subdued than when she'd heard it before. Shortly after, she heard Rob murmuring softly, then two pairs of footsteps approached. She glanced to the side, refusing to turn her head, and saw Jay staggering along in her direction, leaning heavily on Rob for support. Finally he collapsed beside her, and she nearly screamed again at the blood that trickled down across his face and stained his shirt. His eyes were wild and filled with terror. Ami was positive the sight of Eric being nearly decapitated was something Jay would have to live with the rest of his life.

If they all survived long enough to have a rest of their lives.

"Some kind of wire," Rob said, dropping down heavily in front of them. "Thin, but strong. Betting the whole damn tree line's booby trapped with it."

Ami started to ask him something, found herself unable, and cleared her throat. "Is he . . . ?"

Rob nodded slowly, his eyes growing moist. "He's . . . gone. I . . . I think it was quick, but . . ."

"Probably not quick enough," Jay finished for him, his voice thick. "I think he knew what was happening, I think he wanted to stop it, wanted us to stop it, but knew nobody could do anything. I think . . . I think . . ."

His words trailed off into sobs, one shaking hand coming up to cover his eyes. Ami wanted to put an arm around him, comfort him, but she felt too numb to be able to do anything. She looked down at the ground, her vision blurring as tears formed in her own eyes. Eric hadn't been such a bad guy. He definitely hadn't deserved anything like *that*. To have your head damn near cut off, and to know you'd effectively done it to yourself because you got over-excited and didn't see the trap right in front of you . . . It was too terrible to contemplate.

"We can't stay here," Rob said. His voice was shaky, but still firm. "If they set traps, they're probably going to check them now and then to see if they caught anyone in them. We can't be here when that happens. We'll stick to the trees, try to circle around. Maybe we can find a way out, but I'm more concerned about putting some distance between us and this place."

"What about Eric?" Ami asked softly. "We can't leave him there."

Rob sighed. "Ami, we can't take him with us. We've barely got the strength to carry ourselves, much less someone else. Even if we could manage it, we'd leave . . ."

He swallowed hard, unable to finish his thought. Ami looked up at him.

"We'd leave a trail," she said. "He'd keep bleeding out and leave a trail right to us. Is that what you were going to say?"

Rob gave her a miserable look and nodded. She looked away, unable to meet his eyes. This wasn't the first time he'd pointed out the harsh reality to her, but at least this time he seemed as hurt by that fact as those he was telling would be. A part of her wanted to brand him a monster for thinking that way, but some- one had to. As sad as it was to admit, and as much as she hated putting that kind of burden on him for it, Rob was the least emo- tionally invested in their well-being. He had only met them the day before yesterday. He'd only really talked to her and Jay since then. And as much as the thought made her sick to her stomach, she hoped he'd be as rational regarding her if something should happen.

She nodded and started to her feet. Rob rose with her, and together they got Jay up as well. The three of them turned to start moving through the trees surrounding the empty field. Ami turned after a while, hoping for one last look at Eric's remains, but, perhaps mercifully, the spot where he'd died was already hidden by the thick underbrush. Making sure to watch for more traps, she returned her attention to the path ahead of her and trudged onward, no longer believing they were going to make it out alive, but hoping for a miracle just the same.

TWENTY

EUGENE GLANCED UP FROM THE makeshift fire pit and squinted his eyes against the glare of the morning sun off the river. It wasn't often he miscalculated, but seeing the proof others had been here—and recently, judging by the warmth of the ashes—he had to admit it was possible that was exactly what he'd done. It was doubly troublesome that Clint had been the one to suggest searching this way, since it was the direction the girl had come from when they caught her yesterday. Eugene had considered and dismissed the possibility at the time, but Clint had been adamant, if somewhat subdued after already being put in his place. Had he listened to the man who was, despite his proclivities for perversions and violence, a remarkably skilled head of security, this problem would already be dealt with, and he wouldn't have to be out here hoping to catch the intruders before they saw more than was healthy for him.

He trailed his eyes across the woods on the other side of the river and those scattered across the small island, easily accessible in the summer but now distinctly isolated with the added runoff from higher up the mountain. There was no sign of anything, only an occasional rustling as some wild animal scurried about looking for its breakfast. He had proof the girl had friends out here beyond the boy who'd nearly managed to escape last night, but he saw nothing to indicate they were making their way toward the more commonly used access road on the other side of the river. Not that getting to it would be easy, what with the river's current being as strong as it was, but it could be done. He'd done it once himself, long ago. That adventure ended with him running headlong into a new and better life than the one he'd had before getting lost out here. If the girl's friends made it, they stood more of a chance of undoing everything he'd worked so hard for these last fifteen years.

If they hadn't gone back across the river, and since neither he nor Clint had seen them when they started upstream from the docks, either the intruders were heading back upriver themselves or had gone farther inland searching for help. If they'd gone upriver, it was only a matter of time before he and Clint caught up with them. The shore would become so rocky and overgrown after a while they'd have no choice but to come back this way or cut into the woods and move inland after all. Either way, it would amount to the same thing.

Trouble.

The sound of breaking sticks drew his attention back to the clearing where the intruders made camp last night. Clint was emerging from the trees, what seemed to be a nearly permanent scowl etched onto his face. Eugene brushed the dirt from his slacks and stood, waiting for the man's report.

"They're headed right fuckin' for it," Clint said, shaking his head. "Left a path a blind man could follow. They missed the dirt road that leads to the docks, so they're takin' the long way 'round, but they're headed toward the compound sure as shit. For all I know, they done found it."

"We knew that was a possibility," Eugene replied, trying to sound more confident than he felt. "That's why we left Otis there, to keep an eye out just in case."

"Yeah, smart thinkin' there," Clint said. "Leave the dumbass to deal with the big shit instead'a havin' him come with you on this wild goose chase and leave the one what knows how to fuck shit up to stand guard."

"Otis can handle it."

"Jus' like he handled the dipshit last night, huh?"

"Yes, like that," Eugene said, taking a step closer to the man. Clint took an involuntary step backward, but Eugene closed the gap again. "If he hadn't handled 'the dipshit last night', we might have had our throats cut while we slept. And while we're on the subject, whose fault was it the boy managed to get loose in the first place? Was it the one of us who was too worried about getting his dick wet to secure him properly?"

"I've broke plenty of assholes in my time, Gene," Clint said, his eyes narrowing. "And he looked good and broke to me. How was I supposed to know he'd up and grow a fuckin' pair?"

Eugene considered pointing out he was supposed to know because it was his job to know, but there was no use. Arguing with Clint would only make him angrier, and that would keep him from thinking straight. If there was one thing he needed to be able to do right now, it was consider things clearly. Unfortunately, that meant taking advice from the man he wanted so badly to strangle at the moment.

"Their fire hasn't been out that long," he said. "How far do you think they've made it?"

Clint stared at him a moment longer, then his face relaxed as he shrugged. "No tellin'. They left out not long after first light, they could already be at the fields. Maybe not if they was hurtin' after their mishap, but I wouldn't count on that. If they angled either direction, there's a chance they found the road or missed the whole she-bang."

"Suggestions?"

Clint sighed. "You ain't gonna like it none."

Eugene didn't say anything, merely raised an impatient eyebrow at him.

"Fine. We go back to the compound. I'll take the nitwit and check the traps. If they made it to the fields, they probably got caught in one. That'll tell us somethin' at least. If we don't catch up to 'em on the road back, you're gonna need to make a phone call while we're makin' that check. There's the three of us up here for now. Can't do much heavy searchin' that way."

"Fuck," Eugene said, shaking his head. Calling for reinforcements was the absolute last thing he wanted to do, but Clint was right. If they didn't find those intruders quickly, there was every possibility they could end up doubling back and catching them off guard. That wouldn't be so bad in and of itself since three well-rested men against a handful of exhausted and injured idiots would be no real contest. But if they stumbled across the compound, got freaked out and hightailed it, then somehow managed to get themselves rescued? That could mean a whole

172

world of trouble coming down on their heads.

"Take the radio when you and Otis check the traps," Eugene said. "You don't find anything, I'll make the call. If you do, well, you figure out if we can handle it ourselves or not and let me know. I don't want to bring AJ in on this unless there's no other choice."

Clint's lips twitched up into a smirk. "You don't want to look bad for the boss, do you?"

"No, I don't," Eugene admitted. "And you shouldn't want that either. You're supposed to be the one in charge of security up here. Do you really think AJ is going to give you a pass because this happened on my watch, or do you think he might choose to retire all three of us and start fresh with new staff?"

Clint opened his mouth, paused, and then closed it again. He knew the answer as well as Eugene did. He'd been present when Eugene had taken over this particular operation from his predecessor and had seen the methods he'd used to carry out his orders. Clint liked to think of himself as something of a tough guy, and the truth of it was that it was an accurate assessment. But tough didn't mean stupid. Eugene could clearly remember the look on Clint's face the day Eugene turned to him, his own face covered in a mask of blood and bits of flesh, and asked if he'd done a sufficient job of carrying out those orders. The man had been incapable of answering, but the retching noise he made when he emptied his stomach onto the dry, dusty ground had been answer enough.

"That sounds good," Clint said, his voice quiet. "Me and Otis'll check it out, then I'll let you know if you need to make that call."

"Then we need to get moving," Eugene said, turning to head back downriver to where the ATVs were parked at the dock. "We've already wasted enough time. The longer we mess around out here, the further onto the block our necks go."

As he went, he couldn't stop thinking about those intruders. If there was one thing Eugene valued above all else, it was his own ability to remain calm, even when doling out punishments of some sort. He'd been calm when he punished Clint last night, and earlier in the day when the man had challenged him. He'd been calm when AJ explained to him if he took this job, the only way out was death. He didn't much care for the violent aspect of things—not that he had to, since that was more Clint's purview than his own—but he remained calm even when things came to it. His calmness as he'd casually tossed his predecessor's face onto the ground at Clint's feet when he assumed control here was a testament to the fact. He'd even remained calm throughout the entire grisly slaughter that preceded the final act. But whoever these idiot thrill-seekers were, they'd managed to rattle that calm.

If for no other reason, they would pay dearly for that. And once their bodies were dumped into the deep crevice opposite their grow fields, his calm would return and all would be right with the world.

When he'd first seen them coming, Teddy got excited. He could already tell it wasn't his friends, but at least it was a couple of living people. In a way, that was better. People he didn't know meant a potential for rescue. He was disappointed he missed out on the chance to see which of his other friends might've survived whatever happened—and how the hell had he managed to sleep that long after being unconscious the better part of the previous day?—but the chance of getting the fuck out of this wilderness and back to the real world managed to override everything else. Then he'd seen the rifle slung over the one man's shoulder and caught a glimpse of their determined faces and knew rescue was the furthest thing from him this morning.

Luckily, the two men had discovered the spot where the people he assumed were his friends built their fire last night, and stopped to check it out. It bought him enough time to retreat into the trees and hide in the brush, still able to keep an eye on them, but hopefully hidden enough to keep them from seeing him as well.

After a brief and heated discussion where both men raised their voices, but not enough for Teddy to make out what they were saying, the guy with the rifle had disappeared into the woods and the other one had knelt next to the ring of stones at the center of the clearing. At first, Teddy thought the man might be praying, and his hope started to return. Religious nuts would be less likely to shoot him on sight, or at least he hoped that was the case. Then he realized the man was feeling around in the ashes before he started looking around like he was searching for something.

For a brief instant, Teddy was sure he'd been spotted. The man's eyes lingered in his general direction, then moved on. The other guy showed back up, and when the rifle didn't come down and start sweeping toward him, Teddy breathed a sigh of relief. They'd talked some more, then headed back the way they came.

Still, Teddy thought it was best to stay right where he was. He had his doubts those two had anything resembling good intentions on their minds, and it was possible they really *had* seen him and were trying to lure him out for a clearer shot. Maybe it was silly, but he'd seen enough stuff in the movies and on television that the concept of backwoods cannibals was within his realm of reason. Even with as much pain as he was in, the thought of being shot, dressed, and served up for dinner tonight wasn't one he relished.

So he remained hidden. At some point, he slept again. When he awoke, his head felt like it was stuffed with cotton and thinking was harder to do than it seemed it should be. Some deep part of his mind told him he needed to move, to do whatever he could to stay awake, but it was too hard, so he ignored it. Before he knew it, he was asleep again.

This time when he woke up, it was morning again, and while he didn't know it, everything was over.

TWENTY-ONE

NUMB AS SHE STILL FELT following Eric's death, when the scent of cooking meat reached her nostrils, Ami's body responded to it the only way it could, considering how long it had been since she'd had a meal: her mouth began watering and her stomach rumbled and clenched painfully. From the twin looks of confusion on Jay and Rob's faces, they must have been experiencing the same thing. There was no mistaking the aroma, though there was something else just beneath it, something sharper and more pungent that she couldn't immediately place. She was sure she'd smelled it before, she wasn't sure where it had been or under what circumstances. Normally she was good at connecting scents to what it was she was smelling—something that had been both a blessing and a curse at different times in her life— but this time, that undercurrent was too diffuse to come to her.

It wasn't something that worried her; it was a curiosity. Besides, with the way the cooking meat smell took her back to when she was a kid running around the back yard while her dad tended to the grill up on the deck, it made sense she couldn't focus on the other smell now.

She found her eyes drifting closed. Her nose lifted into the air as she turned slowly, trying to determine the direction the smell was coming from. It was an unconscious reaction, and a part of her mind screamed at her to pay more attention to her immediate surroundings for fear there might be another booby trap nearby she could stumble into while she was focused on the smell, but she couldn't help herself. Not even half an hour ago she'd have sworn she wouldn't want to even think about food for a long, long time, but now that she was faced with even the *smell* of potential food, here she was honing in on it like a human radar.

Jay must have been doing the same thing she was because she saw out of the corner of her eye as he started off in the direction she thought the smell was coming from. She opened her eyes completely, fully ready to join him and go after the chance for food, but Rob put a hand on both their shoulders, stopping them.

"Not a good idea," he said, his voice filled with disappointment. "Remember where we are. Remember what just happened."

Ami scowled, annoyed he would ruin their chances for a meal, but then she realized how foolish what she and Jay were about to do had been. After all, it had crossed her mind moments ago that Eric's death made her forget about how hungry she was, and here she was about to run the risk of dying the exact same way.

"But it's food," Jay said, succinctly voicing her own views on the matter. "I don't know about you, but I'm starving, and I'm betting Ami is, too."

"And we could die going after that food," Rob pointed out. "Believe me, I'm starving as much as you two are. But I seriously doubt anything they're cooking is worth risking my life for."

"You think it's the ones who set the traps?" Ami asked, forcing herself to turn away from that wonderful smell.

"I think the odds are good," Rob answered. He looked around as if trying to catch his bearings, shook his head, and sighed. "In fact, I'd say they're better than good. If we were in Vegas, I'd say bet on it. We've been trying so hard to watch for traps by keeping the field in sight that I think we ended up circling around it instead of moving away from it. Stupid."

Ami looked to the side and saw he was right. They were farther into the tree line than they had been when they left Eric's body behind, but the empty field was still clearly visible a few yards through the trees. She could make out some other vague shapes as well that might be buildings on the other side of the field. They hadn't moved away from the potential danger like they thought they had. They'd walked right into the lion's den instead.

"What now?" Jay asked. It was obvious from the look on his face that while he understood the situation they were in perfectly, he wasn't relishing the thought of abandoning the chance for something to eat. "If we take them by surprise, we might could steal whatever it is they're cooking and get far enough away to eat it without them finding us."

"Maybe," Rob said, frowning as he studied the field. "Or maybe we end up eating bullets instead of barbecue. Not a good alternative, if you ask me."

"We've got to do something," Ami said. "It's obvious we're not going to find those cabins any time soon, and we didn't think to bring any water from the river with us."

Rob jerked like he'd been punched and looked over at her with shock evident on his face. "I never thought about that. We can do without food, but we need water. Shit! How could I have been such an idiot? You'd think I'd never done anything like this before, when I was the one you thought had all the experience and should be your guide on the rafting trip. Can't believe I forgot the damn water."

"It doesn't matter," Ami said. "It's not like we had anything we could've carried it in."

Rob nodded, but he still didn't look very happy with himself. He looked back to the field, his eyes scanning it before turning to the edge of the tree line along the path they'd been taking.

"Okay, let's hedge our bets a little," he said. "We go in through that field, assuming we don't kill ourselves on a trap, they're going to know we've seen too much and be less inclined to listen before they kill us all. We keep going the way we were. I'm betting there's a trail or something that leads to those buildings in the distance. We go in that way, tell whoever we find we were staying at the cabins, went out camping a couple nights ago, and a bear tore up our campsite. We got turned around and lost our way, and ask for them to point us in the right direction. If they seem friendly enough to talk to us, we try for some of their food. If not, we at least stand a chance of finding a faster way to the cabins and out of the mess we're in. Thoughts?"

"Maybe one of us should hang back," Jay said. "Keep a big stick or something handy. If it looks like they're going to get mean, that person runs in and whacks them, buys time for the others to get away."

Rob considered, and then shook his head. "Better not. We don't know how many are in there, and if they have guards or a lookout or something that sees us split up, they might decide we're scoping them out to steal their crop or something."

"It's fucking winter," Jay replied. "There's no crop, man. Or didn't you notice that?"

"Not the point I was making," Rob began. Jay held up a hand to stop him from continuing.

"I get what you're saying, never mind," he said. "And a stick probably wouldn't do us much good if they did have guns anyway."

Rob nodded. "Ami, any thoughts?"

She sighed. "I'm starving. If you think that's the best way to try for something to eat, or better yet, to get out of here, I say let's go for it."

"Okay then," Rob replied. "If they ask, we don't have any idea what they're doing out here and we really don't care."

"That's pretty well true," Jay muttered. "Walter White could be standing over the grill and I wouldn't ask any questions."

"Then let's get moving," Rob said. "We get there, let me do the talking, okay?"

He started off, and Ami fell into step behind him. Jay hung back, bringing up the rear. She wondered if he was still considering finding something he could use as a weapon, but when she glanced back at him he was trudging along with his head down. She thought he looked as tired and despondent as she felt and realized he and Eric had spent a lot of time alone together since the accident. She knew there wouldn't be anything romantic developing between them, but being used and rejected by the same woman would've given them a common link they might well have bonded over. She hadn't stopped to consider whether the two of them might've been forming a friendship suddenly cut short a while ago when Eric got caught in that trap. She'd always felt concern for Jay's psyche, since he'd seemed particularly fragile ever since he'd dropped out of college his junior year without warning or explanation, and found herself wondering whether the near-constant stream of bad fortune they were dealing with might be taking more of a toll on him than the rest of them. She'd try and ask him tonight, hopefully after they'd had something to eat and found the cabins so they'd be warm and relatively safe.

As Rob predicted, they soon rounded a corner and saw a dirt trail up ahead of them, leading back through the trees in the direction of the river. She was not a good judge of distance, but she thought it would cut right through the area where she'd seen some sort of buildings across the field earlier. The scent of cooking meat was growing stronger as they neared it, despite the wind no longer blowing the smells into their faces. It was far from concrete proof of much of anything, but at least it was something of a confirmation.

Rob turned and nodded to her before heading directly for the trail and angling so it would appear they'd been on it all along. Ami and Jay followed, likewise adjusting their stride. Ami didn't know whether or not it achieved the effect Rob had apparently been going for, but she was so relieved to have something resembling normal, level ground beneath her feet that she didn't much care, either.

Ahead of them, she could clearly see the buildings coming closer. Two were fairly large and looked to be barns of some sort while the third was farther in and appeared to be a cabin. It wasn't an overly large one, and if Ami had to guess, she'd say it had no more than two bedrooms in it, but it still made her more nervous than she had been at first. She'd seen stories on the news about illegal pot farmers, and in almost every case, they had been living in a tent, or maybe a camper or something. For there to be not only a single permanent structure here, but *three*, they had to be dealing with something beyond the norm. This bespoke a considerable investment, not only in the construction of the buildings themselves, but in the costs of actually getting the materials up here in the first place. The road they were on was wide enough for a pickup to make it without too much difficulty, but that was about it. It would be tremendously difficult to get all the materials up here to build all three of those structures.

Besides the money, though, there was the arrogance to consider. Someone who was afraid of being caught doing something illegal didn't put down roots like this. That was the main reason for campers and tents and the like: easy to break down and move, or cheap enough to abandon if the need was dire enough. There was no moving this, and the investment that could be lost if the place was abandoned was insane to consider. Whoever had built this here was obviously not worried about being caught in the act and probably wasn't concerned about the potential financial loss if the place was discovered. That meant lots of money and lots of power. That meant whoever was running this was not some two-bit idiot hoping to make some extra money selling weed. To whoever set this up, it was serious business.

She was about to point this out to Rob when the first tendrils of smoke came into view. After another couple of steps past the longest of the three buildings, the tendrils became clouds that obscured her view of whatever might lie beyond them. Based on the sheer amount of smoke and the intensity of the cooking smell, it was entirely possible they were about to walk into the middle of a virtual army of drug dealers getting ready for their lunch.

She thought maybe Rob was having similar thoughts, since his pace slowed and he began craning his neck, trying to make something out beyond those billowing, fragrant clouds. Finally he seemed to work up his courage and strode forward confidently again, passing through the haze as if they were in the middle of a city park and he was the mayor.

Ami followed him through and saw not an army on the other side, but a single, large man tending to the fire and whatever was cooking atop it. The man was wearing a stained t-shirt stretched taut over his ample belly and sagging jeans barely holding onto his hips. He was turned so three quarters of his front was facing away from them, giving her an unwelcome glance at nearly half his butt peeking at her from over the top of his waistband. It was decidedly hairy, but more disturbing was what she thought was dried shit knotting several of those hairs together.

If this was their cook, she suddenly wasn't so hungry anymore. At least it was only one person, so some of her nervousness faded away.

"Hey there!" Rob called out. "We're lost and hoping maybe you could help us."

The man jumped when Rob spoke, obviously unaware they had come up behind him. He turned to face them, a confused look on his broad features. He had a long metal rod in one hand, the tip glowing orange from where he'd been poking it into the fire.

Ami couldn't focus on that, though, because what he held in his other hand caused her breath to leave her and her legs to suddenly weaken.

She tried to think of it as having come from an animal of some sort, and she supposed that was true in a sick sort of way, but there was no mistaking a severed human arm dangling loosely in the man's fist. Her gaze moved from the torn and ragged spot where the arm once attached to someone's shoulder, down the loose bicep, to where the elbow bent slightly before ending in another patch of raw meat. She glanced down at the man's feet and saw a pile of more body parts. There weren't many, but she could clearly see the rest of the arm the man was holding as well as another one that hadn't been torn apart quite as thoroughly—it still had the forearm and hand attached to it.

Her eyes went to the fire pit, already knowing what she was going to find there but needing to see it, to prove it to herself anyway. As she feared, the rest of the body was there, the flesh already blackened and starting to melt from the intensity of the heat it was being exposed to.

"You ain't supposed to be here," the giant said, taking a step away from the fire and closer to them.

When he moved, Ami saw the head. It hadn't been on the blaze long, since the hair was still alight, so the features were still recognizable. Ami felt her stomach turn. If she had anything in it, she'd be vomiting all over herself right now. A wave of emotional agony unlike anything she'd ever experienced welled up inside her as she stared at the face she'd seen countless times before, that she'd once lovingly kissed. She focused on the lips that had kissed her in return, lips that had, in better times, given her so much pleasure. Lips that were now opened in a soundless scream.

Benny's lips.

"It's you!" the man said, his voice filled with not anger, but awe.

Ami looked up to see the giant staring at her, his eyes wide, his lips curled up in what would in any other circumstance be a goofy grin.

"You come to *me!*"

It was too much for her to take. Ami screamed.

"What the fuck?" Jay yelled. "What the fuck did you do, you

asshole?"

Ami felt hands on her shoulders, turning her, pushing her back the way they'd come. She looked up to see Rob trying to herd her away, his eyes locked on the giant, the giant's eyes still locked on her. It didn't seem real. The world had gone hazy and dreamlike, though whether it was from the smoke stinging her eyes or her own mind's retreat from the madness, she couldn't say.

Jay wasn't following, and that broke through the haze. He stood stock-still, staring unbelievingly at the remains of her boy-friend—and how horrible she felt about how she'd treated him, how she'd been planning to break up with him but stringing him along first—his hands clenched into fists. She saw what he in-tended to do an instant before he did it and had no time to even consider telling him to run instead.

He threw himself at the giant, fists raised. The larger man saw him coming, dropped the arm he was holding, and slammed one massive hand against Jay's head. Jay wasn't just knocked sideways, he *flew* sideways, his feet leaving the ground before he slammed back into it a few feet away. He tried to get back up, then dropped prone again and remained still.

Ami screamed again before holding out her hands as if she could move him telepathically into them and out of harm's way. Rob stopped watching the giant and grabbed her, hoisting her up into his own arms like a child and trying to run for the woods again. None of them had eaten anything in two days, and they'd last had water sometime this morning before spending the entire day hiking through the woods. He tried, but he didn't have the strength to pull it off. He was moving, but not very fast. If that giant came after them, he was going to catch them with ease.

She somehow managed to pull herself together enough to force her legs back down. Rob stumbled when she thrashed against him and nearly fell, but once her feet touched the ground she managed to keep him upright. There was a roaring sound in her ears now, growing in both volume and intensity that had to be a result of how hard her heart was beating. Nothing else made sense—not that anything about any of this made any sense.

"We can't leave him!" she screamed into Rob's face. They were nearly nose-to-nose, and she was sure he could hear her fine, but screaming at him seemed somehow appropriate. "We can't leave Jay to that monster!"

He nodded at her, his eyes terrified and bewildered, and for a moment, she felt sure he'd lost his own senses and would be frozen by it. Then he turned around and started back to try and rescue Jay. She watched him go, then saw a blur of motion beyond him and understood what the roaring sound was.

A pair of four-wheeled ATVs skidded to a halt before the steps leading up to the cabin's porch, a man seated on each of them. One of the men was yelling, but Ami was too confused and scared, too hyped up from the adrenaline coursing through her to make out what he was saying. The other was standing up and pulling something from over his shoulder. It was a rifle, one like she'd seen people in the military use. Benny had wanted one himself, had gotten to fire one at some gun store and shooting range he'd convinced everyone to stop at on their way to the hotel a couple days ago. She couldn't remember what it was called, but she remembered what the salesperson showed them it could do to a watermelon he'd set up for Benny to shoot at.

Rob must have seen it as well, because he stopped running toward Jay and tried to turn around and run back toward her instead, perhaps to try and get her to safety, perhaps to run right past her and try to save himself. She would never know.

The man with the rifle socketed it against his shoulder and leaned his head over it slightly. She saw a flash from the muzzle an instant before the air split with a massive cracking sound. She felt the air as the bullet passed inches from her arm and instinctively shied away from it, dropping to one knee when her legs would no longer hold her. She looked back to see the man taking aim again, then her view was obstructed by Rob's frightened face. There was another cracking sound, then Rob's face was gone, a red mist of blood spraying out over her head and spattering across her face like a bucketful of warm water had been thrown at her. Rob's body took another staggering step before falling over and mercifully hiding what was left of his head from her sight.

She felt her vision narrowing to a pinprick and had enough time to wonder if she'd feel it when she was shot as well, then sweet unconsciousness claimed her and she didn't care for a while.

TWENTY-TWO

SHE HAD NO IDEA WHERE she was or how long she'd been out this time, but Ami was sure of one thing: her arms were killing her. Her shoulders were pulled back painfully, creating a dull ache deep in the sockets that made it feel as though the circulation to the rest of her arms had been cut off. She tried moving them, searching for some kind of relief, but the attempt made the rope looped around her wrists bite in painfully, tearing at the already-abraded skin there. Her legs felt strange as well, and after getting her mind to focus on the sensation, she realized they were bent backward at the knees, her ankles bound as efficiently as her wrists. She tried to straighten them out and felt her shoulders scream as though they were going to tear free. Apparently, there was another rope connecting her ankles to her wrists, effectively preventing her from finding any position even relatively comfortable.

When she finally managed to open her eyes, she found herself staring at packed dirt almost directly in front of her. She had to be lying on her stomach. How else could her legs be pulled up behind her like they were? It still didn't tell her anything about where she was or how she came to be here, but at least it was one more piece of the puzzle. She found she was able to raise her head slightly with only minimal discomfort, which allowed her to breathe slightly better so her head could clear enough to assess the situation further.

Slowly, the memories of what happened began to come back to her. Their discovery of Benny's mutilated corpse, the giant man who hacked it apart before burning it, the arrival of the other two men on four wheelers. The man standing up, rifle in hand. The gunshots. Rob . . .

Ami fought down the tears that welled up in her eyes at the memory of Rob's head practically exploding from the gunshot. She'd obviously fainted right after, and the men had taken her. There was no way she would be able to figure a way out of this mess if she let herself be torn apart by grief now, especially grief over someone she'd only known a couple of days. She'd held herself together after Eric's death, and after discovering what happened to Benny, so she could do the same now. Rob wouldn't want her to do anything else.

She took in a deep breath through her nose and nearly gagged at the stench that assaulted her. She had no idea what it could be and, considering her position, had no way to see what was causing it, but it was horrid. A strange and vile concoction of shit and piss and rot and weed and something else she couldn't place, something she wanted to describe as metallic, as if she'd been holding a handful of pennies then smelled her hand after dropping them. Then again, maybe it wasn't so hard to figure out what that smell was. Right or wrong, Ami thought it was the smell of death.

Whatever it really was, it was a clear indication she didn't want to stay where she was for very long. She dropped her head again, gathering her strength, and then shifted her weight to one side. She moved, but only slightly. Still, it was progress. She rocked back and forth, trying to use the muscles in her abdomen to give herself more momentum, and finally managed to roll over onto her side. The bright flash of momentary rending pain that shot through the shoulder she was now lying on drew a soft, agonized moan from her lips, but it was balanced by the modicum of relief she felt in her other joints. It didn't manage to buy her any more freedom of motion, but at least she could turn herself enough to survey her surroundings.

Judging from the quality of the sunlight peeking in through the cracks in the walls, it was still daylight outside. She had no idea what time of day it was, so she still didn't know how long she'd been unconscious, but at least she was able to see.

From the looks of things, she was in an old barn. It didn't seem very long, so she didn't think it was the one they'd walked past as they entered the compound, but the other, smaller one across from the cabin. From where she lay, she could see a table with assorted tools scattered across its surface. Another table lay beyond it, with scraps of wood that looked like it was once a chair in a pile in front of it. Chains dangled from the ceiling, a pair of padlocks hanging unclasped in the links. She glanced to the side where the first table was and saw the other end of the chains draped over a massive crossbeam in the wall.

She shivered. The way those chains were set up, there could be no mistaking their purpose. She wondered if that was where Benny ended up, and where he met his end. Her eyes misted over at the thought. She blinked the tears away, refusing to give in to her emotions. She had to find a way out. If she didn't, she was as good as dead herself.

If she craned her neck, she could make out the edges of the doors to the barn at the far end. They were closed, and she was willing to bet they were locked from the outside. She hoped there was some other exit from the building, but she didn't think there would be. Of course, she would need to get out of her bonds somehow before she could even consider a way out of the barn.

She tried to turn herself to get a better look at the rest of the interior, but she couldn't get enough leverage without managing to pull the ropes securing her even tighter and causing more pain to herself than she could withstand. She stopped trying, panting from the effort, unable to stop the groan that slipped from her lips.

"Ami?" a familiar voice behind her asked.

She went rigid, hope flooding through her. "Jay? Is that you?"

"Yeah," he replied. "I thought you were in a different position when I woke up than you were when I dozed off. Are you okay?"

She let out a bitter, humorless laugh. "Not really, but I'm alive. You?"

"About the same."

"Can you see any way for me to get free?"

"No," he whispered after a long pause. "But I see Christy. At least I think it's her."

The words turned her blood to ice. "Is she . . . ?"

"I think she's what's making the smell," he said. His voice sounded choked, and Ami wished she could go to him and comfort him. "She's naked, Ami. And she's got a big fucking hole in her head."

Ami shivered again and winced when it pulled her bonds tighter. She forced herself to relax. "Is . . . is Rob in here, too?"

"No," Jay replied. "Did he make it? The last thing I remember is that big bastard hitting me."

She wasn't sure why she even bothered asking. She knew there was no way Rob could've survived what happened to him. "No. They must have put us here because we're the only ones still alive."

Jay let out a shuddering breath. "I was afraid you'd say that."

"What about Teddy?" she asked, a fresh wave of hope grasping for her. "Is he here, too?"

"I don't see him," Jay said. "I guess we still don't know what happened to him. Unless that fucker out there already roasted him, too."

"There's more than him," Ami said. "There's two more. One of them had a gun. He . . . shot Rob."

"We're next, aren't we?" Jay asked. There was no emotion in his voice, just a flat statement of fact that chilled her to the core. "They're going to kill us, too, aren't they?"

"We don't know that," Ami said, trying to sound more sure of her words than she felt. "After all, Teddy might still be out there somewhere. He might find us, and somehow manage to save us."

It was Jay's turn to let out a bitter laugh. "Have you met Teddy? First off, do you really think he'd stand a chance against whoever's got us? And even if he did, do you really think he'd do anything other than try to save himself?"

Ami sighed. "It's still a chance, isn't it? That has to be better than nothing."

"I'm not holding my breath, if it's all the same to you."

She was about to say something else when the sound of the barn doors opening caught her attention. She craned her neck again and was able to see the doors swing open so the giant man and the one with the rifle could step inside. The guy who shot Rob was holding something in his hand, but she couldn't get positioned well enough to make out what it was.

"Hey!" the man called. "Looks like they done woke up!

Oughtta make this more interestin' if nothin' else. Right, numb nuts?"

There was no response, but from the way the larger man looked at his companion, Ami could tell he wasn't entirely sure what was about to happen himself. There was a distaste in that look that told her there was no love lost between these two, and the giant was not the one in charge of this operation.

The smaller man circled around in front of her so she no longer had to stretch her neck into an uncomfortable position to see him. He tossed the object he'd been holding onto the ground nearby and gave her a lascivious grin.

"Looks like you found the wire we had set up," the man said. "Ain't that a fuckin' shame?"

Ami looked down and found herself staring into the sightless eyes of Eric's severed head. His face still wore the same expression of pain and fear that had been there when he died. At least she had seen it before, and after what happened with Rob, it wasn't the worst thing she'd seen today. If not for that fact, she was sure she would have freaked out more than she did. As it was, she managed to keep a straight face and give him what she hoped was an appropriately hateful look.

"Not a shocker, then?" the man asked, still smiling. "Tryin' to stay tough? I'll fix that soon enough."

He crouched down in front of her and let his eyes trail across her body. She became suddenly aware of the way her back was arched and how it pushed her breasts up so they looked fuller and more pronounced than normal. The man's eyes lingered there as he licked his lips, and then moved back up to her face.

"Who are you?" she asked. She was pleased her voice only sounded frightened when she spoke. Her disgust at how the man was looking at her must have helped offset her fear.

"The nitwit over there's Otis," the man replied, gesturing with his thumb. "He's gonna dispose of ya'll once I'm done with ya. When you get the urge to scream a name here in a little bit, I'm Clint, so that's the one for ya to be screamin'. As to what we want, well, that's easy. I aim to have me some fun with you 'fore I kill you."

Ami fought the urge to shudder. "You're planning on raping me first."

Clint shrugged. "Not unless I got to. No, I'm thinkin' you're gonna beg me to do whatever I want to you."

"You must not be very bright, then," Ami replied, sure the man had to be making what he thought passed for a joke. "Because all I want you to do is drop dead, you murdering asshole."

Clint laughed, as if he really was sharing the punch line to a good joke with her. "You say that now, but that tune'll change soon enough."

He rose to his feet and nodded toward where Jay's voice was coming from behind her. "Hook that one up over there, dummy."

"Don't call me that," Otis replied. "I ain't no dummy."

Clint laughed again. "Whatever. Quit your bitchin' and hang that li'l fucker up like I showed you."

After a series of heavy steps when Otis moved around behind her, Ami heard Jay make a strangled noise, followed by a series of meaty whacks. When Otis reappeared in front of her a moment later, she saw he was carrying Jay by the throat. Jay was smacking at Otis's arms, trying to dislodge the man's grip, but the blows had no discernable effect. Clint moved around behind her, and she felt strong hands grab her under her arms and lift her before planting her on her knees. Her shoulders immediately relaxed, no longer having to take the brunt of the force her legs were exerting by trying to straighten. She was still bound, and the bonds were still secure, but at least she wasn't in such excruciating pain. She found she was actually able to lower her head and watch what Otis was doing with relative comfort.

The large man carried Jay over to the pair of chains and took ahold of one of them. Jay continued struggling in his grip until Otis head-butted him. To Ami it looked like he'd barely nodded his head toward Jay, but the thud she heard, combined with the way Jay went limp, told her the blow had been much harder than it looked. As Jay sagged in his arms, Otis managed to wrap the end of the chain around Jay's limp wrist, looping it twice and then using the padlock to secure it tightly. He let go, allowing the chain to bear Jay's weight while he grabbed the other dangling end and quickly wrapped it around Jay's other wrist and secured it as well. Once both arms were locked in, Otis moved to where the other end of the chain rested against the crossbeam and pulled until Jay was in something resembling a standing position, his arms stretched above his head. Otis gave the chain another couple of tugs, dragging Jay onto his tiptoes, then secured it to the crossbeam and stepped away.

"Strong sumbitch, ain't he?" Clint asked. His voice was almost directly in her ear, making her realize he was crouched behind her with his head leaning over her shoulder. "We had to change a tire on one of them four wheelers once, just had ol' Otis there hold the fucker up while we did it. Big dummy never even broke a sweat, just held on till we said to put it down. I tell him to stomp your fuckin' guts out, you're gonna know what it feels like to get run over by a fuckin' semi, you get me? So I'd suggest you don't give me a reason to tell him that. We clear so far?"

Ami swallowed hard. "We're clear."

"Good!" Clint said, getting to his feet and moving to the table next to where Jay was hanging. He selected a wicked looking knife from the assortment of tools there and used it to cut Jay's shirt away, leaving him bare-chested. Ami was relieved to see Jay's chest rising and falling with each breath. For a while, she'd been afraid that headbutt had killed him.

"You and me's gonna play a game," Clint said, putting the knife down and turning back to her. "Here's how this works. I'll tell you what you want me to do to you, then you ask me to do it. You'll have ten seconds from the time I tell you to ask. You don't ask in that time, or say anything other than what I tell you to, this fucker pays for it. You close your eyes or look away when I'm punishin' him for your fuck-ups, shit goes on till you do watch. Any questions?"

"You're going to kill us anyway," Ami said. She noticed the way Otis's head cocked at that, but kept her eyes on Clint. "So why should I cooperate with your sick game?"

"I'm glad you asked!" Clint said, clapping his hands together like a kindergarten teacher who was amused by one of their students doing something cute and meaningful at the same time. "See, I got a feelin' you actually care what happens to this shit-head here. I'm bettin' you won't want to see what could be worse for him than dyin' would be. You not tryin' to run when we saw you fuckin' around with Otis earlier was a dead giveaway. You'd tried to save yourself, maybe I'd figure this wasn't worth the trouble, so I'd kill him, fuck you till I'd stretched you out too bad to use again, then kill you, too. Since you didn't do that, since you had the other dead fuck try to save him, I know you got a heart under what I'm sure are some nice ol' titties. But maybe

I'm wrong. Maybe you don't give a tin shit what happens to the unlucky fuck. Feel free to resist, feel free to say you ain't playin' along. Once you see I ain't bluffin', you might not even change your tune. Either way, this fuck's gettin' carved on unless you do what I tell you to. You want him to suffer, that's on you. You want him to have a quick and somewhat merciful death, well, that's your call, too."

He leaned forward, that wicked, perverse grin back on his face as he leered at her. "Let's get goin' and find out, what do you say?"

This time, Ami couldn't stop the tears from coming. This man was promising a fate worse than death for both her and Jay, and unless she came up with a way out fast, there was no way she was going to be able to stop him from keeping that promise.

Feeling a part of her dying inside, she nodded for him to begin.

TWENTY-THREE

OTIS KNEW HE WAS UPSET, but he couldn't figure out exactly why. He knew he shouldn't be, at least not to the extent he was. This wasn't the first time he'd had to watch while Clint did all the bad stuff to the people they sometimes caught snooping around. It *was* the first time Eugene asked him to do it, but he wasn't even upset about that. He understood that. Clint got careless and one of his pets nearly got loose. That could've gotten the cops involved, and that would mean all of them would end up in jail. Eugene wanted him here in case Clint got too distracted again. If he did, the people would be less likely to do anything with Otis standing by watching.

He wasn't even really all that upset over the way Clint called him names, either. He was used to it. While he didn't like it, it no longer bothered him the way it did at first. It was like his momma told him when he was a kid and some of the other kids picked on him over how big he was. They only kept doing it as long as they saw they were getting a reaction out of you. Once you started ignoring them, they'd move on to an easier target that would amuse them more. Clint wasn't likely to move on to any other target, mainly because the only other person he could call names was Eugene, who would end up putting him in his place again, but at least if Otis tried to ignore him it never went beyond the childish name-calling.

It had to be something else, and the longer he watched the

girl, the more he thought he might have some idea what it was.

He hadn't been able to stop thinking about her since he'd seen her naked by the fire last night. He'd even dreamed about her after he'd fallen asleep. He'd found her again, but this time she'd been by herself. She was naked again, and when she turned and saw him standing there, she'd smiled and motioned for him to come closer. She'd let him touch her, run his hands across those perfect breasts and then down her sides until he was able to cup her rump in his palms and pull her against him. He'd awoken then, sweating and with the biggest and most painful boner he could remember having. He'd been unable to resist touching himself again, and he considered himself pretty lucky he'd managed to remove his soiled sheets and dump them in the fire pit when he was done without Clint or Eugene waking up and catching him.

When Eugene told him to stay behind and guard the house while he and Clint went looking for the intruders, Otis felt a mixture of disappointment and relief. He wanted to go, to see if his dream might actually happen, but he knew that wasn't likely. He was afraid if he did go, he might not be able to stop himself from snatching her away before Clint could get his hands on her. She would probably scream, which would alert Eugene and Clint, and then he'd be caught. Clint would get her anyway, and he'd be punished for doing something so foolish. It was better for him to stay behind, away from the temptation.

Besides, he had the pet who'd attacked him to get rid of. Eugene had a standing rule: you kill them, you get rid of them. Clint had been hopping mad that Otis had killed his pet, and while Eugene seemed to blame Clint for what happened, Clint insisted Otis obey the rule. Eugene finally gave in, probably to make Clint stop arguing about it, and Otis ended up having to burn the body. He hated doing it because of how bad they smelled when he first threw the parts in, but rules were rules. He killed the pet; he had to get rid of it.

Then he'd looked up and seen *her* standing there in the middle of the compound, staring at him. She'd been upset, that much was clear, even to Otis. He wanted to tell her it was going to be okay, but then one of the boys with her had tried to attack him and he'd been forced to defend himself. It had been over quick, but not quick enough for him to calm her down. She'd panicked, along with the other boy, then Eugene and Clint came back and everything happened too fast to react to.

After Clint shot the other boy and she fainted, he'd yelled at Otis for standing there doing nothing while people were wandering around looking at stuff they had no business seeing. Eugene had been the one to point out Otis had already knocked one of them out, and may well have not had time to deal with the other two yet before Clint started shooting. Then he'd pointed at the girl, told Clint at least he had a new toy to play with, and Otis's heart sank. He never even got the chance to *try* and keep her out of Clint's sick hands.

And now, as he stood watching Clint tease and threaten the girl and her friend, Otis realized why he was so upset. Clint was going to mess with her, just like he did all the others they'd caught since they'd been working up here. He was going to hurt her and make her scream and cry and beg and any chance Otis might have to make his dream come true would be gone. The only chance he'd ever get to be alone with her would be after Clint was through and she was dead as dead could be. Otis could pretend she wasn't, do whatever he wanted to with her then, but that would be *nasty*, and he didn't want her to think of him like that, even if she was dead.

He couldn't leave. Eugene told him not to go anywhere until Clint was done and they were both sure the intruders wouldn't be getting away. He didn't want to stay and watch, either. The girl was too perfect for him to bear seeing what Clint would do with her. All he could do was hope Clint would tire of his game sooner than normal and leave the girl for later. He'd done it a couple of times, always saying something about how the fear was sweeter as it grew. If that happened, Otis could sneak in here later and talk to her, maybe even convince her to let him look at her again.

Or maybe, if he was extremely lucky, she'd let him do more than that.

Ami watched as Clint moved around beside Jay's limp form and grabbed a pair of pliers from the assorted tools on the nearby table. He bounced them on his palm a couple of times as if testing their weight, shook his head, and traded them for a larger pair instead. He nodded, smiled, and turned back to her before raising the pliers to Jay's side.

"Tell you what," he said. "This one's too out of it to feel much of anything right now, so let's start small, just so you can get a feel for how the game's played. Tell me you want me to slap you. Ten seconds."

She stared at him, refusing to play along. She knew it was what he was expecting, and probably even hoping for, but she didn't care. She was positive if Jay were able, he'd tell her not to do anything this asshole said, no matter what the cost. They were both his prisoners, true, and she had no reason to believe he was bluffing, but she was determined to do what she thought Jay would want her to at all costs.

Clint's lips moved silently as he counted down her ten seconds, and then stopped. He gave her a quizzical look, and when he saw she wasn't going to give in, he shrugged.

"Okay," he said. "Time's up, here we go!"

He opened the pliers, positioned them against the sensitive skin along Jay's side, and clamped down with both hands. Jay's eyes shot open as he let out a piercing scream that rattled Ami's teeth in her head. He bucked and writhed beneath the grip of the tool on his side but couldn't get enough leverage to break free. Clint's smile grew wider as he held on for a little longer before finally letting go and taking a step back.

Even from here Ami could see how red and swollen the spot on Jay's side was growing, could hear how much his breath shuddered when he drew it in and expelled it. She had her confirmation Clint hadn't been bluffing—as if she'd really needed it to start with—and knew she was going to end up giving in to whatever he asked, if it would keep him from doing that to Jay again. The knowledge both of them were going to die no matter what did nothing to alleviate that sudden desire. Clint promised a quick death for Jay if she complied, and she had to hope he was a man of his word, crazy as that hope might be.

"See how this works?" Clint asked her. "Your refusal brings him pain. So let's try it again: tell me you want me to slap you."

"I want you to slap me," she said without hesitation. The muscles in her neck began tensing against the blow before she even finished speaking.

Clint took three long steps toward her and slapped her with his free hand as hard as he could. The force of it was nearly

enough to send her sprawling, but somehow she managed to remain upright. Her eye on that side immediately began to water,
and her cheek felt like it was on fire. She was trembling slightly,
but she managed to keep from screaming out in pain, so that was
a victory, no matter how small.

"So you understand," Clint said as he returned to his position
next to Jay. "If you'd agreed the first time, I wouldn't have done
it so hard."

He tossed the pliers casually back onto the table and picked
up a long metal cylinder. It had a black rubber handle at one end
before a thumb switch of some sort and a pair of copper-colored
prongs at the other. Ami had never seen a cattle prod before in
her life, but she was fairly certain she was looking at one now.
Clint returned to her and tested his reach with the thing. To her
dismay, he was still able to press it firmly against Jay's bare belly.

"I probably oughtta move you closer," Clint said. "But long as
you're doin' what you're s'posed to, shouldn't be no need. Looks
like I need to drag you over there, not like I can't do it then,
right? Anyway, on to round two. Tell me you want to kiss me.
Before your clock starts, let's be clear. I don't mean no pussy-ass
kiss on the cheek, or a peck like you'd give yer fuckin' daddy or
somethin'. I mean a real, passionate, get the juices flowin' kiss,
understand? Now, ten seconds."

Ami could feel her bottom lip starting to tremble and struggled against the urge to cry. She didn't want to give him the satisfaction, for one thing, and she felt like there was going to be
much worse to go for another. She cleared her throat and forced
herself to meet his eyes.

"I want to kiss you," she said, forcing her words to come out
calm and even.

Clint winked at her. "Well, yes, ma'am. If you insist."

He grabbed her by the hair and the back of her head and
pulled her up toward him. It felt like he was either trying to pull
her hair out by the roots or pop her head right off her shoulders.
She was able to balance herself somewhat on her tiptoes, but doing so required her to lean against him, which, in hindsight, was
probably his intention all along.

She felt a wave of nausea sweep over her the moment her dry,
cracked lips touched his. His breath stank of fetid meat and stale

beer, and when he jammed his tongue forcefully into her mouth, it was all she could do to not gag at the taste. It was every bit as bad as the smell had been. Not wanting to, but knowing she had to, she flicked her own tongue against his, squinting her eyes closed tighter as she fought her revulsion.

The kiss seemed to go on forever, but finally he shoved her away and stepped back. Her shoulders screamed as she leaned backward and forward, fighting to regain her balance before finally settling back onto her legs again.

"God *damn*!" Clint exclaimed. "Not bad at all! Got me harder'n a fuckin' *rock*! Tell me you want to see it. Ten seconds."

This time she was unable to stop the tears from trickling down her cheeks. She swallowed hard, tasting bile, and tried to form the words, but they wouldn't come. After ten seconds passed without her being able to reply, Clint raised an eyebrow at her.

"Okay, then," he said. "A little reminder."

He jammed the end of the cattle prod into Jay's belly and hit the thumb switch. The air came alive with the crackling sound of electric current passing through the device's battery and into Jay's flesh. Jay screamed again, louder and shriller than the first time, and his entire body went rigid. Ami could see the cords standing out on his neck as he was forced to endure the voltage running through him.

"No!" Ami screamed, suddenly able to find her voice again. "Stop it! Please! I want to see it! I want to see it!"

"See what?" Clint asked, grinning. He didn't let up on the switch, and now Ami was starting to smell cooking meat again.

"Your . . ." she began, before swallowing the lump forming in her throat. "Your penis."

"Don't you know how to talk dirty, girl?" Clint asked, laughing. "Better say it again the right way 'fore this boy gets his innards cooked."

"*I want to see your cock!*" she screamed, desperate to make him stop. "*I want to see your hard cock! Show me your fucking cock!*"

Clint broke down in gales of laughter, but at least he let go of the switch on the cattle prod. Jay sagged in his chains, his head lolling on his shoulders.

"Hell yeah!" Clint said between his laughing fits. "Knew you had it in ya!"

He tossed the cattle prod to one side before peeling his shirt off over his head and then undoing the buckle on his belt. He stopped, head cocked to one side, watching her.

"You can't see it with your eyes closed," he said. "Open 'em and look at it, or I'll do him again."

Ami didn't even realize her eyes had drifted closed as soon as she saw Jay's torture stop. She opened them and forced herself to stare directly at Clint's crotch. At least she didn't have to look at his leering face anymore, temporary though she feared it would be.

He had his pants unfastened quickly, but took his time peeling them down over his hips, as though he were trying to perform some sick, sadistic striptease for her. Her eyes filled with tears again, blurring her vision; she'd never been so thankful to be crying in her life.

She still saw enough to know he hadn't been lying about being aroused. His penis stood up straight like an exclamation point, the tip bouncing almost directly in front of her. She was no virgin, but once she understood the sheer size of the manhood in front of her, she found herself both terrified and morbidly curious as to how she was supposed to have such a thing inside of her. She knew where all this was leading, had been trying to prepare herself for it the moment he and the one he called Otis walked through the barn doors, but now it was becoming more real to her and not just an intellectual exercise. If she thought Clint would be gentle, maybe she could let her mind drift away until he'd done whatever it was he wanted, but she knew he wouldn't be. He wasn't just going to rape her, he was going to try and *bludgeon* her to death from the inside out. It was the type of thing a sick pervert like him would do. The world started to grow dim and she forced herself to remain conscious, at least for now.

"Tell me you like what you see," he said. "Ten . . ."

"I like what I see," she repeated, acting on sheer autopilot. That one had been too easy to refuse.

"Good," he replied. He moved to the table again and started rooting around for something. "Let's see if you're as quick with the next one. I'm bettin' you won't be. Otis, get that one's pants off while I find this."

Otis hesitated. Ami didn't think Clint noticed it, but she did.

She didn't know what it meant, but it was there. Could it be possible the giant wasn't as into this as Clint was? She supposed it made sense. After all, he wasn't the one who was getting to be hands on with her, and by the way he'd been looking at her since he came in, even when she'd first encountered him along with Rob and Jay, he apparently wanted to. He still did what he'd been told to, though, moving to Jay and practically tearing his pants from his body. Jay barely moved as he was undressed, and the one time his head came up, Ami could see how glazed his eyes had become. The shock must have done more of a number on him than she originally thought.

"Here it is," Clint said. When he turned around, he was holding a small butane torch in his hands. He smiled at her as he clicked the button that set it blazing, and then adjusted the flame until it was a low, tight blue cone at the end of the nozzle. He angled it in the direction of Jay's genitals and focused his gaze on her. "You fuck this one up, I turn your buddy here into a girl. It's a three-parter, so you better listen close. Tell me you want me to see your tits, then feel how turned on you are, then you want to suck it. Ten seconds. Go."

So this was how it was going to end, with her begging this redneck asshole to rape her. Her eyes watched the torch's flame dance closer and closer to Jay's genitals, close enough the ends of his pubic hair were starting to singe. He was making a high-pitched whining sound and trying to shy away from the heat he must be feeling, but he had nowhere to go. Clint had been right about how death would've been the easier choice. He was able to make both her and Jay suffer at the same time.

When Clint's eyebrows went up, she knew her time was nearly at an end. She couldn't hold back any longer; she burst into tears.

"I want you to see my tits," she said, hoping he could understand her through her sobs. "Feel how turned on I am. Then I want to . . . suck . . ."

She couldn't get the last of it out, but apparently, it had been enough. The torch went out and Clint tossed it back onto the table before heading toward her, his massive erection leading the way. He took hold of the edges of her shirt and yanked it open, sending buttons flying in all directions. She closed her eyes when she felt his rough hand take hold of her bra and tear it away as well. He must have leaned closer, because she could feel his hot breath against the sweat between her breasts. Her nipples hardened—he would think it was from excitement, but she knew it was out of fear.

"Knew they'd be fuckin' awesome," he muttered, his unshaved face brushing against her skin with every word. "Fuckin' knew they would."

One second his fingers were tracing the waistband of her tights, and then his hand was plunging down the front of them, his fingernails taking streaks of hide as he shoved his way into her panties as well. Then his fingers were probing at her, spreading her, rubbing at her before he began to force one of them inside her. She clenched her teeth, tears stinging her chapped lips as they ran down her face.

Then, suddenly, it stopped as a massive roar tortured her ears and something shoved her roughly away. She hit the ground and skidded before coming to a painful stop several feet away. Her eyes instinctively flew open, just in time to see Otis throw Clint across the room by his throat.

TWENTY-FOUR

CLINT HIT THE WALL AND rebounded, staggering forward a half step before his wobbly legs gave out and dumped him unceremoniously on his ass. As she watched Otis stalking methodically toward him, Ami tried to scramble back out of the way, but the position she'd ended up in made any attempt at leverage pointless. Finally, her knees found some purchase, digging painfully in the dirt floor as she used them to shove herself along, but it was slow going. If whatever was happening between the two men came in her direction, there was no way she'd be able to get clear in time to avoid being caught in the crossfire.

By the time Otis made it to where Clint landed, the smaller man had managed to roll over onto his hands and knees. Clint's head came up in time to meet Otis's fist. The blow was like a wrecking ball crashing into the side of a building, knocking his head sideways and sending him rolling onto his back once again. It must have cleared some of the fog away, too, because he managed to scoot out of the way when Otis tried to stomp a large foot down on his belly, but it was a close thing.

He kept moving, finally managing to scramble to his feet and start backing away from the man stalking him. He had begun to smile again, but this time it was not the leer he'd been wearing while dealing with her. This time, that grin was nothing more than a predator telling the tone, challenging his alpha status to bring it on.

"You done fucked up now," Clint said. He spat to the side, and Ami was sure she saw a couple of teeth land in the dirt amidst the mouthful of blood. "Pretty chickenshit thing to do, hittin' a man in the back like that. Not to mention the whole bit about attackin' one'a your own, you traitorous fuckin' retard."

"You're not hurting her," Otis said, walking at an even pace that kept him gaining ground even as Clint speed-walked backward away from him. "You're not doing none of that bad stuff to her."

Clint laughed, but his eyes were no longer only on Otis. They were flicking back and forth, looking for some kind of weapon to use against him. He started angling toward the table full of tools. "So that's what this is all about, huh? You got a hard-on for that bitch over there?"

"Don't you call her that!" Otis bellowed. Ami clearly saw how red his face was getting and wondered if Clint had any idea exactly how mad his former companion had become. "Don't you never call her that!"

"That fuckin' split-tail ain't never gonna love you, you dumb fuck," Clint said. One hand reached out behind him and Ami heard the sound of tools being knocked against one another as he felt for something appropriate to use. "But you want to think otherwise, be my fuckin' guest. You can talk to the Devil about it when I send you to Hell here in a minute."

"You know better," Otis said. He had stopped moving forward, apparently working himself up for what he expected to be his final assault. "Eugene said you can't do nothing to me, or he'll get you for it. I heard him."

"Uh-huh," Clint said, his smile growing wider. His hands had stopped moving, and Ami knew he'd found something, even if she wasn't sure what it was. "You keep thinkin' that. Once I tell Gene what you done, he's gonna see you had this comin'. And if he wants to try and get all pissy about it, well, he ain't gonna have you there to save his ass this time. Might be tough explainin' to AJ why you're both fuckin' dead, but I'll manage it."

Otis roared at him again and charged. Right before he tackled Clint around the waist, the other man swung his arm around in a wide arc, burying the large knife he was holding in the thick of Otis's neck all the way up to the handle. Ami expected it when Otis's scream of rage turned to one of shocked pain, but she didn't expect to hear it in stereo as Clint started screaming as well. Once Otis turned, she understood why.

Clint hadn't had time to pull his pants back up and get himself tucked away. As Otis moved enough for her to see what was going on, she saw the big man had one meaty hand clamped onto Clint's crotch. She felt a twinge of vengeful gratitude when she saw the head of his penis and one swollen testicle sticking out around Otis's hand. As she watched, Otis tightened his grip and stood up straight again, taking Clint along with him. Clint rained frantic fists down on the big man's arm, but however hard those blows were, they weren't enough to make Otis let go. Ami looked down and saw that his feet were dangling a good three inches off the ground.

With a resounding, cracking boom, Otis slammed Clint against the wall of the barn hard enough to send dust billowing through the room. He maintained his grip on Clint as he reached up with his free hand and slowly pulled the knife free before tossing it away over his shoulder. It was like pulling the drain plug from a bathtub. Blood flowed down Otis's shoulder and back like a waterfall, drenching his shirt a crimson red in the process. He didn't seem to notice, didn't even hesitate as he put one hand against Clint's chest, holding him against the wall, and began pulling steadily with the other. Clint's screams grew more frantic, even as they went up in pitch, until he was making a sound unlike anything Ami had ever heard in her life. She would never have believed a man capable of making such a sound. Clint's eyes were nearly bugged out of their sockets, his head thrown back so far his forehead was nearly brushing the wall he was pressed against. Another massive cracking sound filled the room, just audible beneath his wails, and Ami found herself almost hoping the wall would give way before Otis finished what he was trying to do.

The wall held. Clint reached a crescendo in his screeching as Otis's hand suddenly came away from his crotch. Gore sprayed out almost all the way to where she was lying, and a veritable river of it flowed across Clint's legs before pattering on the ground beneath him. Ami turned her head away and vomited a thin stream of bile onto the dirt floor, not even caring that it was pooling around her mouth and getting all over her face and hair, just thankful she no longer had to look at that gaping wound where Clint's genitalia used to be. Even the random thought that at least he would never rape anyone else wasn't enough to calm her rebelling stomach. It was one thing to say or even believe it was a just punishment for a man like Clint, it was something else altogether to bear witness to such a punishment meted out.

Clint's screams grew muffled before a faint snapping sound cut them off completely. Ami heard a meaty thud as his body hit the ground, but she couldn't bring herself to look and confirm her suspicions. Not yet. She was too afraid she'd see his groin again and didn't want to add to how badly her stomach was already hurting. When she heard Otis's thudding footsteps growing closer, she closed her eyes and fought the urge to scream.

The footsteps stopped. She didn't look up but could feel Otis standing over her, watching her. Finally, she felt the heat from his bulk as he leaned over her and snapped the rope holding her wrists to her ankles as easily as she'd seen her mother snap a thread after she finished sewing something. Her arms were still pulled painfully behind her, but the immediate relief in her shoulders and being able to straighten her legs was enough to elicit a gasp of joy from her. She quickly scooted away from both Otis and the small pool of bile, purposefully scraping her face along the dirt to try and clean as much of it as she could without the use of her hands.

She stopped when her fingers touched something both metal and wood, and her heart leapt. It had to be the knife. She felt along it, wincing as her fingers encountered a warm and slightly sticky coating over the entire length of the blade that could only be Otis's blood. How he was still standing was beyond her comprehension, but since he'd stopped that agony in her shoulders and inadvertently put her so close to a chance for freedom, she supposed she should be grateful for it. She managed to get her hand closed around the handle about the same time she heard those footsteps approaching again.

A pair of hands took her firmly but not forcefully by the shoulders, lifted her into the air, and then set her gently onto her feet. Her balance was still unsteady since she couldn't spread her legs to distribute the sudden application of her weight, but she still managed to stay upright after a couple of steadying hops. Once she had the grip of the knife reversed in her hand and found she was able to slowly move part of the blade's edge up and down against the bonds on her wrists, she finally opened her eyes to look at her savior.

Up close, Otis was every bit the giant she'd thought him to be. If she stared straight ahead, she found herself looking at the center of his chest. She had to hop back a step and look up to see his face. On the way there, her view paused at the gash on his neck. It was still bleeding, but it had slowed to barely more than a trickle. His entire upper body was covered in blood, making him look like he'd been caught out in the world's most grotesque rainstorm. When she met his face and saw an expression of dopey affection so plain it was nearly heartwarming, the contrast was enough to disorient her for a moment. She forced herself to look him in the eyes, amazed at the awe and curiosity she found there. He had to be feeling pain—as bad as he was bleeding, there was no way he couldn't be—but there was no trace of it in his eyes.

"Why?" she managed to ask. Her voice was barely loud enough to be heard, hoarse and shaking, so she repeated herself. "Why?"

He raised a hand easily as large as her head, maybe to caress her face, maybe to snap her neck as easily as he'd apparently snapped Clint's, then paused. She followed his gaze and saw the blood running across his palm and between his fingers and felt her gorge rise again. She knew what he seemed not to understand: that wasn't his blood covering his hand, it was Clint's; the reminder of the forceful castration he'd performed minutes ago. The hand lowered again slowly.

"You came to me," he said, surprisingly tender considering what she'd seen. "I couldn't let him do bad stuff to you, make you all broken. You came to me."

She looked away from his hand, back to his eyes, but they were no longer focused on her face. She felt her cheeks grow warm as she realized her shirt was torn beyond repair and hanging open, and all that was left of her bra was one shoulder strap flapping stupidly against her armpit. She was basically standing here topless before the giant who'd taken a liking to her, exactly as Clint said when he taunted the man. For some reason, she felt more exposed before Otis than she had before the man whose intention had been to violate her in every way he could think of. Otis went to his knees in front of her, his eyes never leaving her breasts.

"Pretty," he said, raising that blood-stained hand again. This time, he didn't hesitate, but carefully cupped her breast in it and squeezed gently.

Ami bit her lip and stared at the ceiling, willing the knife to cut her bonds faster. She had been spared from one man who wanted to defile her, but it looked like Otis was going to do the same thing, only out of some misguided sense of love rather than malice. It would be no less rape than what Clint intended, and while she had no desire to allow it to happen, she also had no way to stop it, either.

The hand moved away, trailing down her body and leaving a sticky red streak in its wake. His fingers carefully took hold of her pants and began tugging them down her hips, just as the rope around her wrists gave way. Her first instinct was to jam the blade into Otis's temple, but this was the man who'd saved her, and she had a feeling he didn't fully understand what he was about to do. Instead, she put her hands on his shoulders and tried to push him away, knocking herself off balance. She fell backward and landed hard on her ass, but at least it accomplished what she'd been attempting. The movement put her out of his grasp, even if it was only briefly.

His face grew hurt and confused as he raised his eyes to her. "I'm not gonna hurt you. Why'd you do that?"

"Look," she said, hoping she sounded soothing and not terrified. "Thank you for saving me, but you can't do that. Not without permission. That's as bad as Clint."

He nodded, his expression more understanding. "Can I . . . can you . . . we . . . that?"

Ami wasn't sure if he truly didn't know what to call sex, or if he didn't know how to ask what he was trying to, but she got the gist of it all the same. "No, that wouldn't be right. My friend's hurt, remember? He's hanging right over there. Can you let him down?"

"No?" he asked, the hurt returning. "But I saved you. You came to me, and I saved you."

"I understand that," she said, trying to keep her anger in check. "But that doesn't mean this should happen. Like I said, I appreciate you saving my life, but I don't even know you. This can't happen."

She felt a chill as the hurt in his eyes deepened and something else sparked to life there. From the way his face started to grow red like before, she knew the other thing was probably anger.

"But I saved you!" he yelled, and that was definitely anger she saw in his eyes alongside the hurt of her rejection. "You came to me and I saved you! You! Came! To! Me!"

"That doesn't mean . . ."

"*You came to me!*"

"*That doesn't give you the right to fuck me, you dumb shit!*"

She regretted it as soon as she yelled it, knew she didn't have a good enough hold on her own anger and fear, but the way he was screaming at her triggered something primal inside her mind and she snapped. It was brief, and she knew her folly immediately, but the damage was already done.

Otis recoiled at first, surprised by her outburst, but he recovered quickly. The pain of rejection fueled the spark of anger within him until there was nothing left but rage. He roared as he came for her, seemingly no longer considering rape, but now entirely focused on killing her for refusing what he probably saw as his just reward. She tried to scurry away, but his reach was too long. His hands closed around her throat and started to squeeze.

Her body went into autopilot, thinking of nothing other than trying to restore the flow of air to and from her burning lungs. She couldn't even draw enough air to wheeze or whisper pleas for him to let her go. Her arms hammered at his, but had no effect. His muscles were rock, while she was barely more than clay. As her vision began to dim, she saw a flash of light near her hand, brighter than the spots forming across her view. She fought to stay conscious, to focus on the light, and felt a spark of hope.

She was still holding onto the knife. She stopped trying to beat at his arms, reversed her grip on the handle, and with the last of her fading strength slammed the blade into what she thought was his head. A roar of pain broke through the sound of her heart beating in her ears as if speeding through a long tunnel, a train growing closer as the roar's volume increased. Suddenly, she could breathe again. She rolled away and held herself up with her hands, gulping lungsful of horrible tasting, but oh so sweet air.

Little by little, her vision cleared and her heartbeat slowed to a fast clip that, while not exactly normal, was at least reasonable under the circumstances. She realized she was panting and forced herself to take deep breaths and hold them in for a slow ten count before letting them out to take the next one. When she no longer felt like she was about to hyperventilate, she pushed herself to her knees and turned, trying to prepare herself for her attacker's next salvo.

It wasn't coming any time soon. Otis lay on his back a few feet away, one hand grasping weakly at the air a good six inches from the handle of the knife now sticking out from the side of his head. His other hand convulsed at his side, and his legs occasionally kicked out as if he were trying to keep the Devil from rising up from Hell to claim him in person.

Ami shuffled toward him on her knees, making sure to keep a safe distance between them, but coming close enough to see his face. Blood was bubbling up from his lips, and the eye on the same side as the knife was filling with it as well. She tried to say something, but her throat hurt too badly to let her do anything more than let out a choked cough. Otis stopped thrashing about and turned his head toward her, both hands dropping to his sides and going still.

"But . . ." he said quietly, his words slurred. "But I love you."

His eyes focused on something over her head as he let out one last gurgling breath and went still. He was dead. Ami covered her face with her hands and wept.

TWENTY-FIVE

GIVEN THE CHOICE, AMI WOULD'VE preferred to stay where she was until she either passed out from exhaustion and hunger or someone wandered in to find her, whichever came first. It did not even matter the latter option was more likely, considering there was still one more person somewhere in the area who probably wanted her dead, it would be easier than trying to get up and get moving and keep fighting to live longer. She'd heard the cliché of someone being ready to lie down and die before, but she'd never understood how anyone could get to that point until now. If not for Jay's increasingly frantic attempts to get her attention, she might very well have curled up on her side and waited for it to be over.

Instead, she raised her head and looked over at him, nodding slightly to let him know she was okay even though she really wasn't. He seemed to sag in the chains holding him up, his head dropping back to his chest. He was still breathing—she could see that much—but as to how badly he was injured after Clint's attentions, she had no idea. He would need to be set free from those chains in any event. If he was able to help her try to sneak out of here or confront their remaining captor, she would welcome it. If he wasn't, well, at least he could die on his own two feet, same as she would.

But first, she had to finish freeing herself.

She could feel the knot when she reached behind her ankles,

as well as the strand of rope connecting them to her wrists, but she could not get it to break loose no matter how much she tried to work her fingers into it. All the attempts she'd already made, along with how she'd been manhandled and moved all over the place, had tightened the knot into something resembling steel instead of coarse rope. If she wanted to free her ankles, she would have to do it the same way she'd freed her arms: by cutting through that rope.

Her heart sank when she realized the only thing reasonably close to her she could use for such a task was the knife buried in Otis's head. She looked longingly over at the table filled with tools, but the sun had shifted too far in the sky for her to make out more than dim shadows. This surprised her. She'd had no idea so much time had passed since they saw Otis burning Benny's body around lunchtime, but she supposed it made sense. Things happened fast when they finally did happen, but there had been a lot of time spent unconscious in between those events.

It wasn't like she couldn't hobble or hop her way over there and feel around, but from the way her legs felt, she wasn't sure she'd be able to get back up and try again if she should stumble and fall in the attempt. Scooting would take forever and run the risk of whoever was still out there catching her before she could get there, and when she attempted to hold herself up and use her arms to help speed her along, they began to tremble from her shoulders all the way to her hands, threatening to stop supporting her weight at any second.

The table would have to be a last resort, then. She had to try for the knife.

After what felt like an almost superhuman effort that left her panting for breath, she finally managed to maneuver her way around Otis's head to the side where the knife was. From this angle, she could see that it wasn't buried as far into his skull as she'd originally thought. Several inches of the blade were visible above his blood-matted hair. Nowhere near as deep as the wound Clint had made in the man's neck, but apparently, it had been enough. She didn't want to touch the thing, but since she didn't have any telekinetic powers she was aware of, there was no other way to retrieve it. She reached out, not knowing whether the tremble in her hands was from her aching muscles or from fear, and wrapped her fingers around the handle. She took a deep breath to steady herself, and then pulled as hard as she could.

If the knife moved, she couldn't tell. Otis's head canted to the side, forcing another small trickle of blood and some purplish-gray fluid to run out around the edge of the blade to join the puddle already formed next to him. She let go of the handle, both hands covering her mouth as she gagged. Her stomach calmed after a few seconds, and she forced herself to take hold of the knife again, this time with both hands. She pulled as hard as she could, and once more, the knife barely moved.

She leaned closer and was able to make out shallow, serrated ridges along the back of the knife's blade. She'd seen that kind of blade before. She was fairly sure Eric had brought one along when they'd gone camping. If she remembered right, their purpose was to prevent the knife from being easily dislodged by whatever prey it had been stabbed into.

After bracing her feet against Otis's skull, she grabbed ahold of the knife and pulled at the same time she pushed out with her legs, using her entire body for leverage. She heard a soft snapping sound, as though someone was breaking toothpicks nearby, and then the knife was free, tracing a sharp line of pain up the inside of her calf before she had presence of mind enough to let go of it before collapsing onto her back.

Her hand went automatically to the cut, making her wince as it closed over the long slice up her calf. She could feel her tights had been slit neatly a half inch above the inseam, but when she brought her hand back up to look at the palm, only a thin line of blood was visible. She let out a shuddering breath. It could've been a lot worse than it was. She probably wouldn't even have a scar from the cut. As if such a thing was worth caring about anymore.

It took mere seconds to grab the knife and slide the blade through the ropes around her ankles. It took longer to unwrap them, but the sensation of blood flowing into her feet again made it worth the wait. She lay back on the dirt, spread-eagled, and savored the feeling of freedom for a moment before getting to her feet and making her way to where the chain holding Jay was attached to the barn's crossbeam. She glanced over to see his head was raised again, his eyes watching her eagerly. She offered him what she hoped was a reassuring smile, and then started unwrapping the chain.

It came loose quicker than she'd expected, whipping around the crossbeam as Jay's weight pulled on it, catching her in the center of her palm with a massive blow that made her fingers go momentarily numb. She wondered briefly how big a bruise it was going to leave, then let out a series of mad chuckles that even scared her. Scars and bruises held little meaning for her anymore. She wasn't going to live long enough for any of her injuries to matter.

When she looked back to check on Jay, she found him on his feet, watching her with a strange look on his face that was almost enough to set her off again. She fought the laughter down and waved a hand at him.

"I'm okay," she said, more for her own benefit than his. "Really. I'm way beyond exhausted. It's been a long day. I'm not losing it or anything, I promise."

"Never said you were," he replied, but his tone definitely indicated he thought otherwise. At least he didn't seem to want to press the issue. "Didn't happen to see what happened to the key for these locks, did you? They're pretty tight, no way I'm just sliding my hands out."

Ami tried to think back to when Jay had been put in the chains to start with, then turned and looked at Otis, a sinking feeling in her stomach.

"He was the one who put you there," she said, nodding at the massive bulk on the ground. "I don't know if he had the key or not. It would have to be him or Clint, if they even brought the key with them."

Jay glanced over at Clint, then to Otis, then sighed. "You check the little one, I'll check the big one."

Ami nodded, at first relieved to not have to look at Otis's corpse any longer than she already had, then realized she was going to be closer to the gaping wound where Clint's junk used to be, and began to feel she'd gotten the worse end of this arrangement after all. She started toward him then stopped when she noticed his pants must have come all the way off during his fight with Otis. She hadn't noticed it at the time, but she vividly remembered they were down around his ankles while he'd been feeling her up. Whenever it happened, he wasn't wearing them any longer.

She also could clearly see how the skin around his neck was bunched and twisted from how forcefully Otis had wrenched his head around. Had the big man turned it any farther, Clint's head would have come off like a bottle cap. The only thing she could see of his face was one bulging eye staring sightlessly at the wall. It was more than enough.

It took a couple of minutes searching to find his pants bunched up on the ground a good five feet behind where she'd originally been kneeling while he molested her. She had no idea how they'd flown so far from him, but they were the only discarded clothing she could see somewhat out of place. She crossed to them and felt around in the pockets, her imagination making the cloth feel slimy and disgusting on the backs of her hands and fingers. The pockets were empty. Clint didn't have the key. That, or it had flown out of his pockets as well, and was lost until they could get more light in here.

She looked over to Jay and saw him kneeling next to Otis, a look of disgust on his face. He reached toward the man's far pocket and suddenly pulled his hand away as if something had stung him. He began shaking his arm vigorously, and then stopped when he noticed her watching him.

"Bastard pissed himself," he said. "The whole front of his pants and the bottom of his shirt's soaked with it."

"Clint didn't have it," she replied. "If you want that key, his pockets are your best bet, so get on with it."

He sighed and gritted his teeth before reaching for the pocket again. His face scrunched up as his arm touched the front of Otis's clothes again, but he didn't pull away. He probed the inside of the pocket with his fingers for a minute before pulling his hand away and sighing, then reached for the other side. After another minute his face broke out in a grin as he pulled out the object he'd found and held it up so she could see it.

A small key, like the kind used on padlocks.

He held it out to her and she moved to take it, quickly slipping it into the lock on his chains and saying a silent prayer before turning it. The hasp snapped open. She laughed.

"Finally, some good luck," Jay said, laughing along with her. He took the key from her and unlocked the other side himself. "God, feels like I dropped twenty pounds."

"Might have been," she told him. "Those weren't little chains, you know."

"Yeah," he agreed. "So what now? Run like hell?"

As appealing as the idea was, Ami knew they couldn't do it. They would have no idea where they were going and no guarantee the other man she'd seen come in on one of those four wheelers would stop hunting them, especially once he'd seen what they did to his friends. Beyond that, they hadn't eaten for two days and wouldn't last very long in the woods without food or water. The cabin they'd seen was bound to have both, as well as a warm place to sleep for the night.

But that meant doing something she wasn't particularly looking forward to.

"See if your pants aren't too torn up to wear, and then find something you can use as a weapon," she said. "We're going to finish this."

Eugene stared down at the cover of the book he'd been reading, his index finger sandwiched between its closed pages to mark his place, and considered picking up the satellite phone next to him and making that call he'd been trying so hard to avoid. He had a bad feeling in his gut, his instincts warning him shit was about to go down, but he tended to not be ruled solely by instinct. He was a creature of logic and analysis, and he would not make such a potentially life-threatening decision without careful consideration.

He hadn't paid much attention when the screaming started out in the barn. Clint wasn't exactly known for his subtlety when he was "playing" with someone and screams were a natural byproduct of that. Besides, he'd made sure to send Otis to keep an eye on things so there wouldn't be a repeat of last night's near-disaster. When the screaming calmed down some, Eugene was positive Clint had managed to break one or both of their captives. Faster than normal for him, true, but still nothing unusual.

Then he'd heard that roar. He'd recognized it as coming from Otis, which was somewhat unusual, but he still hadn't worried overmuch about it. Without knowing, or even really *caring*, what Clint was up to out there, that angry roar wasn't enough to be concerned about. After all, the girl was prettier than many of those who happened to stumble into their operation unawares, so it was quite possible Clint let his guard down while messing around with her and let the other one nearly get the drop on him. Otis would do his part to make sure nothing happened to Clint, and it was likely that would be preceded by a roar like the one he'd heard.

It was only when the unholy shriek had come that Eugene actually started paying attention. He couldn't remember ever hearing anything like that in his entire life, and he'd heard plenty of screams and cries from people in pain over the years. It had stopped suddenly, a sure sign whoever had been making it was good and dead, but it hadn't relieved the dread that settled into the pit of his stomach.

There had been other sounds since the shriek, and once he was sure he'd heard Otis bellow in rage again, but nothing conclusive. Glancing out the window told him nothing, only that the sun was starting to disappear over the mountain and Clint hadn't yet bothered turning on the lamps out there. Still, it was troubling. He'd gone back to his seat, determined to read his book and let Clint do whatever sick shit he felt like doing, but he hadn't been able to shake the feeling of impending disaster.

The longer he looked at the sat phone, the more sure he was that something had gone terribly wrong out in that old barn. If it had, he would need to do something. The only question was exactly what that would be.

It was possible one of their captives could've managed to get the better of Clint. The man was good at what he did, but he was overconfident to the point of sloppiness on occasion. He'd been challenging Eugene's authority for nearly a week now, sometimes subtly, sometimes not, so it was easy to see that overconfidence getting him killed when his back was turned. It was also possible, if extremely unlikely, they could've overpowered Otis as well. The man was built like a Mack truck, and just as strong, but there were two of them out there and he wasn't the sharpest knife in the drawer. Their captives didn't particularly look as though they had much fight or cunning in them, but people did strange and desperate things when you backed them into a corner. Clint's overconfidence combined with a possible adrenaline-fueled last-ditch effort to stay alive could've given them the perfect opportunity to outsmart Otis as well.

Eugene had to admit, if Clint or Otis had been the ones to

come out the victor in whatever happened, one of them would've already come back to the cabin to tell him about it. Otis to rat out Clint for whatever stupid thing he'd done, and Clint to bitch and moan about how shit didn't go his way. Since neither of them had done so, he had to assume their captives were the ones who'd prevailed.

Which meant if they acted at all logically, they'd be heading for the cabin as soon as they worked up the nerve. He was going to need to be ready for them. Ignoring the phone—after all, there was no way he'd be able to get backup here in time to do anything and would catch hell from AJ for being unable to deal with two weak punks on his own—he headed for the storage room attached to the cabin's kitchen. He had no idea what was about to happen, but he intended to be fully prepared for it when it came.

TWENTY-SIX

AS FAR AS THEY COULD tell, there was only one person in the cabin. Ami had waited by the window to what they assumed was the living room while Jay circled the building, and when he returned, he shook his head, indicating he hadn't seen anyone other than the single man sitting in the armchair near the fireplace with a book opened on his lap. The place was much larger than they'd originally thought, so it was entirely possible someone else they hadn't seen was hiding somewhere inside, but they would have to take the chance if they wanted to finish this once and for all.

She let Jay lead the way back up the porch to the door, hanging back out of the way while he tested the knob. He gave her a surprised look when it turned easily in his hand. She shrugged. They were way out in the middle of nowhere, and the man was more than likely waiting on Clint and Otis to come back in once they finished the two of them off, so why would he bother locking the door? He nodded, mouthed a silent three count, then opened the door and rushed inside with her close on his heels.

The man glanced up briefly at them before returning his gaze to his book. He seemed utterly unsurprised at their sudden appearance, and utterly unconcerned about it as he flipped to the next page and continued reading. It was so unexpected that it caused Ami to freeze in her tracks while she tried to figure out what the man might be up to. From the look on Jay's face, he was obviously as confused as she was.

"You're not Clint or Otis," the man said calmly, not looking at them. "I assume they're both dead?"

Ami glanced over to Jay again, but he was of no help. All he did was shrug and nod for her to take the lead.

"They are," she said, not sure what else to add.

The man nodded. "May I ask how that came to be?"

This was going nothing at all the way Ami was prepared for it to. She'd expected a fight, some kind of violent outburst from the man that would end with someone else dead on the floor, be it him or one of them. That he didn't react other than to remain sitting placidly in his chair, reading and asking questions with a note of what she thought was genuine curiosity, kept her from reacting at all. She knew this man was allied with the men who'd killed her friends and tried to rape and kill her and Jay, so by all rights, she should be attacking him, but she'd been taught for so long to be respectful to those who were being respectful to her she couldn't bring herself to raise the knife in her hand and attack him.

"Clint was about to rape me," she said, trying to match his tone and failing. He was confident and assured; she sounded like she was about to wet herself. "Otis apparently wanted me for himself, so he attacked Clint and snapped his neck."

"After he ripped his dick off with his bare hands," Jay added. Ami frowned at him, wishing he'd remained silent. By stating it so bluntly, he'd inadvertently caused the image to spring back up in her mind's eye for her to watch all over again.

The man sighed and closed his book, finally looking over to them. "Otis never did care much for Clint's methods. I warned Clint he'd go too far and make Otis mad one day, but he wouldn't listen. But you said Otis wanted you for himself, which doesn't make any sense. What happened to him?"

"He tried to rape me after he killed Clint," Ami said. She held up the knife so the man could see it. "So I put this in his skull before he could get very far."

"Huh," the man said, surprise coming to his face for the first time. "I'd never have believed it. Ah, well. Who can say what a simple mind might do? Done is done, I suppose. So you're here now to do . . . what, exactly? Kill me as well? A little added revenge for you to finish your evening? I might point out I was not one of the ones trying to rape or kill you out there in the barn."

"Doesn't look like you were doing a whole hell of a lot to stop it, either," Jay replied.

The man gave him a half-shrug. "Semantics, but true enough, I suppose. Enough to make me an accessory in any case."

"Who are you?" Ami asked. "What is this place?"

The man chuckled, the honest amusement in it sending a chill up Ami's spine.

"Do I look like a Bond villain to you?" he asked. "We're in the real world and I have no desire to outline anything about who I am or what I'm here for to the likes of you two. I'm sure you've seen enough pieces of the whole while you've been wandering around to have some ideas. You figure it out."

"You're a pot farmer," Ami said. "Pretty big-time one, too, I'm betting. You probably can't leave the place unattended for very long because of the danger someone might stumble into it and call the cops on you, so you and your friends out there were here to guard it through the winter until time to plant again."

The man gave her a round of slow clapping, sarcasm dripping from every slap of flesh on flesh. "I hope you're not expecting a prize or anything. Check the kitchen, maybe you earned yourself a cookie if you can find Otis's stash."

"You're pretty confident for a guy sitting there running his mouth while two of his victims are ready to kill him," Jay said.

"Oh, please," the man scoffed. "You're hardly *my* victims. If you were anyone's victims it would be Clint, but you've already said Otis killed him, and in particularly grisly fashion. I was in here reading, and did nothing to interfere one way or the other with what he chose to do to you. As you've already pointed out, I might add."

"Fine," Jay said, his voice growing angrier. "You're innocent. That mean you're going to let us use your phone and call for help?"

The man laughed again. "Absolutely not. You know as well as I do I can't let you leave after all you've seen. You two were as good as dead the moment we found your friend down by the river, the girl who couldn't seem to do anything other than cry and beg for mercy."

"You killed Christy, too?"

"Pay attention, dear, I'm getting tired of repeating myself," the man said. "*I* didn't kill anyone. Clint killed her. As I understand it, he blew her head off while anally raping her, but no one ever said he was very smart. *I* was reading my book."

He held it up and shook it, as if to emphasize how stupid they were for thinking anything different.

"You're a fucking dead man," Jay said, taking a step toward him.

"No, I'm not," the man said, sighing. "But you are. See, when most people break into a house and find someone sitting around doing normal things, they tend to forget the most important considerations about confronting that person. Oh, they look for any immediate danger, but then they stupidly keep their eyes on their target. If they're particularly paranoid, they'll look to their sides, maybe even at the floor under them. What they never do, and what you didn't bother to do, was look *behind* them."

Everything happened so fast it felt like time had to have slowed for it to all occur at once. The man lifted a small metal box with a wire running from it with the hand that wasn't holding the book as Jay began to turn around. Ami didn't bother turning. She dove to the side and scrambled away as quickly as she could, trying to stay as close to the floor as possible. She heard a soft, electronic clicking sound, then a concussive boom that felt like someone kicking her eardrums.

Bits of metal tore at her legs and peppered the floor around her. None of the injuries felt too bad on their own, but the sheer amount of them made her wonder if there would even be anything left to her from the thighs down once she recovered enough to look. She started to check and saw the mangled body lying in pieces on the floor where Jay had been standing only moments before. He'd caught the full brunt of the explosion, and the force of it had shredded his flesh as effectively as if he'd been shoved through a meat grinder. His entire upper body was gone, pulverized into the consistency of ground beef and spread across nearly the entire living room area. The only things left to identify the pile of gore as having once been human were his legs and hips, resting at the end of a long trail of blood across the pockmarked floor.

Ami started to get to her hands and knees, but a kick to her stomach sent her rolling back onto the floor again, all the air driven from her lungs. She looked up and saw the man pulling his leg back for another strike. He was saying something to her—at least his lips were moving like he was—but all she could hear was the constant, ringing after-effect of the blast that killed Jay. She tried to back out of the way, but her reflexes were slowed by her inability to catch a breath. The man's next kick caught her below her ribcage and sent her sliding backward. It was the direction she'd wanted to go, but she could've done without the man breaking a rib to help her along.

The man closed the distance to her and reared back for another kick. Just as he threw his foot forward, she instinctively held her hands out in a vain attempt to block it and found herself gazing in amazement at the knife still clutched in her hand. Somehow, she'd managed to hold onto it. She flipped the blade around as quickly as she could and braced it against her chest. The man must've seen it as well, but his momentum was too great to pull back in time. The sole of his foot impaled itself on the blade of the knife, and when he jerked his leg away, the knife was plucked from her grip as well.

He hopped backward several steps, then slid in Jay's bloody remains and fell onto his ass. When he pulled his foot up and reached for the knife embedded in it, Ami knew she had to take advantage of the situation now or he would kill her for sure.

Unable to breathe or even *see* clearly, she pushed away from the floor, ignoring the crushing pain in her chest, and leapt at the man. He saw her coming and tried to brace for her assault, but she'd managed to catch him enough by surprise he couldn't react in time. She landed on his belly, wincing when his knees slammed against her back, but relieved when he tried to double over as he lost his own breath. She rose slightly, intending to ram her knee into his face, but he managed to shift sideways enough that she slammed it into the floor instead with a great deal of her weight behind the blow.

She screamed in pain and scrambled away, terrified by the tingling sensation that suddenly broke out along her lower leg and foot. She'd done some kind of massive injury to herself, that much was obvious, but if she'd done something that would prevent her from being able to stand and fight back, she'd managed to turn the upper hand into a losing one in a single failed attempt. She stopped when her back hit the man's chair and reached behind her, hoping to use it as leverage to get to her feet so she could try to do something else in the limited time she had before he recovered enough to come after her again.

When she tried to apply weight to her injured leg, it buckled beneath her immediately. Had she not been holding onto the chair for balance, she'd have ended up right back on the floor again. She looked over and saw the man had managed to regain his breath and was slowly—and apparently *painfully*—extracting the knife from his foot. Sweat stood out on his face as he inched the blade back, and Ami remembered the serrated edge on the back. She might be too injured to run very fast, but he would be as well, considering the damage the edge was doing to his foot as he pulled it out.

She glanced up to the remains of the explosive device mounted above the door to the cabin, angled downward enough that whoever was standing directly beneath it would take the brunt of its detonation. If there were things like that in this cabin, there had to be other weapons as well, things she could use to defend herself. After one final check on the man's progress in removing the knife, she hobbled toward the rooms at the back.

A quick glance into the first was enough to let her know it was a barracks of some sort. She could see three of the cots were fully set up in a line along one wall. Through a partition set up midway across the room, she could make out several other steel-framed bunks with rolled-up mattresses atop them, space for the rest of the crew to sleep when this place was fully operational. There were lockers and chests at various points, but all of them appeared to be locked, and she didn't have time to try and break into them before the man would be after her again, this time with a weapon she knew could kill her quickly. She pushed away from the doorway and moved on.

Another door was attached to the cabin's small kitchen and dining area. She moved toward it, heart racing. Worst-case scenario, she might find another knife she could use in the kitchen. It wouldn't be as effective as the one she'd lost in the man's foot, but it would be better than nothing. She grabbed ahold of the doorknob and tried to use it for balance while she looked for a butcher's block or something, but it turned in her palm and the door opened, sending her spilling into the dark room. She hit the floor hard and saw spots dancing in her eyes from the impact.

"You're fucking dead, you little cunt!" the man bellowed from the living area. Her ears were still ringing, but she could clearly make out what he was saying. *"I'm going to carve bits of you off, a little at a time, and when you think I can't possibly do anything more, I'm going to cut off a little more! It's going to take you fucking weeks to finally die, but before you do I'm going to cut your fucking face off and wear it like a fucking mask while I laugh at you and you beg for me to fucking kill you!"*

Her time was running out fast. She looked around wildly, hoping to find something she could use to get back to her feet or, better yet, something she could use to defend herself against the attack she knew would be coming at any second. Her eyes finally landed on the large, glass case at the back of the room and she froze, unable to believe that her luck had finally turned around.

Rifles filled the case, leaning against a molded rest at the back of it. They looked like the one Clint used when he killed Rob, and all of them had clips inserted so they were ready for fast use. She crawled to the case as fast as she could go, dragging her injured leg behind her. She'd managed to reach it when she heard the man let out a long bellow of pain from the other room and knew she had minutes—maybe even seconds—left before he came for her. She had no doubts he would make good on his promise to make her death take a long time. His words carried absolutely no hint of a bluff.

She screamed in frustration when she found the glass door of the case was locked. She looked around, her eyes frantically scanning the shelves and boxes stacked along the room's other sides, finally spotting a large can of what looked to be crushed tomatoes. She grabbed it, spilling the shelf's contents to the floor around her and wincing as another can roughly the same size and weight slammed into her uninjured thigh hard enough to make the leg start to tingle. It was obvious from the pain she wasn't going to be going anywhere quickly. This was to be her last stand, it seemed.

A triumphant laugh escaped her as she slammed the can against the glass door and saw cracks spider-web their way across the surface. She hit it again and more cracks joined the first, further weakening the glass. With one final, herculean effort, she hammered the can against the glass door as hard as she could and actually screamed with joy when the glass exploded inward. She barely noticed as several shards propelled outward to slice her cheeks and forehead. She grabbed the bottom of the door and pulled herself closer, screaming again as the jagged glass knifed into her palms, digging out great chunks of flesh. It didn't matter. Nothing mattered save getting her hands on one of those rifles.

She managed to grab the butt of one of them, terrified once it started to move it was going to overbalance and slam into her head. If that happened, it would more than likely knock her out, and wouldn't that be a fitting way for her to end up? So close to victory and stopped by her own carelessness. She managed to get a better grip on it and caught it when it fell before turning it over and wrapping her hand painfully around the pistol grip.

She'd fired guns before, but it had been a long time. She wished idly now she'd taken part when Benny stopped at the shooting range on their way into town a couple days ago, but she hadn't, and now she had to try and remember what to do in the middle of all this chaos. Her thumb found a lever right next to the trigger guard and she pushed against it until it clicked as far as it would go in the opposite direction. She assumed it was the safety, but whether she'd flipped it on or turned it off she didn't have the chance to check.

A shadow blocked the light trickling in from the living area and she looked up to find the man standing in the doorway, all his weight planted on his good foot, knife in hand and at the ready with a look of unadulterated hatred burning on his shadowed face. She didn't give him time to act, didn't even give herself time to think, just braced the rifle against her shoulder and pulled the trigger. She was shocked to discover not only had she turned the safety off, she'd apparently set the rifle to fire on its fully automatic setting. It jerked wildly in her hands, threatening to throw itself from her like a horse might throw a troublesome rider, but she redoubled her grip and held on for all she was worth.

It looked like fire shooting from the end of the barrel, lighting the room in a deadly strobe as the rifle slung bullets at a rate faster than she could even hope to count. Not all of them hit her intended target, a fact clear to her by the amount of splinters and wood chips flying from the area around the doorway, but some did. The man's body twitched and jerked as the bullets tore through him, driving him backward and finally toppling him like a felled tree. She didn't let up on the trigger even after he went down, but kept holding it until the only thing she could hear was the rapid click-click-click of the firing pin hammering against an empty chamber. Only then did she release it, holding onto the rifle with trembling hands as she watched the slumped form.

It lay still and did not move.

After almost a full five minutes of waiting for him to rise up like some boogeyman out of a horror movie, Ami finally managed to get herself turned around and started inching her way back out of the room. She knew the rifle was out of bullets, but she couldn't bring herself to put it down. Not yet. It was like a safety blanket she wasn't quite ready to part with, even though she knew she was past the age she actually needed it. Only when she finally saw the man's eyes, open and staring at the ceiling with a series of wounds bisecting his face in a neat, diagonal line, was she willing to drop the rifle to the floor with an abused-sounding clatter.

Somehow, she managed to get back to her feet, thankful the tingling in the leg the can hit was subsiding and it was able to support her. She hobbled out of the kitchen and made her way to the chair where the man had been sitting when she and Jay came in, pointedly not looking toward the door or the mess of shattered tissue and bone that had once been her best friend. She would grieve later. For now, she wanted to sit down and catch her breath. She made it to the chair and worked her way around it before finally collapsing into it and letting out a relieved sigh.

She numbly stared at the crackling flames in the fireplace before her, something relatively normal amidst the chaotic hell she'd just endured. Her gaze drifted to the table next to the chair, and when she saw the satellite phone resting there undisturbed after everything that happened, she finally began to weep.

TWENTY-SEVEN

Agents from the Drug Enforcement Agency, the Bureau of Alcohol, Tobacco, and Firearms, the National Park Service, and the Federal Bureau of Investigation descended on a remote area of the Great Smoky Mountains National Park this week to take control of what many of them have described as the largest marijuana grow operation in the eastern United States. This endeavor is the result of a months-long investigation following the discovery of a compound approximately three miles inland from a branch of the Pigeon River that flows through the mountains on the North Carolina side. The compound itself was discovered during rescue operations related to the survivor of a river rafting expedition that stranded them in this unsettled area of the park.

In the weeks that followed the rescue, forensic technicians were able to determine the compound also was used as a slaughterhouse for unlucky park visitors who happened to stumble across it. Authorities have determined through extensive testing that evidence suggests the demise of at least twenty separate individuals in the area surrounding the compound, including the discovery of what appeared to be a mass grave at the bottom of a crevice approximately half a mile away.

At the time of the rescue, the bodies of Eugene Raymond Schwartz, 51, Clinton Matthew Barnes, 46, and Otis Ralph Odenmeyer, 44, were found in the compound's barn and cabin, killed by the lone survivor and her friend as they attempted to defend themselves while seeking rescue following their raft overturning on the river. Schwartz and Barnes had lengthy criminal records, including multiple charges of assault, battery, and assorted drug-related offenses. Barnes further was listed as a registered sex offender who had failed to check in as directed by law for the last five years, and was suspected in several instances of theft involving firearms. It is suspected the three had ties to a larger drug cartel and were in their employ at the time of their deaths, a fact the continuing investigation seeks to confirm.

Confirmed among the dead were Christy Lynn Gilles, 25, Benjamin Lee Wilkes, 26, Eric Nathaniel Ray, 26, and Jason Troy Harrison, 25, all residents of Nashville, Tennessee, and Robert Lewis Richards, 38, of Boulder, Colorado. Another member of the rafting party, Theodore Edward Anderson, 23, is still missing, but is presumed dead as well. The group had been rafting down a relatively obscure branch of the Pigeon River when they encountered extremely rough waters and their raft capsized, leaving them stranded near the drug compound. Authorities have withheld the identity of the lone survivor citing safety concerns, considering the potential far-reaching connections for the grow operation itself.

A representative of the DEA, speaking on condition of anonymity, stated it is believed more of the discovered remains will be identified as belonging to park visitors who have been listed as missing for quite some time, and hoped the families of these additional victims will soon be able to find some closure.

In the wake of this discovery, authorities are finding themselves under intense scrutiny and pressure to explain exactly how an illegal operation of such magnitude could have run for so long without detection. A joint proposal is currently being drafted for presentation to the National Park Service and Congress to allocate funds for increased aerial patrols over the area in the hopes of preventing operations of this type from setting up shop in one of the nation's most treasured National parks.

It wasn't yet spring, but it was already hot as hell out here. Part of that was due to the unseasonably warm weather that persisted since the end of January, and some was due to the increased altitude, but a lot of it probably stemmed from having to wander around the woods in full tactical gear, waiting for the arrival of an army of cartel enforcers that most likely had better things to do than throw their lives away trying to regain one of their compounds currently so overfilled with law enforcement that the effort would outweigh the potential gain.

Gary Wilcox glanced around to make sure no one was watching him, then propped his rifle against a nearby tree and unsnapped the chinstrap on his helmet. He lifted it off, sighing with relief as the added weight disappeared from his neck and the gentle breeze finally got the chance to ruffle his sweat-matted hair. He couldn't wait to get off duty so he could take off the bulky ballistics vest and nearly ten pounds of assorted gear hooked up to it, and then have a nice, refreshing shower and a cold beer before settling down to peruse the hotel's meager video on demand selections. Considering how it would be on the government's dime, he was thinking about hitting up some of the more adult-oriented fare instead of the generic, too-old-to-care-anymore movies on offer. His girlfriend would be pissed if she ever found out, but she was still back in DC. Besides, he needed something to distract him from this shit job he'd ended up with.

When he first joined the DEA, he'd been hoping he'd get the chance to make a difference and have a little excitement in the process. Visions of raiding meth labs or squaring off against cartel flunkies along the Mexican border raced through his head, a real-life version of *Breaking Bad* with a touch of the Wild West thrown in for good measure. It was a disappointment to learn the reality was much more mundane. He had a rifle, but it was more a symbol of force than an actual weapon. Aside from the range, he hadn't even had to flip the safety off, much less shoot the thing. Raiding meth labs required highly skilled technicians in haz-mat suits paired with an insertion team also in haz-mat suits. The lowly grunts like him got to stand outside and keep John Q. Public from getting too close while those other guys did all the heavy lifting. His exciting career was more boring than the security guard gig he'd worked through college.

This assignment was more of the same. Here he was patrolling the woods for any potential traps the first guys missed and watching for anyone wandering too close like at the lab raids. At least with those, they were close enough to civilization he actually got to talk to people on occasion. Out here in the middle of fucking nowhere, the only thing he had to talk to was the wildlife, and with so many people wandering around, even the bears were steering clear.

That he'd been doing the same thing for a good six weeks only made the situation worse.

He ran his gloved hands through his hair, scratching furiously at his scalp to dislodge the dried sweat making it itch like crazy. He felt like he was roasting in all this gear, and the fact every stitch was as black as midnight wasn't helping any. He knew he was going to have to put the helmet back on before too much longer. If he sat around here too long, someone would eventually cross paths with him, and unless it was one of the other guys who drank and bitched about it with him after they got off duty, he was liable to get reported and then he'd be in a world of shit over it. He couldn't bear to do it yet. The breeze wasn't very strong, but it was somewhat cool and was doing an incredible job of keeping him from feeling like he was going to pass out from heat exhaustion in barely seventy-degree weather. Besides the embarrassment that would cause him, he'd end up being sent back through physical evaluations and might even get pulled out of the field until he was cleared for normal duty again. Boring as it was, a desk job would be a thousand times worse.

He checked his watch and figured he had under five minutes before anyone might come by. He could always say he'd been checking what he thought was a tripwire that turned out to be nothing more than a thin blade of grass bent down low. It happened all the time, especially since they were trained to be paranoid when looking for booby traps, and since they were encouraged to take their time with such things, no one would think anything of why he'd been in one place for so long.

He was about to sit down next to his rifle when he heard a snap from the woods behind him. He turned quickly, heart racing as he scanned the foliage for movement, but saw nothing. He waited, remaining as still as he could, and finally heard the sound again, a little to the left of where he thought it came from initially. There wasn't any movement he could see, so it was probably a small critter of some sort and nothing to be concerned over, but it was still too early to say for sure.

"Cooper?" he asked, his voice loud enough to be heard a ways off but not so loud as to carry far. "That you, buddy?"

There was no answer, and after a slow count to sixty without the snapping sound repeating, he finally allowed himself to relax. Probably a rabbit or a raccoon or something. Nothing at all to be worried about. After all, these woods were lousy with them.

He turned and shifted his weight to start back to his intended resting spot when something slammed into his back hard enough to knock him over onto his face. Something was on his back, thrashing wildly at the neck of his fatigues, trying to dig into the padded collar to get to his bare skin. He had no idea if there were any mountain lions in this part of the country, but on the off-chance there was and he was being attacked by one, he needed to do something to get away from it, and fast.

Luckily, his training gave him some considerable upper body strength, so he was able to shove himself up hard enough and fast enough that whatever was attacking him was dislodged and thrown to the side. He immediately dropped back down flat and rolled away from where he thought it landed before trying to scramble back to his feet again. He had enough time to see he hadn't been attacked by some animal, but rather a skinny-looking man, naked, with red welts and scrapes covering his entire body. The man's nose was canted at a strange angle and one arm looked slightly misshapen, as though both had been broken at some point and never set so they'd heal properly. Before he could make out any more details about his assailant, the man leapt at him again.

He hadn't been expecting it, so his center of gravity wasn't set properly. When the man slammed into his chest, Wilcox was knocked backward, hitting the ground hard enough to drive the air from his lungs. One of the man's flailing hands caught his bottom lip, and Wilcox grimaced as the attacker's long fingernails sliced through it as easily as a knife through butter. He tried to get his hands up to shove the man away, but his arms were pinned beneath the man's scrawny knees. Wilcox would've never expected someone that looked so malnourished to possess such strength, but that appeared to be the case.

The man slashed at his collar, and Wilcox heard the fabric tear an instant before he felt a breeze cooling the sweat on his throat. He had no time to savor it, for the man leaned in, teeth snapping at his face like a dog ready to kill. His hot, fetid breath filled Wilcox's nose, making him fight the urge to gag.

As they struggled, Wilcox realized the man was muttering something under his breath over and over like an insane mantra. He strained to hear what it was while still trying to keep the man's teeth away from his face.

"Teddy hungry, Teddy eat," the man muttered. "Teddy hungry, Teddy eat."

Wilcox had time to wonder with amazement if this was the missing member of the rafting group, then the man's teeth found his throat and sank in before tearing a chunk of flesh away. Wilcox felt hot liquid soak his neck and run across the side of his face and down his shirt, his mouth making desperate gurgling sounds, then his vision dimmed and he felt no more.

If you ask his wife, John Quick is compelled to tell stories because he's full of baloney. He prefers to think he simply has an affinity for things that are strange, disturbing, and terrifying. As proof, he will explain how he suffered *Consequences*, transcribed *The Journal of Jeremy Todd*, and regaled the tale of *Mudcat*. He lives in Middle Tennessee with his aforementioned long-suffering wife, two exceptionally patient kids, four dogs that could care less so long as he keeps scratching that perfect spot on their noses, and a cat who barely acknowledges his existence.

When he's not hard at work on his next novel, you can find him on Facebook at johnquickbooks, Twitter @johndquick, or his website, johnquickauthor.blogspot.com.

Other Grindhouse Press Titles

Made in the USA
Columbia, SC
13 June 2021